Amelia Found

by
Millicent Stone
with
Derrick Chilton

Cover and interior illustrations by Mim Aylett
www.mimaylett.com

ISBN 978-1-671-00781-9

v1.2

Dedicated to Linda Robinson.

We are bound together by our children.

We would like to acknowledge the contributions of Graham Stuart, Lisa Gresseinger, Jane Grimshaw, Elizabeth Lyon, and Patrick Diggnes whose kind and generous assistance and encouragement helped make this book possible.

"May you have the hindsight to know where you've been, the foresight to know where you are going, and the insight to know when you have gone too far."

[An Irish blessing]

INTRODUCTION

I had done what I had always promised myself I would – I had written a book. And now the whole world was going to see it for the first time. And see me for the first time too. What would they think? I was about to find out. I was sitting in a less than comfortable armchair in a badly air-conditioned hall at my first literary festival facing rows of book readers. I had to remember they could also be book buyers, and I was looking into the eyes of a man called Jeremy who was about to interview me. We had spoken before and I had told him how I had written my book. But had he been listening? Did he like my book? What would he think of me? I was anxious. It seemed to me that I had a strange effect on men, they either loved or hated me, no in-between. Jeremy had the look of a man who had interrogated a lot of writers and might be getting a little bored of what they had to say. How could I change that? The only way I knew. Be myself and tell the truth...

CHILDHOOD

Jeremy: "Amelia, the first thing I have to say is that your book is not like anything I've ever read before. The most striking aspect is that it has a completely different rhythm. Short sentences, bursts of dialogue, and an almost dizzying pace throughout. And then I realised where it came from - it is so close to the way you tell stories. So, what made you write it?"

Amelia: "Well, Jeremy, I wrote this book because I actually love telling stories. It's 'the seanchaí' in me, the storyteller, all part of my Irish heritage you know. From when I can first remember, I was told I had a way with words. And in my life so many crazy, bizarre, at times funny, and yet tragic things seemed to happen to me. I loved recounting stories about it all and people loved listening to them, especially my kids. But it was only when my daughter got seriously ill, and during the long bedside vigils she begged me to retell her all my little stories, that I decided to write them down and create this book."

Jeremy: "What intrigued me from the start was the structure of the book and the storytelling."

Amelia: "Well, the storytelling was something we used to take our minds off the really tough times we were having. We started by making a little list of all her favourite stories that I'd been telling over the years. She would then pick one, ask me a prompting question, and I would record the telling of the story on my cell phone. For example, one of the first stories she picked, she asked me, 'Mummy, tell me the story of you walking home alone from school'. And so I did..."

Walking Home Alone

When you are three years old the world is full of challenges, but for a strong-minded and resourceful child like Amelia Alice Allen, challenges were there to be met and overcome.

Her day at playschool had come to an end. The schoolroom echoed to the sound of chairs being pushed under tables, and children being told not to run.

Had everyone put on their shoes and coats? Had anyone forgotten anything?

There was much to think about, and much on everyone's minds.

Amelia was feeling impatient, waiting around in her stiff buttoned-up coat, scuffing her shoes against the parquet flooring.

Mothers collected their children, but there was no sign of Amelia's mother. And then she had a thought. She walked up to her teacher and tugged at her patterned dress.

'Oh, my mummy's here,' said Amelia smiling brightly.

'OK, off you go,' replied her distracted teacher.

And so off went Amelia. She had decided to walk home by herself. An adventure. She wanted to do it, and she was going to do it.

Beyond the wrought iron school gates there was a tall hill, a really tall hill, but Amelia was determined, and set off on her journey, her brown-flecked eyes wide to the world.

At the top of the hill she reached the crossroads and the shop. She looked left, and she looked right, as she had been told to do.

'Gosh, this is easy,' she thought.

The shop had fruit and vegetables displayed outside, stacked and crated for easy viewing, labelled and priced with hand-written signs.

Amelia continued past.

No one seemed to take much notice, even when she tripped and fell.

She picked herself up, and did not cry, she was not going to cry even though her hand hurt. She was proud of herself for making the journey, and carried on past the terraces of slate-roofed houses and the tall trees that lined her route home.

'I don't know what all the fuss is about,' thought Amelia. 'Walking home alone is easy. I could do it every day, all by myself. There really is no need for my mummy to come and collect me.'

Amelia's mother knew she was late, she didn't like being late, she considered punctuality to be a virtue. But today, for some inexplicable reason, she'd just lost track of time. She didn't want to let Amelia down, she wanted to be there for her.

She hurried through the school gates, up the stone steps and through the main doors. She looked around the empty space, and saw Amelia's teacher sat down, leafing through some papers.

'Hello, Mrs Allen, how can I help you?' inquired Amelia's teacher, looking up.

'I'm here to collect Amelia,' said Mrs Allen, politely, removing her elegant white gloves.

'Mrs Allen, your daughter has already gone,' stated Amelia's teacher.

'What! My daughter can't have gone, I'm here to collect her,' declared Mrs Allen.

'But, Mrs Allen, your daughter's left with you...' faltered Amelia's teacher.

And in that moment both teacher and mother realised. 'Oh my God!' exhaled Mrs Allen.

Quick to react, Amelia's teacher leapt up and raced to the school office, her papers tumbled in a flurry behind her, and scattered across the floor. In the office she grabbed the black telephone receiver and dialled frantically.

'Police?'

Walking home was taking a long time, but Amelia was not tired. It was her adventure. There were horses in the field. Amelia really liked horses, she thought they looked so free and happy. If she stood on tip-toe, she could see them up-close over the dry-stone wall. They were really big, their coats glistened in the sunlight.

Past the field, Amelia saw her home in the distance, a large white house with a large garden, set in a street of large houses and gardens.

'Just keep going,' she told herself.

As Amelia arrived at her house, she could see through the dining room window. She noticed a lot of people.

'Oh, my mummy must be having a party,' she thought excitedly. 'Oh goody!'

Amelia raced up the driveway and knocked on the front door. The door swung open, and her mummy dashed out, and just wrapped her up in her arms, hugging her tightly.

'Wow, this is a big hug,' thought Amelia, 'she's clearly impressed with me.'

Mrs Allen stepped back, and looked her daughter up and down.

'Sacred Heart of Jesus, Mary and Joseph, child!' she wailed. 'You scared the living daylights out of me, Amelia Alice Allen. Don't ever do that again. Do you realise how worried I was?'

'But Mummy, I'm fine, I'm fine. I'm a big girl now.'

Jeremy: "Amelia, I read the book with the benefit of having met you and having heard you tell some of your life stories, like the one we've just heard. This made discovering those tales on the page even more fun. But, what was your inspiration behind telling these stories?"

Amelia: "Look Jeremy, my daughter told me to write a book that was inspiring, that was funny, that would make people laugh. She said to me it wasn't to be about her, her illness, but that it was to be about me and my life. So it got me thinking about my life, my mother, and my children..."

Mothers and Children

Amelia's mother hardly saw her husband, William, these days. The demands of his feed distribution business and the livestock farms he managed for the Harringtons, a local land-owning family, meant he barely had time to wave goodbye to the children in the morning or kiss them goodnight in the evening.

Had she seen William, her first thought would have been to hand Amelia and her brother, Alex, over and say, "All yours", and go and get some much needed sleep quicker that he could say, "But Audrey, I'm too busy".

Amelia was awash with boundless energy and limitless questions. And Alex, well, he was off wherever took his fancy. It was as much as she could do to keep up. Sometimes, if she managed to finish a cup of tea, then that was a good day.

And to add to the mayhem there was William's dog, Jack, a very silly dog, a dog the children simply loved. Supposedly he was the family guard dog, but to the children he was just one wonderful, loveable dog, who bounded up on their beds in the morning, and licked them awake. He was a big, grey Weimaraner, with the most beautiful of blue eyes.

Amid all this, though exhausted, Audrey could not have been happier. The fun and the joy and the laughter and the love that the children brought fulfilled her life. It was all that she wanted. And if Audrey ever needed help with the children there was always William's aunt, Aunty Bea.

Aunty Bea was a sprightly, stoical, retired ex-school teacher who wore a white blouse under a cashmere cardigan with a matching tweed skirt below her knees. Her grey hair was fixed into a bun at the nape of her neck. She had always lived next door, and had raised William since the age of three after his mother had died from a brain tumour.

Though it was never said, Audrey came to realise that William's father had not been able to come to terms with his wife's death, and had turned to alcohol. It wasn't that William's father had neglected William, he had loved William very much, it was just that the daily routine of raising a child didn't fit easily with the pressing needs of running a business.

Aunty Bea adored children, and had that timeless patience and interest in them that made them adore her. "Going to see Aunty Bea" was always a treat, and even when she was strict with them, they just adored her more.

But it wasn't only the children that Aunty Bea helped Audrey with, she knew William better than anyone. Over afternoon cups of tea, Aunty Bea would tell stories of William as a child. She gave Audrey the insight into his past that William never had and never would.

Today Audrey led her children and Jack the dog down past the shopfronts of Loch Garman's Main Street, towards the opera house on her way to morning Mass.

Audrey was always glamorous, well dressed. Motherhood had not altered her fashion sense or figure. Style was key, and she wasn't about to change who she was for the sake of practical, maternal wear.

Though a newcomer to the town, Audrey was welcomed and quickly drawn into conversation by passers-by, for William and his family were well-known, and highly respected merchants. She was shy when talking about herself, and always sought to say as little as she could, to understate. While this was seen generally as a commendable personality trait, some wondered whether Audrey thought of herself as a little superior, a cut above.

However, Audrey knew that Loch Garman was indeed a small town, a town that you could shake hands across. And after morning Mass, the mothers gathered, as they always did, in the shadow of the church. And while their children ran and played, the mothers talked. Everyone knew everything about everyone, and everyone was more than happy to tell.

Of course, the silent hum of conversation was all about Amelia's little adventure yesterday, though no one ventured to speak directly to Audrey.

Audrey simply smiled through the unsaid accusations as she circulated among the mothers.

Jeremy: "Well, we can certainly see you get your sense of style from your mother, Amelia. So how about you and your father, were you a daddy's girl?"
Amelia: "Ah Jeremy, it's often said that every Irish girl wants to marry a man like her father!"

Our Father

Amelia's father was a fiercely intelligent man. The grey of his eyes matched the steel of his resolve. He was a kind and generous man too. However, a wife, two children, three farms and a feed supply distribution business, not to mention the family dog, made for a busy life, and a life that wasn't always balanced. But what free time William had, he spent with his children.

There were not-to-be-missed annual events.

William would take the family in the car to the New Bridge to watch the firework display that opened the Loch Garman Opera Festival at the end of October. Every year, he would buy raffle tickets from the Loch Garman Arts Society raffle, and give one to each of the family. This year, top prize was to have your portrait painted by Sean O'Meara, a well known local artist.

Amelia won!

It was on that occasion that William turned to Amelia. He just smiled and shook his head.

'Amelia, do you know what? You're the luckiest little soul. If you threw a penny up in the sky, a fiver would come down.'

And each Christmas, William would drive the family to Dublin to see St Martin's Moving Crib. The family would then walk hand-in-hand, crossing the Liffey, to look at the fantastic festive displays in Switzers' shopfront windows.

However, the annual event that was not-to-be missed most of all was the family summer holiday, camping. Though it was an event that generally did not pass without difficulty. Typically, Audrey, the children and Jack would be stood on the drive, with bags that had been packed by Audrey weeks before, awaiting the arrival of an always late William. There was always something or other last-minute that had to be done. Audrey's frustration would then become compounded when some drama, a puncture, a wrong turn, a forgotten wallet, would mean they would arrive invariably late at their destination. Putting the tent up in the dark, while fun for the children, did nothing to soothe her temperament. It would often take a day or two for Audrey to no longer be cross with William.

But the family holiday often proved to be the best time for all. Alex, though younger than Amelia, was Amelia's best friend, and the opportunity to play together at the seaside was just wonderful. The children would even manage to persuade their father away from his newspaper and to join them in the water, splashing and messing around with Jack.

Audrey and William even found time to talk.

'I've been approached by Gerry Hanlon,' remarked William.

'Gerry who?'

'You know, Gerry Hanlon, the big property developer from Dublin.'

'Oh. Approached to do what?' Audrey shaded her eyes from the sun.

'Well, somewhere down the line he's heard about the work I've been doing with the Harringtons, and he wants me to do something similar for him, but on a much larger scale,' explained William.

'But won't that be in conflict with your business with the Harringtons?' asked Audrey as she placed her book by her side and sat up.

'Not if I handle it properly. There could be big money in this, perhaps enough to afford that house in the country you so admired,' suggested William.

'I don't know, William,' said Audrey. 'You seem to have more than enough on your plate. The children and I barely see you as it is.'

'If you want to succeed you've got to take risks, that's what I've learnt,' replied William. 'Haven't we done well these last couple of years?'

'We have,' agreed Audrey and then added, 'what do the Harringtons think?' 'I, um, haven't spoken to them yet.'

'Don't you think you should, after all, they've been a big part of your success, and I would always trust what they have to say.' Audrey picked up the book and lay back down again.

'Come on Amelia, Alex,' beckoned William. 'I'll race you. First to the sea wall gets an ice cream.'

And in a spray of sand, William flicked his matted wavy hair off his face, and sped off down the beach followed by the two excited children and one large wet dog.

Jeremy: "Having read your book cover to cover, I really thought the Irishness is so well handled. You show real affection for the people and the way of life. What surprises me is how much religion eventually matters to Amelia in the later part of the book. She is so quick to make light of all the Catholic ways throughout her childhood."

Amelia: "Well, religion was so much a part of life in Ireland when I grew up. I remember going to mass three times on a Sunday in my best bib and tucker, and being told to be good, and quiet and restrained, because Holy God was looking down on me. We had the fear of God put into us, the 'Irish Catholic guilt' we all call it. I couldn't understand what everyone was praying for when I was a child. And yes, I was quick to make light of some of the Catholic ways."

Mass Pishwishing

With their parents away in Dublin, Amelia and Alex had been left in the care of Aunty Bea, and Aunty Bea was a lady of daily routine, the most important part of which was morning Mass. She had never failed to attend Mass in all her born days. She had taken William to the church religiously when he was a child, and she was now going to take Amelia and Alex.

Aunty Bea inspected the children, you had to be clean and dressed properly to go to Mass. She stood them in a line, if two children standing next to each other can be described as a line, and carefully examined their outstretched, upturned hands. They had been given clear instructions to wash, and that was to include both soap and water! The children giggled, they thought Aunty Bea was funny.

'This is no laughing matter, now,' she impressed upon them with a wry grin. Next she checked behind their ears.

'That tickles!' exclaimed Alex.

'Does it, now?' And as Alex tried to pull away, Aunty Bea checked his ears some more.

'Right then, you'll do,' concluded Aunty Bea. 'Now, we are going to visit Holy God's house and he'll be watching you and everything you do, so I expect you to be on your best behaviour.'

Amelia and Alex looked up and nodded.

It was a fine day, cold, but fine. They arrived a little later than Aunty Bea normally did, however morning Mass hadn't yet started. Aunty Bea hurried the children through the doors and went to her usual seat to the left of the altar.

The church was, as always, full. The congregation consisted almost entirely of elderly men and women, all known unto Aunty Bea. In addition, there were a few mothers with children, also known unto Aunty Bea.

She leant across and told Amelia and Alex to be quiet in a hushed, stern tone, though the children had said nothing.

The Mass started.

Prayers.

More Prayers.

Aunty Bea gestured to the children to kneel down.

Alex and Amelia dutifully knelt, pressed their hands together and looked heavenwards.

All that could be heard was the rustle of rosary beads and the whisper of prayer.

It was a congregation intent on receiving forgiveness, though what for was known only unto the sayer of the prayer and God. However, it was doubtful whether any of the congregation had committed a sin in their entire lives, but that didn't stop the prayers from being recounted, or the ritual of Mass from being attended every morning. It was said that some of the congregation had "worn their knees away" they prayed that hard.

Amelia listened to the collective tone of the pious congregation. All she could discern was "Pishwish, pishwish, pishwish..."

She wondered what they were saying, and looked up to Aunty Bea.

'Aunty Bea, what are they all pishwishing about?' she asked.

'Shh, child,' ordered Aunty Bea. 'If you are not quiet you'll go outside. Now, say your prayers.'

Amelia considered this, playing outside seemed much more fun than kneeling inside, however she remembered that she must be on her *best behaviour*.

'Pishwish, pishwish, pishwish,' mimicked Amelia.

Alex muffled a laugh.

Aunty Bea took a breath, and called on her reserves of patience.

'What are you doing, child?' she said.

'I'm just doing what all the old women are doing,' responded Amelia, 'saying my prayers.'

'Child, they are not saying, "Pishwish, pishwish, pishwish",' said Aunty Bea.

'What are they saying?' asked Amelia.

'They are saying their prayers. Now, return to yours. This is your last chance.' Aunty Bea closed her eyes and prayed.

Amelia pondered this for a while. However, still unclear, she decided to stand and tap the lady in front of her on the shoulder.

'Excuse me, do you mind telling me, what are you pishwishing about?' enquired Amelia.

Several in the congregation turned, and at this, a truly exasperated Aunty Bea, grabbed Amelia by the scruff of her neck and dragged her, with Alex in tow, outside for a good telling off.

Jeremy: "Amelia, for a child who walked home alone at the age of three, who was such a mischievous little rascal, it amazes me that you were so reticent in other ways. Why so?"

Amelia: "Well, Jeremy, <pause> you see, you have to understand that I grew up in the seventies in rural Ireland, in the era of the Magdalene Laundries. Are you familiar? There was a culture of conformity, to be seen to be doing the right thing. We were always afraid of getting into trouble, especially with the nuns. In school, they wielded so much power over us, and we were terrified of them. It was deeply ingrained in our psyche not to question authority, and this made us very reticent in some of the simpler things of life, from when we were little kids 'til adulthood. For example, I remember being even afraid to put my hand up in class to ask the simple question: 'An bhfuil cead agam dul go dtí an leithreas, más é do thoil é!'"

Jeremy: "Sorry, what did you just say there?"

Amelia: "Ah, Jeremy, let me recount you a little story to explain..."

Waterpants!

Amelia was struggling to concentrate in class, which was most unlike her. She had other things on her mind. Well, that's to say, she had just one thing on her mind, and she couldn't think about anything else.

Amelia needed to go to the toilet. However, Amelia was afraid to raise her hand and utter the phrase that the nuns had drummed into them all from day one: "*An bhfuil cead agam dul go dtí an leithreas más é do thoil é*". She whispered it to herself over and over, but she couldn't say it out loud. Stupidly, she was afraid she might get into trouble for disturbing the class, and anyway, she rationalised, she never went to the toilets in school if she could help it, they stank.

'It must be near lunchtime now,' she thought, as she crossed her legs.

Amelia was sat next to Ryan.

Ryan was always quiet.

She liked Ryan, but she really liked Ryan's friend, Dermot. She fancied Dermot.

It was no good, she was bursting to go. She clenched her bottom, and started to rock back and forth on her chair.

She was absolutely bursting to go.

13

'What's wrong with you?' whispered Ryan.

'Oh, I don't know... I think I... I need to... I need to go the toilet,' blurted out Amelia, clearly embarrassed about what she'd said.

'Why don't you put your hand up and ask to go?' he suggested.

But Amelia had never, ever put her hand up to ask, and she wasn't about to now.

'Oh, the bell'll ring, the bell'll ring,' was all that Amelia could think, wishing that it would be lunchtime soon.

She closed her eyes.

And then she felt a trickle, warmth, release. Oh, the agony and the ecstasy of release.

She couldn't stop it. It was too late. It was like a fountain of shame gushing out of her all at once. It just kept coming, and coming, and coming.

She opened her eyes and looked down. There was more, and more, and more. It went under her chair. Then it went under Ryan's chair. He lifted up his legs. And then, it went under Dermot's chair, and the girl beside him, and the boy beside her. And then there was steam rising, and the smell...

Everybody started looking at Amelia. She just went red.

'Oh no, I've wet my pants,' she said quietly.

And Amelia looked across at Ryan.

'Don't worry, I'll tell teacher it was me, you're not to worry,' he assured.

And Ryan raised his hand.

Jeremy: "School then was clearly not like school is today. It must have been tough for you, and yet you seem like such a confident, personable individual now. There must have been love and nurturing at home."

Amelia: "Oh thank you, Jeremy. And yes, there was a lot of love at home when I was little, but my life became difficult with the onset of my mother's illness because it went undiagnosed and hidden for such a long time. My poor mother struggled so much and so unnecessarily..."

A Struggle

Audrey sat in the kitchen listening to the radio, though she wasn't. The radio was on, she knew words were being spoken, but what she heard seemed a little jumbled, unclear. She cradled a cold cup of tea in her hands, and looked through the window at cars passing over the distant hill. First there was a black car, then a white one, followed by a blue. Then a black car again. There were definitely more black cars than any other colour. She didn't like black.

She wondered who was in each car, what they might be doing, where they might be going. Her mind drifted. She'd yet to put her make-up on, yet to get dressed.

Someone pulled at her dressing gown.

'Mummy, when are we going to school?' asked Amelia.

'School?' repeated Audrey

'Yes, school, Mummy,' insisted Amelia and then added, 'I could go by myself and take Alex if you like, Mummy.'

Audrey blinked, and turned to look at the kitchen clock.

Nine-thirty.

'Oh my goodness, we're late!' she exclaimed. 'What could I have been thinking? I'd better go and get ready.'

Minutes later Audrey reappeared as smart and as elegant as ever, perfectly put together on the outside.

She rounded up Alex and Amelia. Bag, shoes, coats, all there. Time to go. As she started to pull the door to, she checked she had her keys, she didn't. She darted back inside and searched for them on the hall table. She found the keys next to the vase of red carnations that William had given her the day before, and was caught momentarily in their bittersweet aroma.

Outside, they all proceeded up the road, hand-in-hand, tallest first, dragged by Jack the dog, who was ever-eager for his morning walk.

At the school gate Audrey was greeted by the stern smile of Sister Aloysius.

Audrey could only apologise.

'Don't worry yourself, Mrs Allen,' reassured Sister Aloysius.

'I'm sorry, Sister,' repeated Audrey.

A shadow fell in front of Audrey, as Sister Aloysius loomed forward in her black habit.

'Come along, children,' barked Sister Aloysius, ruler in hand.

As the children were marshalled into the darkness of the doorway, Amelia turned and ran back to Audrey.

She pressed her hand.

'Bye-bye, Mummy,' she said, feeling that something was wrong with her mother, wanting to comfort her.

Audrey looked down at her daughter and smiled.

'Bye-bye, Amelia,' reassured Audrey.

Audrey then looked up and saw her son disappearing into the black.

'Bye-bye, Alex, see you later, after school,' she called.

Audrey could still feel Amelia's hand in hers.

'Now, go on, Amelia, go with your brother,' she instructed.

Amelia nodded, and joined her brother.

Audrey stood and waved, anxious for her children.

Jeremy: "Though your mother was struggling, you clearly had a very important, stabilising female influence in your life in Aunty Bea."
Amelia: "Yes, we loved and adored her, and she us, but I'm sure we drove her crazy too, especially when my mother went away for respite…"

Swimming

With their parents away on a well-deserved holiday, Amelia and Alex had been placed in the care of Aunty Bea. She had duly arrived at their home, struggling with two over- laden suitcases, even though she only lived next door.

The children were under strict instructions to behave and do as they were told, given that Aunty Bea was over seventy years old. Their mother said there would be consequences if they didn't.

The day was hot, there was a heatwave. Jack had taken to the shade, head resting on his outstretched paws.

'Aunty Bea, can you take us to the beach, please, Aunty Bea, please?' insisted the children.

Aunty Bea had a car, a Morris Minor, which she drove on occasion. Though people who had experienced her driving thought she shouldn't be allowed behind the wheel, for Aunty Bea had rather poor eyesight.

She considered the children's request.

'No, I can't take you to the beach,' she said.

'Oh, but Aunty Bea, please,' pleaded the children.

'No, I can't, I'm too busy,' she replied. 'Maybe tomorrow.'

'Please?' repeated the children.

'No,' said Aunty Bea, firmly. 'Now run along outside and play, I've got things to do.'

Amelia followed Alex out into the garden. Alex marched round and round, Amelia remained a few steps behind. Jack watched, wondering quite what was going on.

Alex was thinking. He thought about the beach and the sea and what fun it would be. He thought about the cold water. And with each thought he would stop and stand still, only to begin marching again when the thought had passed. And then Alex turned, walked to the middle of the garden, by his mother's newly-planted shrubs, and pointed to them.

'There, that's where we'll build it. It's the perfect place,' he said.

'Build what?' asked Amelia.

'The swimming pool,' declared Alex.

Amelia's face beamed.

'Fantastic, great idea, Alex, you're so clever.' Amelia could just imagine leaping and splashing about in her own pool.

And so the children set about their task. They went inside the house and looked up "swimming pool" in their encyclopedia. They were able to work out how big it needed to be, and how deep it needed to be.

They returned to the garden, and with their school rulers, marked out the pool's shape on the ground. Their mother's shrubs would have to go, but they knew she would love the pool.

Alex found two shovels in the garden shed. Firstly they pulled up the shrubs and put them in a bonfire-shaped heap against the garden wall. And then they began to dig, aided by Jack. They piled the earth around the pool's edge.

As evening came, they looked at the hole they'd created. An afternoon's digging had resulted in a very small hole. The pool was going to take quite some time to build. Two weeks without Mum and Dad didn't seem so bad after all.

Aunty Bea called them in for tea, pancakes, their favourite.

'I haven't seen you all afternoon. Are you having a nice time?' she asked. 'We're having a great time, we're playing in the garden,' replied the children innocently.

'Oh my, you're the best children ever,' remarked Aunty Bea.

Every day, Alex and Amelia, and Jack, dug and dug and dug. And every day, the pool got a little larger, and a little deeper.

Their parents were due back later that afternoon, so Alex decided it was time to finish digging and time to fill the pool.

All the pools in their encyclopedia were lined with blue tiles. Alex remembered seeing some blue plastic sacks in the garden shed.

'They would be perfect,' he thought.

The children carefully placed the blue feed sacks across the hole they'd excavated.

And then Alex got the garden hose and began filling their swimming pool, much to Jack's delight, who tried to jump and catch the streaming water.

It looked wonderful, a perfect pool.

'Me first!' shouted Alex, as he made ready to run and jump in. 'No, me,' demanded Amelia.

'Together then. One, two, three...'

And in a splash the children were submerged in the pool.

However, clear blue water soon turned to muddy mire as the plastic sacks slid away and became detached from the pool sides.

Undeterred, Amelia, Alex and Jack were having a ball.

There was a knock on the kitchen window.

'We're home,' called Audrey.

Aunty Bea opened the kitchen door.

'So lovely to see you,' she said. 'Now, did you have a nice time?' 'Oh yes, it was wonderful,' replied Audrey.

Hugs were exchanged.

Then Audrey and William stepped in through the open door. 'And how about a nice cup of tea?' offered Aunty Bea.

'Now that would be brilliant, thanks a million,' replied Audrey. 'How are the children?'

'They're fantastic, they're the best children in Ireland,' declared Aunty Bea. 'Well, that's good to hear,' said Audrey.

Aunty Bea switched the kettle on, and got some cups from the cupboard.

'You know, I never heard so much as a whick out of them for the last two weeks,' she said. 'They have been out in the garden all day long playing, as good as gold. I don't know what kept them so amused.'

'Great. Thank you, Aunty Bea,' said Audrey.

And Audrey went to the back door to look for her little darlings in the garden. 'Um, Aunty Bea,' remarked Audrey. 'What is that big hole doing in the garden?' 'What big hole, child?' questioned Aunty Bea. 'You're imagining things again.' 'Aunty Bea!' exclaimed Audrey, raising her voice. 'There's my children and the muddiest dog I think I've ever seen, and they're in a big hole in the garden. And where have all my shrubs gone?'

'Where is there a big hole, child?' asked Aunty Bea.

'There, see!' panicked Audrey.

Audrey ran out of the back door.

Jack barked.

Alex and Amelia, who were covered from head to toe in muck, looked up.

'Hello, Mummy. We've made a swimming pool. Do you like it?' ventured Amelia.

'How could Aunty Bea not see this huge hole,' exclaimed Audrey. 'She must be getting as blind as a bat in her old age!'

'Don't say anything bad about Aunty Bea,' defended Amelia. 'We love her!'

Shocked, Audrey calmed herself and bit her lip.

'I love her too,' she agreed.

Jeremy: "Yes, I can see that Aunty Bea was a lynch-pin in your family."
Amelia: "Jeremy, in Irish culture at the time it was not unusual for the unmarried female members to take on a matriarchal role and help the next generation. I guess it holds true for many societies. But the extended family was very important in Ireland."

News

The children were sat on the sofa, somewhat formally, their legs together, arms by their sides, dressed in Sunday best, admiring their shoes. Their father was stood, hands behind his back, facing the fireplace. And their mother was leant forward in the armchair. She held out her hand, nudged their father. He reached to hold it as he turned to face the children.

Amelia was a little anxious, she wondered what she'd done wrong. Occasions like this were normally held for serious telling-offs. Generally it didn't matter who did wrong, they both got the telling-off, and they both got the lecture, and, more-often-than- not, they both got the punishment.

'Children,' began William in a considered tone, 'your mother and I have something to tell you.'

Amelia looked up.

'This wasn't starting like a normal telling-off,' she thought.

Usually their father would begin shouting, and their mother would try and calm him down.

'We are going to have a new baby,' he said.

There was silence.

'You are going to have a new baby brother or sister,' added Audrey.

'I want a sister,' said Amelia.

'I want a brother,' said Alex.

'Well, we'll just have to wait and see,' replied Audrey.

'Can I feed the baby when it comes?' asked Amelia.

'Why of course you can,' agreed Audrey.

Audrey beamed.

'When are we getting the baby?' inquired Amelia.

'Soon love, in a few months,' answered Audrey.

'Where do babies come from?' continued Amelia.

Audrey had prepared for this.

'They come from the love that Mummy and Daddy have for each other,' she explained.

'Oh,' said Amelia, digesting the answer she had been given. The words "love" and "baby" were now connected in her mind.

'Come and give your mother a hug,' ordered William.

The children tumbled down from the sofa and threw their arms around Audrey, and she put her arms around them.

'What is the baby going to be called?' Amelia was just full of questions.

'We haven't decided yet,' said Audrey. 'Have you got any ideas?'

'Let me think.' Amelia scrunched up one eye and rested her chin on her palm, 'Oh, I know, I know... If it's a girl we call her Ermintrude!'

'And, if the baby's a boy, we could call him Zebedee and he could bounce around the house just like this!' Alex started bouncing up and down.

Audrey shook her head. 'Ermintrude?' she asked.

'Yes, after the cow on the television,' replied Amelia. 'She's really funny!'

'I'm not sure that the baby would appreciate being named after a cow, even a funny one,' said Audrey.

Amelia began to moo, just like Ermintrude.

'I think we should give the baby a good Irish name,' said William.

Audrey grasped William's hand a little tighter.

'You're right, William, we should,' she agreed.

The children were now chasing each other around the room in a frenzy of excited bouncing and mooing.

'Are you sure you're going to be able to cope with another one?' asked William.

'After these two, it'll be a doddle. And...' Audrey clasped William's hand between hers, adding, '...I'll always have you to fall back on.' William smiled.

'And there's always Aunty Bea,' he added.

'Yes, indeed, there's always good old Aunty Bea,' agreed Audrey. They both laughed.

'It was good to hear William laugh,' thought Audrey. 'It was good to be together as a family, something that seemed to be a rare event these days. Perhaps the baby would bring them closer again.'

'Come on, children, time to visit Aunty Bea, let your mother get some well earned rest,' said William.

'Hurray!' exclaimed Alex.

'See you later, Mummy. Get a nice sleep,' said Amelia.

Amelia blew Audrey a kiss.

Not to be outdone, Alex went across to the armchair and gave Audrey a hug. 'Come on, Alex, time to go,' called William as held the door open.

Alex paused and bit his lip, clearly a little unsure.

'Mummy?' he said.

'Yes, Alex,' replied Audrey.

'Mummy, if we don't like the baby, can we give it back?'

Audrey smiled.

'No Alex, we can't,' explained Audrey. 'You see, a baby is for life, you can't just give them back.'

'Oh,' said Alex.

'I'm sure the baby will be fine and lovely,' assured Audrey. 'Now be off with you.'

Alex turned and ran past William, through the open door.

'Give the baby back! Whatever next?' reflected Audrey. 'Where do these children get their ideas from?'

'Who knows?' replied William. 'I'll see you later, get some rest.' And he too blew Audrey a kiss.

Jeremy: "I want to be a bit critical now, Amelia. There are some stories that don't seem to have a resolution, for instance Alex and Amelia waiting for their father to come home to face the consequences after the dentist scene, and the rather unconvincing tale of the swimming pool being dug in your back garden."

Amelia: "Jeremy, I know, some of the things that happened to me are often a bit unbelievable, which is why friends over the years have been constantly telling me to write a book to share these funny scenarios. And of course I have taken poetic license here and there in the retelling. Who wouldn't, but I totally see why you would critique the dentist scene in this way, however, bizarrely it's true fiction!"

The Tooth Fairy

Alex had decided he was going to become a dentist, well, for today anyway. Quite how, or why, he'd reach this decision at such a young age, no one could be quite sure. Amelia had agreed to be the patient, after all you couldn't be a dentist and not have a patient.

Anyway, Amelia sat patiently on the chair in her bedroom, her feet swinging back and forth.

'Hurry up!' she called.

'Hang on, I'm coming,' replied Alex from behind the door.

The door edged open, and Alex stepped into the room wearing one of his father's nicely ironed white shirts over his clothes.

'Open wide,' he said.

Amelia dutifully tipped her head back and opened her mouth as wide as she could and closed her eyes. Alex peered in.

He prodded and poked Amelia's teeth with his fingers and found one that was a little bit loose.

'Right, we're going to, em..., em..., do a tooth extraction,' he declared.

Amelia wondered quite what an extraction was. Clearly Alex knew what he was doing as he knew all the right words. She trusted him, and kept her mouth open, head back and eyes closed.

Alex disappeared out of Amelia's room. Amelia heard the sound of rummaging and something falling over. A few moments later Alex came back into her bedroom.

Unknown to Amelia, he'd found a fishing rod and reel. He'd made a small loop at the end of the line, and had dragged it in behind him.

He stepped forward and managed, by no mean feat of dexterity, to hook the loop around Amelia's loose tooth.

'Amelia, go sit in the wardrobe,' he ordered.

'Why?' she asked.

'So we can do the extraction,' explained Alex.

'OK,' she replied. Amelia got down from the chair and clambered up into her wardrobe as instructed.

Alex closed the door, and went back to his room.

He picked up the fishing rod.

'On the count of three,' he shouted.

'OK.' Amelia's voice was muffled behind the wardrobe door.

'One, two, three...' With considerable force and speed, Alex whipped back the fishing rod.

There was a scream and a loud thump.

Alex dropped the rod and ran back into Amelia's bedroom to find the wardrobe door open, Amelia sprawled on the floor howling, and blood everywhere.

And there, amid it all, was the tooth.

He bent down to pick it up.

He felt a little hot... and fainted.

Thud.

Amelia began crying out for help. At which, Alex came round, and started to sob uncontrollably.

He stood and looked at Amelia's tooth in his hand.

'Successful extraction,' he managed to utter between sobs, and then added, 'I hate the sight of blood, and there's no way I'm going to be a dentist!'

Amelia was about to say something, but Alex ran out of the room, clutching her tooth, just as Audrey was clambering up the stairs to find out what all the commotion was about.

'Alex, love, what's wrong with you?' she asked.

Alex cried and cried.

Audrey hugged him and then led him to his room. She sat next to him on his bed.

'Alex, poor Alex, what's wrong darling?' pressed Audrey.

Audrey cradled him in her arms.

He looked up, tears streaming from his eyes.

'There's all blood in that room,' he said and pointed to Amelia's door, adding, 'and I'm not going in there to be a dentist anymore.'

'There, there, I'm sure it's going to be all right,' comforted Audrey.

After Alex had calmed down, Audrey stood up and walked across to Amelia's bedroom. She opened the door to find the wardrobe open, blood on the floor and Amelia sat, rocking back and forth, holding her jaw.

'Alex!' she shouted.

She then she turned to Amelia and loomed over her.

'Amelia Allen what have you been doing?' demanded Audrey, as she crossed her arms.

'But Mummy...' was all Amelia could get out before Audrey continued.

'What a mess you've made, young lady,' declared Audrey, 'and your brother's in tears. I can't leave you alone for five minutes without mayhem breaking out.'

Audrey knelt down and pulled Amelia's hand away from her mouth.

'And what in the name of God Almighty, what have you done to your mouth?' demanded Audrey.

She lifted Amelia's head up.

'What have you done to your teeth?' she shrieked. 'But Mummy...' ventured Amelia.

'Don't you *Mummy* me!' retorted Audrey. 'Wait until your father gets home. You are in one whole lot of trouble, my girl. And what have you done to scare your poor brother so, and look at what you've done to your bedroom carpet.'

Audrey was beyond reason, she was furious.

And Amelia was in trouble, afraid of what her father's wrath might be.

Jeremy: "I want to explore with you now, Amelia, the important and very topical issue you raise in the next sequence. We have been hearing a lot of late about postnatal depression, many celebrities have been coming forward to talk about their experiences. Clearly, it touches the lives of so many, and you have given us an insight in your book about how it reaches inside to the very heart of the family."

Amelia: "Jeremy, I had no idea at the time what was happening because I was so young and nobody really talked about these kinds of things. You must remember that 'little girls should be seen and not heard' was the cultural philosophy that I grew up with. We were taught not to ask questions about grown-up issues. It is only since I have had a child of my own that I am beginning to understand what a big impact postnatal depression can have, not just on the mother, but on the whole family dynamic. It was important to me to highlight this issue in the book. And I am so glad that other people feel the same way."

Third Time...

Aisling Aileen Allen was born to Mr and Mrs William Allen in the same private nursing home in the heart of Dublin that her siblings had been. Named after William's mother, Aisling was a healthy baby delivered on time without major complications.

Audrey was tired, and struggled to find the energy to mother Aisling. The nurses helped, it was their job and they did it very well. Audrey didn't have to worry.

William held his newborn child in his arms and could think of no happier day. How lucky he was to have three delightful children and a wonderful wife.

Amelia and Alex fussed over mother and baby. Audrey tried to smile, but just stared to space.

The doctor told William that he shouldn't be concerned about Audrey, it was just "baby blues". It was common, particularly in the first week after giving birth.

Aunty Bea minded Amelia and Alex.

William, as ever, was endlessly busy, but made time whenever he could to visit Audrey and Aisling.

Aisling was doing well.

The following week the doctor said that it could be the first signs of the onset of postnatal depression. The doctor suggested that it might be best if Audrey and Aisling continued their stay. He would prescribe some medication, antidepressants.

Weeks passed.

Audrey did not respond to the medication.

She did not dress, her make-up remained untouched.

She did not hold Aisling.

She did not talk about Aisling.

When William asked, she talked about the black cars she'd seen, the ones she could see outside, through the window. She didn't like black.

Audrey stared to space.

The doctor said he had spoken to a psychiatrist. Audrey's condition would be best treated in a psychiatric unit.

Condition?

The doctor looked straight at William from across his large, tidy desk. He leant forward and rested his arms on its edge, his hands held together, fingers interlinked.

'The psychiatrist has yet to make a full diagnosis, Mr Allen,' said the doctor. The doctor paused.

'However, Mr Allen,' he continued, "Audrey is very sick. Her postnatal depression is severe.'

William sat silently, still, his mind full of a thousand thoughts and feelings tumbling over and over, vying to be said, vying to be expressed. But in the end he thought that there was little that could be said. He would just have to do the best he could do for Audrey and the children.

'Postnatal depression can be treated, Mr Allen,' reassured the doctor. 'Mothers get back to normal lives, given time and support, and the right type of care, but I won't pretend that it will be easy, far from it.'

William nodded, then looked to the ground, lost in thought.

'We propose to transfer your wife across to the psychiatric unit later this week,' said the doctor. 'I have arranged an appointment for you to meet the psychiatrist to discuss and agree matters. He will be able to explain things much better than I, but I thought it was important for you to be aware as soon as possible. I know this must come as a shock. It isn't easy to understand, but rest-assured, your wife is going to be in the best of hands. We will do everything we can to make her better. It will, however, take time, Mr Allen.'

William recognised his name being spoken, but the rest of the words escaped him. His beautiful, lovely, wonderful, elegant, charming Audrey. It didn't seem possible.

'Mr Allen?' prompted the doctor.

William looked up, drawn back from his thoughts.

'Yes, Doctor, I understand,' he replied.

But the truth was he didn't.

Amelia: "And my father struggled to cope also. I honestly don't know how he managed. Most of the time he was full of such good humour. I remember him waking us in the morning with a steaming bowl of porridge and a smile on his face. Everyone loved him, and they still do. And that's the truth."

You Do What You Can

William had a household to arrange. Aunty Bea and he had never been so busy with three children and a dog to care for. The hospital had said that it would be several months before Audrey would be ready to come home, and that was if everything went well.

When asked, he would reply that Audrey was recovering from complications after Aisling's birth. He never talked about Audrey's condition, not even to Aunty Bea. But he was always positive, saying that she was on the mend and would be back home soon enough.

Prayers were said at Mass, all hoped for a speedy recovery, and many asked if there was anything that they could do to help.

Dr Martha Walsh offered for Amelia to come round after school each day and do her homework with Sara Jane, Amelia's best friend. William accepted, and Amelia was overjoyed, she and Sara Jane would have a great time.

But most surprising of all was Kathleen Hanlon, the wife of William's business partner Gerry Hanlon. Though she had no children of her own, and lived just north of Dublin, she would travel down frequently to help with the children. She would tell them the most outrageous stories, stories that children shouldn't hear. And she would play with them for hours, running them and Jack round the garden until they could run no more. Amelia was captivated.

'You're a lucky man, William Allen,' declared Kathleen in her smoker's voice, 'to have such gorgeous children. Young Amelia's an absolute delight, she's a special little girl.'

William nodded, he was thankful for the support, his business interests were becoming evermore demanding. He knew that without Aunty Bea, Martha, Kathleen and others he wouldn't be able to manage.

With time, a routine became established. Without Audrey, Amelia and

Alex just seemed to be that little bit more grown-up, independent. It didn't take them long to accept that Mummy wasn't well, and once they had accepted that Mummy wasn't there for them, they got on and did things, not that they had much choice now that Aunty Bea was in charge.

Aunty Bea just doted on the children and particularly Aisling. This was the second generation of Allens that she had been called upon to bring up, and she had never been happier. For many women of her age the responsibility would have been a great strain, but for Aunty Bea it was invigorating, life-affirming, and she tackled the challenge with complete dedication.

Each weekend William and the children would travel up to Dublin to visit Audrey. As time passed, Audrey began to smile as she cradled her baby.

And each week the children would tell her what they had been doing and ask when she was coming home.

'Soon, my loves, soon,' was all that Audrey would say.

William would sit and look on, thinking that everything seemed so normal, and he would wonder why Audrey couldn't come home now. But the doctors would say that, though Audrey was responding well, it wasn't time yet, it was too early for them to be sure that her condition had been treated and that she had stabilised.

To William, Audrey just looked a little off-colour, pale, but that was no surprise given that she wore no makeup, nor was dressed in her usual finery.

All too quickly the visits would end. William would rest Aisling from Audrey's arms, and Amelia and Alex would have many hugs and kisses.

There were never tears, not in front of the children.

Amelia had a close bond with her father, but it was not the same as having her mother at home. She missed her mother sat on the end of her bed, at the end of the day, telling funny bedtime stories about her life, and listening to Amelia's little worries.

Amelia: "And I became even more independent as time went by."
<Jeremy steals a glance at Amelia>

My Little Mushroom

With her mother still in hospital and her father busy at work, Amelia resolved to do more to help. Amelia decided she would cook her own dinner, not that she'd cooked dinner before. How difficult could it be?

Mushrooms. Amelia adored mushrooms. She searched the kitchen, but could not find any. She'd have to go to the shop to get some. Amelia wanted dinner to be a surprise, so she thought it best not to say where she was going or what she was doing. She would slip out of the house quietly while Alex was next door helping Aunty Bea with baby Aisling.

Amelia jumped up and took down her coat. She checked and found the pocket money her father had given her. She hoped it would be enough to buy the mushrooms.

Amelia didn't forget to close the door behind her, and to shut the garden gate. At the road she looked for cars, and then crossed.

The shop that sold fruit and vegetables was near to school. Amelia knew how to get there. She enjoyed the walk, there were fields and trees and animals. She particularly liked looking at the cows. Her father said there was a lot you can tell from a cow. If a cow is sat down it means that it is going to rain. If a cow's tail is tucked between its legs it means that the cow isn't happy, it is cold or sick or frightened. She tried to remember what else her father had said you could tell from a cow, but couldn't. Anyway, she was sure it was a lot.

The bell rang as Amelia pushed on the glass-panelled door. She had been inside many times, though this was the first time she was by herself.

The shopkeeper was chatting to an old lady by the counter. Amelia searched the aisles for mushrooms. She found them with the other fruit and vegetables, they were in little blue cardboard boxes. She chose the box with the biggest mushrooms, and took it to the shopkeeper.

Amelia reached up and placed the box on the counter. The shopkeeper and the old lady continued to talk, neither had noticed her. Amelia waited, patiently.

'I'll make sure that they're ordered for you, Mrs Nolan,' said the shopkeeper.

'Thank you, Mr Healy.' At which the old lady turned and stumbled into Amelia.

'Child, what are you doing there?' she demanded. 'You shouldn't sneak up on people like that, you'll give them a fright.'

'Sorry, I...' stammered Amelia.

'Save your apologies, child,' said the old lady. 'Just make sure you don't do it again!'

Amelia dropped her head as the old lady gathered her bags and strode off.

The bell over the door rang, loudly.

Amelia looked up tearfully at the shopkeeper.

He smiled.

'Don't worry about Mrs Nolan,' he said. 'She can be a bit grumpy sometimes. She doesn't mean anything by it, it's just the way she is. Now what can I do for you, Miss Amelia?'

Amelia was a little surprised that the shopkeeper knew her name.

'I would like to buy these mushrooms.' Amelia edged the box of mushrooms forward, 'I have some money.'

Amelia pulled the change from her coat pocket and let the coins tumble onto the counter.

Mr Healy carefully selected a shilling's worth, and pushed the rest back towards Amelia.

'Thank you, Miss Amelia,' he said, and with a ring of the till he put the money in the wooden drawer.

Amelia gathered the remaining coins and took the box of mushrooms.

'Thank you,' she said, remembering that it was important to be polite.

'Thank you,' replied Mr Healy.

It took a little effort, but Amelia managed to pull the door open. The bell rang, quietly.

'Goodbye,' she beamed.

'Goodbye, Miss Amelia. Hope your mother gets better soon,' he added.

Mr Healy felt sorry for the child, it couldn't be easy for her with her mother being ill for so long.

At home, Amelia stood on a kitchen chair, tipped the box of mushrooms into the sink and proceeded to wash them, just like she'd seen her mother do. They were very mucky, water went everywhere. She put the mushrooms into the frying pan with some butter. She then moved the kitchen chair next to the stove, and put the heavy frying pan onto it.

She turned the dial.

The butter began to melt, and then sizzle, and then spit and spatter. It hurt when it landed on her, but she stood by, watching the mushrooms cook. And when the mushrooms looked like they were ready to eat, she lifted the frying pan off the stove and put it down onto the kitchen table.

They were delicious, best she'd ever tasted.

She ate every one until she could eat no more.

Amelia was tired. It had taken a lot of effort to cook her own dinner. She decided to go to bed.

At the top of the stairs she turned and went into Alex's bedroom. She preferred his bed to hers, it was much more comfy, and Alex's curtains were much darker. It was so much easier to get to sleep in his room. When she slept in Alex's bed, she felt like she could sleep forever.

Amelia awoke. She felt really bad. Her tummy ached. She climbed out of bed and rushed to the toilet. Her stomach convulsed, and she was sick.

Tears streamed down her face.

She convulsed again, and was again sick. Her mouth tasted of mushrooms. Her tummy hurt so. She threw up again, drool hanging from her cheek. She called out, but no one heard her.

Amelia decided she was never, ever going to eat mushrooms again.

Jeremy: "Tell us did you ever eat mushrooms again?"
Amelia: "Jeremy, to this day, even the smell of mushrooms sizzling in a pan brings back so much emotion."
Jeremy: "Amelia, It does strike me though, that there were intervals of normality and harmony in your family life, but then it seemed decisions were taken that shattered those fragile periods."
Amelia: "Yes, you're right, there were lovely periods in my life, and I'm so glad I can remember them and retell them. Looking back now on the darker moments, I do remember feeling lost and afraid at times. I had no control over my life, as a child I was at the mercy of the grown-ups and their decisions. I guess it's the same for all children, although perhaps less so nowadays."

Home and Away

The children couldn't wait, they scampered across the garden, through the front gate and straight to the car, ignoring Aunty Bea's calls for them to come back.

'Mummy's home, Mummy's home!' they shouted.

Jack bounded after them, seemingly equally excited.

Amelia pulled open the passenger door and flung herself onto her mother. Alex dived in afterwards. Jack barked.

Audrey just held them in her arms.

Even Aunty Bea relented, and began walking down the path with a toddling Aisling in hand.

Audrey's homecomings had now become part of the routine.

Sometimes several months would pass, before Audrey would need to return to hospital, other times it would be just weeks.

Something would happen.

Audrey would return to black.

Colour and reason would simply vanish, chased by voices.

And while Aunty Bea and the children seemed to take it in their stride, William couldn't.

Just when he thought his beautiful Audrey had returned, just when she was there to touch and hold, just when they had started to settle to a normal family life, it would happen.

Audrey would become motionless, still, empty.

Or there would be ranting, baseless accusation. It wouldn't make sense. It didn't make sense.

What possible sense could it make?

William had decided that Alex was to be sent away to boarding school. It would be good for him, it would good for Aunty Bea. Asking her to look after all three children was too much, she wasn't getting any younger.

Amelia was to stay at home, she would need to help Aunty Bea with Aisling, and she could help a little around the house when her mother wasn't well enough.

She couldn't be a child forever.

The fact that Alex was to be sent to boarding school, came as a shock to Amelia.

Alex was Amelia's best friend, they played together, shared in each other's adventures. Alex was as close to Amelia as any brother could be.

She cried. Her brother wrapping his arms around her.

'I'll be back for holidays,' said Alex. He didn't like to see his big sister upset. 'We can play then.'

It didn't help stem the flow of tears.

Her father was hardly ever there, her mother kept going away, and now, Alex was gone too.

Amelia felt like she was losing her family, one-by-one.

Tears turned to sobs, and sobs turned to heavy breaths.

'Well, that's settled then,' concluded William, who was clearly in a hurry. 'I need to go, I need to supervise the delivery.'

William leant across, and kissed Audrey and Amelia. He patted Alex on the head.

'You'll have a great time at school, son,' he said.

William spotted Aisling out of the corner of his eye. She was playing hide and seek, though she had neglected to tell anyone. It was her favourite game.

'And where is my naughty little daughter?' he asked.

He turned, she giggled and ducked back behind the chair.

'I wonder where she might be? Under the table?' toyed William. He bent and looked.

'Not there. Hmm, perhaps she's behind the sofa,' he suggested.

There was another muffled giggle.

'Not there, either. She must be...' declared William, as he reached over the chair and lifted Aisling high up into the air, spinning her round and round. 'Right here!'

Aisling's giggles were infectious.

Everyone smiled and laughed, even Amelia.

Jeremy: "As I read your book, I wondered, do you now cringe at some of the things you got up to as a child?"
Amelia: "Sure, I now realise that from a young age I did take advantage of others to get what I wanted."
Jeremy: "Go on so, tell us more."

I'll Tell You, If You Give Me

Amelia had become used to Alex being away at boarding school, reluctantly. She missed him, it wasn't the same. Meanwhile, Aisling had grown to become her little sister, her little shadow, irritating at times, amusing at times, but always there. Little sisters did have their advantages though.

Their mother was home. She had been home for many months, and the girls were so happy. Every child wants their mother, and Amelia and Aisling were no exceptions.

On this day, pocket money weighed heavy on the girls' minds. They asked if they could go to the shop, and were told they could, but they had to mind the traffic, and Amelia had to hold Aisling's hand all the way there and all the way back.

For Amelia, going to the shop with Aisling was an opportunity to get what she wanted, and for Aisling it was an adventure with her favourite big sister.

As they passed the crossroads, Amelia stopped and took out her change. She returned the silver to her pocket, and held out her pennies and halfpennies for Aisling to see.

'Show me what pocket money you have,' instructed Amelia, smiling.

Aisling duly did as she was asked and held out a handful of assorted coins.

'I'll swap you two of these big coins for that small silver coin,' proposed Amelia, pointing to the sixpence.

Aisling swayed from side to side, considering the offer. Two big ones for one small one, that had to be good trade.

'OK,' agreed Aisling.

Amelia quickly swapped the coins and pocketed the sixpence.

The girls continued on their journey to the shop, and crossed the road.

They walked past rows of houses.

'Have you ever wondered why some people paint their front doors red?' asked Amelia.

'No,' said Aisling.

'Well, I'm not sure you're old enough to know,' said Amelia, and continued walking, pulling Aisling along with her.

'I am too, tell me,' insisted Aisling, tugging at Amelia's hand.

'No, I don't think Mummy would want me to,' replied Amelia.

'She would, she would. Go on tell me,' demanded Aisling.

Aisling rooted herself to the spot, clearly not going anywhere until she was told.

Amelia bent down and looked Aisling directly in the eyes.

'If I tell you, you've got to promise not to let Mummy know I've told you,' said Amelia in her most serious adult voice.

'I promise,' replied Aisling.

'And...' continued Amelia.

'And?' Aisling was hanging on Amelia's every word, desperate to know. 'And it'll cost you,' spelt out Amelia.

Aisling put her hand in her pocket and pulled out a penny.

'Is this enough? It's my biggest coin,' she said.

'OK,' and Amelia took the coin. 'Now lean in close and let me whisper in your ear, we don't want anyone else finding out do we?'

'No,' agreed Aisling.

'Well, what I'm about to say may save your life one day,' explained Amelia.

'Oh,' said Aisling.

Amelia made a show of standing taller and looking all about, just to check in case anyone else was listening. She leant forward again and pressed her mouth to Aisling's ear.

'People paint their doors red to warn adults with young children that there's...' Amelia stood up again as if she'd spotted something.

'What, what? Tell me.' Aisling stamped her foot in frustration.

Amelia paused.

'People paint their doors red to warn that there's a big bad wolf hiding in the house ready to gobble little children right up!' concluded Amelia.

Aisling squealed with horror.

And then Amelia grabbed Aisling's arm and sank her teeth into it, slobbering and howling like a wolf.

Amelia: "So Jeremy, I became a manipulative little minx to get my own way, and I loved being the centre of attention."

Jeremy: "Indeed, that's what we see in your book, Amelia, but what I miss with Amelia is what is life like inside her head, hearing what she thinks and feels, what motivates her."

<Pause, Amelia leans forward, takes a sip of water>

Amelia: "Well Jeremy, I was a little girl who was hurting inside. I wanted my family to be there. But, they weren't, and so I was insecure. I guess I tried to compensate by being overconfident on the outside."

Talking My Way Out Of Mass

Amelia yawned and slumped her head against the window of the coach as it bounced its way along the winding country road. She was already bored and they hadn't even arrived at the convent.

The annual retreat was the school trip she looked forward to least. Prayers, prayers, prayers and more prayers. Boring, boring, boring! But, like last year, she knew she would make the effort because it was, after all, God's time.

The one thing that Amelia was looking forward to, though, was seeing Father Rafferty. At least he tried to make the day fun. He would laugh a lot, tell humorous stories. Even his big red curly hair would make the children smile. Everyone liked him. Well almost everyone. Amelia sensed that Sister Aloysius was not impressed.

Finally the coach lumbered onto the gravelled courtyard of St. Mary's Convent and crunched to a halt under the imposing frontage of the grey-stoned building.

The children were counted off two-by-two. Amelia looked up at the stacked rows of arched windows. They were all dark. All she could see was the reflection of the surrounding trees and fields in the glass.

'Silence!' commanded Sister Aloysius.

The hubbub of anticipation stopped immediately. Even the coach driver, who had been about to have another cigarette, lowered his head and drew his hands together.

'Today is a most important day, for it is God's day. I expect each and every one of you to treat it as such.' She paused and surveyed all those before her. Her gaze was not met.

'You will be on your best behaviour or you will have me to answer to,' she said, ruler in hand.

Amelia stared straight at the ground, not daring to look up. She already felt guilty for thinking that the day was going to be boring, and she began to worry that Sister Aloysius might find out.

'Follow me children.' Sister Aloysius turned and led the children towards the waiting nuns and Father Rafferty.

And so the day began. Prayer followed prayer. And the nuns and the priest talked about God, sin, hell and heaven. Then the preparations began for Mass. The children were being allocated jobs. Some had to bring the votive offerings, some had readings to do. Much to Amelia's delight, the preparations were being led by Father Rafferty.

Amelia dreaded the homily. It took forever and was the most boring part of the Mass, particularly as the priest usually droned on and on about things he thought were interesting, but nobody else did, in the most dull voice ever.

But, Amelia had a plan.

She walked up to Father Rafferty and stood with a smile, her arms folded. It took Father Rafferty a while to notice.

'Amelia, my dear child, what can I do for you?' he asked.

'Father Rafferty,' began Amelia, 'I don't want to do any of these jobs.'

Father Rafferty drew breath, and with as much patience in his manner as he could muster, turned and faced Amelia so that they could have an eye-to-eye conversation.

'And why might that be, Amelia?' he queried.

'Because I've done all these jobs before,' replied Amelia.

'Oh, is that right, Amelia. Well, you know, in our devotions to Our Lord not everything can be fun and games. Sometimes we need to be serious, we must open our hearts and minds to his words as spoken through his son, Jesus Christ.'

'Yes, Father Rafferty,' agreed Amelia, 'but I have an idea. Please may I tell you?'

Amelia's answer wasn't quite what Father Rafferty was expecting.

'You do?' he wondered.

'Yes, I do,' she said. 'What I'd really love to do, is that I'd really love to give the homily.'

Father Rafferty scratched his head. No child had asked to give the homily before. What harm could it do?

'Yes, I don't see why not,' said Father Rafferty. 'Amelia, you can give the homily.'

'Brilliant.' Amelia smiled. Her homily would be much more interesting that the priest's homily. She was going to talk about things that people are interested in, and most important of all, her homily would be short!

The Mass had been going on for what seemed like an eternity to Amelia when, almost without warning, Father Rafferty held up his hand and said.

'And now it is time for the homily.'

There was an almost audible groan from the children.

'Today's homily will be delivered by Miss Amelia Allen.' At which Father Rafferty waved Amelia forward.

The almost-groan turned to an almost-gasp as the children craned to see what Amelia would do next.

For the first time in her life Amelia walked to the lectern, and faced the congregation. She could see rows of expectant faces.

'Dearly beloved...' Amelia paused. 'And Sister Aloysius.'

A few children stifled their giggles.

'We are gathered here today to give thanks to the Lord for his son and our Saviour, Jesus Christ, and to hope that he comes again... soon.'

There were many smiles and not a little laughter.

'And also,' added Amelia, 'I'd like to thank Father Rafferty and all the nuns for making our day out fun and enjoyable.'

At this, a smattering of polite clapping began, though this was soon hushed by the nuns.

'But most of all, I'd like to thank all of you for listening,' said Amelia. 'And now, if you could please stand and join me in a little prayer of thanks giving.'

The congregation stood.

'In the name of the Father, the Son, and the Holy Spirit,' began Amelia, 'Amen.'

'Amen,' repeated the congregation.

And with that, what had to be the shortest homily in history, ended with stunned silence.

Amelia grinned, bowed and returned to her seat, all eyes upon her.

After an uncertain pause, Father Rafferty gathered his papers and returned to the lectern.

'Well, I'd like to thank Amelia for her most... interesting and, um... to the point homily,' said Father Rafferty, gesturing in Amelia's general direction.

All turned to look at Amelia.

It was clearly the best homily ever.

But the children's grateful smiles faded all too fast when Father Rafferty continued. 'As Amelia has explained,' he said. 'We are gathered here today to give thanks to the Lord for his son and our Saviour, Jesus Christ. And for this we must consider what we can do in return to show our devotion.'

Father Rafferty leant forward, rested his arms astride the lectern and surveyed his audience.

'Let us consider the fable of...' he began.

And then Amelia realised, Father Rafferty was going to give the homily after all.

Instead of the Mass being the shortest ever, it was going to be twice as long!

Jeremy: "I saw there were key moments in your life, Amelia, like what happened with your dog. Tell us what happened and how you felt."
<Amelia drops her head, opens her book, and starts to read to Jeremy>

The Best Dog

To his credit, Jack fulfilled his role as protector of the family and its territory with absolute dedication and gusto. Indeed, Jack considered that his family extended to the whole street and everyone who lived in it. If there was an outsider he would bark loudly, and if he thought that outsider was an intruder, he would run, leap, and knock them to the ground. In fact, he was often found pinning down some hapless visitor, growling and slobbering over them.

Sunday came as Sundays do in summer, with a warmth that caused the residents of Jack's street to leave their doors open to catch the cooling breeze. And for Jack this meant a greater opportunity to explore his territory, and more importantly a greater opportunity for titbits from people's tables.

The O'Connors, a couple in their nineties, lived a few doors down from Amelia, and used to like to take a nap on a Sunday afternoon before eating their Sunday roast.

Mrs O'Connor had put the roast beef out on the kitchen table to stand for half an hour or so, while she went to wake her husband.

Jack's timing was impeccable, for he knew when dinner time was in the O'Connor household. Drawn in through the open back door, he followed the scent of roast beef all the way to the kitchen table. With one effortless bound, he jumped up. This was more than just a titbit, and in less than a moment it was gone.

After devouring this unexpected meal, Jack decided he needed to rest to digest. He got down from the table, and searched for somewhere to lay his head.

Quite how Jack missed Mrs O'Connor, as she came down the stairs, remains a mystery, but miss her he did. And upstairs, in the front bedroom, Jack found a big comfortable bed. The bed was warm, and occupied by a dozing Mr O'Connor. Jack clambered in beside him.

Mr O'Connor rolled over and put his arm around this body in the bed.

'Oh Honey, have I told you I love you today?' he declared.

The body in the bed said nothing.

'Honey, you're feeling a little skinny,' commented Mr O'Connor, 'you'd better eat up your Sunday dinner.'

Mr O'Connor, who was half-blind, opened his eyes in shock to find that it wasn't Mrs O'Connor beside him, but a dog! After momentary paralysing panic, he used a few choice words and with both hands, he managed to eject the dog from his bed.

'Ahhh, our dinner's gone, the joint's gone,' shrieked Mrs O'Connor from downstairs.

Mr O'Connor heard his wife, but as he stood up frailly, he staggered and then fell, his body wracked with pain.

Mrs O'Connor, who had now managed to calm herself down, wondered what all the noise was coming from upstairs. She went to investigate.

As she put her hand to the bannister, Jack scampered past.

'Dog, you...' she began.

But before Mrs O'Connor could finish telling him off, Jack was long gone, tail wagging behind him. She turned, climbed the stairs, and made her way to the front bedroom.

The whole street heard Mrs O'Connor scream when she discovered Mr O'Connor's body.

Amelia's parents were told that this was the last straw, Jack had to go. And so Jack was banished to the family's farm. Amelia missed him terribly, and frequently asked when was Jack going to be allowed to come home again.

Winter came, and so did the family's Christmas outing to the opera. For Amelia this was a big treat, she loved the whole event, the dressing up, the crowds, the performance. And she didn't have to go to bed until half past ten.

Amelia sat next to her mother, watching and listening to the hubbub of people finding their seats, savouring every moment. A neighbour happened to pass along the row. She looked at her ticket, and then sat down on the other side of Amelia's mother.

'Hello, Mrs Allen, how are you?' she asked.

'Fine, Mrs Brennan, and you?' replied Audrey.

'Well, can't complain. Have you still got that brute of a dog?' inquired Mrs Brennan.

Amelia's ears pricked up, sharply.

'Oh no, fortunately the dog is dead,' said Audrey.

Mrs Brennan nodded sympathetically.

'Yes, a couple of weeks ago, a truck ran over him at the farm and he was killed,' explained Audrey.

Amelia froze, she felt as if she was going to die with sadness, and poked her mother.

'Mummy, is Jack dead?' she asked.

'Oh, yes, yes, yes, em, don't worry,' replied Audrey.

'But why didn't you tell me?' gasped Amelia.

Audrey turned and looked at Amelia. This wasn't how she'd meant for Amelia to hear about Jack, but she couldn't think what to say.

'Shhh, shhh, the music is about to start.'

Amelia cast her head down to stare at the floor.

The audience hushed, as the lights dimmed, waiting for the opera to begin.

It was as if this woman, Mrs Brennan, had got a knife and had cut Amelia's heart into pieces.

Amelia cried in the silence without tears, so hard it hurt.

< Amelia stops reading, closes her book>
Amelia: "I choked to death with sadness that night throughout the whole performance. I had been shocked by my mother's revelation about my dog. Every time I've been to the opera since, Jeremy, I'm back at that night."
<Pause, Jeremy looks to Amelia>
Jeremy: "But you bounced back from that, Amelia Alice Dorothy Allen."

The Original Dorothy

For Amelia, coming of age was defined by her confirmation in the Catholic Church. And as part of this holy sacrament, Amelia had to select a name, a Christian name. She had been given a book on saints and told to choose one. Now all the others chose Anne, or Mary, or Bridget, or Catherine, but for Amelia, who had read the whole book, there was only one name that stood out, and that was Saint Dorothy.

Amelia had always loved the name Dorothy since being taken to see the film *The Wizard of Oz*. And now, how she wished that she and Jack could have been be whisked away on that wind to the Land of Oz, then she could have saved him and he wouldn't have died.

'Amelia?' called Audrey from the bottom of the stairs.
'Yes, Mummy,' answered Amelia.
'Amelia, have you chosen your name?' asked Audrey.
Amelia leant over the banister and nodded.
'I hope you've chosen a sensible name now,' said Audrey.
Amelia nodded again.
'Oh yes, Mummy,' she replied. 'My saint is the best of all.'
'And what's the name you've...' But before Audrey could finish, Amelia had disappeared back into her room.

Amelia wasn't going to tell anyone about her choice. She knew that if she did, she'd be made to change it to Mary or something equally boring. It was her choice, her name, and she had decided.

The day came, and the house was a fluster of activity. Amelia sat, neat, upright in her elaborate, white dress amid the scurry of people trying to get ready for her big day.

It was time to go.

Alex was sent to collect Aunty Bea as they all assembled outside. Audrey wanted a photograph taken of the whole family and so William went to find his camera.

'Say "cheese", everyone,' prompted Audrey, as she tried to arrange her extended family into a picture-perfect pose.

William, always one for the latest gadget, set his camera to automatic, and jumped back into the photograph.

In church it was Aunty Bea's responsibility, as Godmother, to escort Amelia to the altar. Amelia knelt with the other girls, awaiting the Bishop's blessing. Aunty Bea stood behind.

Amelia listened to the roll of names her friends were taking. "Anne...", "Mary...", "Catherine...", "Mary...", "Mary...", "Anne...", "Bridget...", "Mary..."

Amelia thought her turn was never going to come.

And then it happened.

'And what is your chosen name, my child?' asked the resplendent Bishop in a matter of fact way as he drew up in front of her.

'Dorothy,' stated Amelia.

The Bishop appeared to pause. He looked at Amelia, and then he looked at Aunty Bea. Aunty Bea looked as white as the Bishop's vestment.

He leant forward, and smiled.

'You know, my child,' he said, 'in all my years as Bishop, I have never, ever had anyone who picked the name Dorothy.'

And then, much to everyone's surprise, he burst out laughing.

Amelia glanced back at Aunty Bea. Aunty Bea was not smiling, though colour had returned to her face, if thunder could be described as a colour.

'Can you tell me about the name Dorothy? Is she a saint?' asked the bishop.

'Yes, she is,' replied Amelia, remembering to add, 'Your Excellency.'

And then Amelia told the Bishop the story she had read in the book about saints.

'She was tortured and executed for not making a sacrifice to the Roman gods,' explained Amelia. 'And she sent some flowers and apples to someone who laughed at her after she'd died. She's the patron saint of brides too. She has the best story ever, far better than the others.'

'Well, so she is,' confirmed the Bishop. And he blessed Amelia Alice Dorothy Allen, adding with a smile, 'Good luck, not that you'll need it, you're sure to do just fine in life, my child.'

The Bishop moved onto the next child. At which point Amelia felt a firm grip on her arm. Aunty Bea pulled Amelia to her feet, and dragged her down the aisle.

'Wait until you get home, young lady,' she said. 'You're in such big trouble! Why couldn't you pick a nice, sensible name like all the other little girls?'

Amelia was unrepentant.

'Well, the Bishop liked it anyway,' she retorted. 'And I like it, and that's all that matters!'

And as Amelia Alice Dorothy Allen passed her family, she saw that her mother had dropped her face into her hands, trying not to be noticed, her father was shaking with laughter, and Alex beaming the biggest smile at her. His sister had just made the dullest of dull Masses fun. She had even made the Bishop laugh!

ADOLESCENCE

Jeremy: "But, did you think your family life was normal at the time, Amelia?"
Amelia: "Jeremy, I was a teenager, I didn't think too much about it at the time. I really didn't know any different, that was until I started going to my friends' family houses."

Best Friends or Not

After primary school, all the girls from the surrounding district went to Loch Garman's one and only secondary school. Amelia had wanted desperately to go to boarding school like her brother, but it was not to be. Anyway, for Amelia this was a chance to make new friends.

Amelia liked Mary O'Farrell, but Mary O'Farrell was very popular, and Mary already had a best friend, Sheila Maloney.

Now Amelia had her own best friend, Sara Jane, but they'd known one another forever. Amelia thought that perhaps another, new best friend might be fun, and Mary O'Farrell seemed so confident, there was something about her, and her family life.

And then one day, quite unexpectedly, Aunty Bea said there had been a phone call from a very nice lady called Mrs O'Farrell asking whether Amelia might like to come for a sleepover at Mary's house in Rosslare.

Amelia was so excited, and practically begged her father into letting her go. Eventually he agreed. Dr and Mrs O'Farrell were well respected in the area, and, frankly, anything that eased the burden on Aunty Bea, while Audrey was in hospital, could only be a good thing. And if it took Amelia's mind off things, then all the better.

The day was set. Amelia was to travel with Mary on the train to Rosslare after school. Just the two of them! Amelia had never been on a train before on her own, well with just a friend, no adults. And though it was only a twenty minute journey, for Amelia it was an adventure on her journey through life.

The train came, and the girls found seats. Amelia hadn't stopped chatting since they left school.

On board, when she wasn't talking nineteen to the dozen to Mary, she had her face pressed to the window, watching the Irish Sea pass by.

After disembarking at Rosslare railway station, the girls walked to Mary's house. It was set on the hillside, not far, with the most wonderful of views, a fine family home.

Mrs O'Farrell stood at the front door waiting for them.

'Well, hello, Amelia,' greeted Mrs O'Farrell. 'It's lovely to meet you. Mary's told me so much about you. Come on in.'

Amelia beamed.

'Thank you, Mrs O'Farrell,' she said.

Mary leant up and kissed her mother on the cheek, grabbed Amelia by the hand and dragged her inside.

'Come on Amelia,' she urged, 'I'll show you to your room.'

Two giggling faces peered down from the landing, but disappeared as soon as Mary and Amelia began to climb the stairs.

'That's Colleen and Deirdre. Ignore them, they're annoying pests,' pointed out Mary in an over-loud voice.

'No we're not!' they exclaimed. 'Mummy says we're her beautiful little angels.'

As Mary and Amelia reached the top of the stairs, the two faces reappeared, curiosity overcoming shyness.

'Colleen, Deirdre, come and say hello to Amelia,' instructed Mary.

'Hello, Amelia,' they chimed in unison.

'Hello, Colleen, hello, Deirdre,' replied Amelia, unsure as to who was who.

After Amelia dropped her bag off in her room, Mary, with the ever-inquisitive twins in tow, gave her a tour of the house. It was spacious and modern, with all the latest gadgets, not like old-fashioned An Diadan back in Loch Garman. Amelia was full of compliments. It smelt like a proper home.

In a room next to the living room, Mary's older brother was watching TV, his feet resting on the coffee table in front of the sofa.

'And last of all, this is Shane,' said Mary with her arm outstretched.

Shane dropped his feet to the floor and looked up.

'And this is Amelia,' introduced Mary.

Shane stood, walked over and offered a handshake.

'Hello, Amelia,' he said. 'Nice to meet you.'

He smiled. Amelia had never seen such an attractive white smile.

'Em, nice to meet you too, Shane,' replied Amelia, a little lost for words as she shook his hand. Amelia felt her ears burn the reddest shade of red ever.

Everyone was sat at the dining room table, and grace was said by Mary's father.

'How are you enjoying the secondary school, Amelia?' asked Mrs O'Farrell amid the passing and serving of food.

'I love it very much, Mrs O'Farrell, thank you,' replied Amelia, enthusiastically.

'Good, good,' said Mrs O'Farrell. 'Going to a new school is not always easy. What with new rules, new teachers, and new friends to make.'

Dr O'Farrell nodded in agreement.

'There's a lot more girls to get to know than at my last school,' said Amelia, and then added as an afterthought, 'and a lot more teachers too. Some of the teachers are quite nice though.'

The conversation about schools continued.

Shane talked a little about the boys' school he went to, and Colleen and Deirdre said they loved their playschool.

It was after the twins had been excused, and Mary and Shane were taking the dishes to the kitchen, that Mrs O'Farrell turned to Amelia.

'How's your mother, Amelia?' she asked.

At first Amelia didn't know what to say.

'She's in hospital at the moment,' replied Amelia, 'but she should be getting better soon.'

'Well, that's good,' said Mrs O'Farrell. 'It can't be easy not having your mother at home.'

'Aunty Bea looks after us when Mummy's away, and my daddy does too, when he can.' Amelia dropped her head. She stared at the table. She said nothing more.

Mrs O'Farrell came across and put her arm around Amelia.

'Now, don't you worry, darling,' reassured Mrs O'Farrell. 'I'm sure your mother will be home soon and everything will be alright.'

Amelia looked up. Her eyes held just the faintest trace of a tear.

'Mary tells me you are doing very well in school. She says you're top of the class,' complimented Mrs O'Farrell.

Amelia smiled.

'Why don't we go and help the others in the kitchen,' suggested Mrs O'Farrell, 'and then, perhaps, we can play a family game. Have you ever played scrabble?'

The game was raucous, everyone played.

Dr O'Farrell kept putting down, silly, rude words which had the twins in hysterics, and Mary dying from embarrassment.

Amelia laughed.

Mrs O'Farrell kept putting down long words that no one understood, and had to keep taking them back because they weren't in the dictionary.

But best of all, they had fun.

It had been a while since Amelia had enjoyed such family fun.

And also, Amelia won.

Jeremy: "With your mother's illness, you were increasingly drawn to your father as you grew up, and we see this most clearly through the bond you formed over the horses."

Amelia: "Yes, Jeremy, my mother used to say to us, jokingly: 'The two of you have a great bond over those old nags!' However, the reality was my father was very ambitious for me, and pushed me to compete and to win in everything I did, especially with the horses. I always wanted to impress him, and this was the perfect way to do so, but I think my mother felt left out, and that made me feel quite conflicted."

Naughty Tabitha

William had decided, after much pestering, to take Amelia to Úll Feirme Crann Equine Centre. It was close to Loch Garman and had been recommended by Kathleen Hanlon. Kathleen was such a help with the children.

William had enrolled Amelia on a two week course.

Each day, William would drive Amelia to the centre, and each day William would pick her up.

Amelia saw more of her father in those two weeks than she'd seen of him all year. She enjoyed the car journeys. Somehow, when she was travelling, she felt cocooned from the world, just her and her father. They didn't talk much, a smile or a glance, a passing word. Simply, she was happy.

On the first day, Amelia was greeted by Mr and Mrs Delaney. They owned and ran the equine centre, and had broadest of country smiles and the sort of conversation that made people feel instantly at ease. If ever there was a picture of two people born of the land, then it was of the Delaneys, standing by the five-bar gate to their yard, set against a backdrop of paddocks and fences, outbuildings and horses pulling at being led.

When the last of the students had arrived, Mrs Delaney opened the gate and gestured for the gathered children to follow. A short walk and they were in one of the outbuildings surrounded by the smell of horse riding and all of its paraphernalia. And it was here that Mrs Delaney introduced them to their riding instructor for the next two weeks, Mr Montforth.

Mr Montforth was a gentleman all the way from England and he spoke with the most refined accent that Amelia had ever heard. It was a voice that made her think she should bow and curtsy every time he entered the room. She wondered whether she address him as "My Lord" or "Your Highness" or some such like. But no, he said they were all to call him "Giles". Though, even his name had an aristocratic sound to it.

Giles explained that he was going to teach them to ride the English way, the proper way. A show of hands made it clear that few of the students had ridden before, and even fewer had heard of the "English way".

And so the day began. Giles described the basics of horse riding to the students, introducing them to the horses and the equipment, telling them about the do's and don'ts.

To make sure everyone was paying attention he would snap a question at a student when they least expected it. If the answer was right, praise would be given. If the answer was wrong, the student had to carry a bale of hay from one side of the yard to the other and back again. Often the student was no bigger than the bale, which caused much laughter if the student stumbled and fell. No one wanted to be laughed at, everyone paid attention.

Amelia was transfixed, she couldn't wait to ride. Her pony was called Tabitha, and she was beautiful. She seemed to have such a spirit about her, and her coat positively shone in the sunlight.

One by one the students were helped onto their horses. And as each got onto their saddle, Giles examined their posture, adjusting those who sat incorrectly.

'Posture, posture, posture!' exclaimed Giles as he walked among the students with a critical eye. 'One cannot expect to ride properly if one's posture is incorrect.'

He turned to Amelia and pointed at her with his riding crop. 'You, girl, what is your name?' he demanded.

'Amelia, sir...' she replied.

'Sir? I am not your father,' he retorted. 'Call me Giles, young Amelia.'

'Sorry, sir... I mean Giles,' stuttered Amelia in a flush of embarrassment.

'Amelia, have you ridden before?' he asked.

'No... Giles,' she stuttered.

'Are you sure?' he asked. 'Well, your posture is excellent. Your shoulders, hips and heels are in a straight, vertical line. You are sat true and square on your horse, leaning neither too far forward, nor too far backwards. Excellent, Amelia, well done,' you're a natural.'

Amelia fed off his praise.

'Students, look at Amelia,' instructed Giles. 'There is a lot you can learn. And pay particular attention to how she is holding her reins, she has a good set of hands.'

Everyone looked at Amelia. She beamed.

Within a few days, the students were rising to the trot with a degree of confidence. Amelia absolutely loved horse riding, and Giles had also told her father that she was a natural.

It turned out that Mrs Delaney was fantastic at baking. Irish scones were her speciality. They smelt wonderful, Amelia couldn't get enough of them, they were simply delicious.

The Delaneys had three sons who helped out around the equine centre. Andrew and Robert were much older, men really, but Peter was about Amelia's age. Peter didn't have his brothers' rugged good looks, and his teeth were much too big for his mouth, but he was always terribly nice and polite to Amelia.

William teased Amelia about Peter.

After several days, Giles said that it was time that they learnt to jump.

Wooden fence poles had been laid out on the ground and the students had to get their horses to step over them.

They led off in turn with Amelia following at the rear. Each horse did as requested without a problem until it came to Tabitha. Tabitha stopped and no amount of coercion was going to entice her to step over.

Everyone looked on, bemused, as Amelia tried her hardest to get the motionless Tabitha to cross. Eventually Peter came to Amelia's aid. He rested the reins from her and with the slightest of tugs, led Tabitha and Amelia over the poles.

There was a round of applause, and some stifled laughter, as Amelia rejoined the others. She sat upright on Tabitha, her arms crossed, struggling to see the funny side of things.

'Don't worry, Tabitha does it to everyone,' whispered Peter. 'She's got a mind of her own, she has. And if Tabitha decides she's not going to do something, then she's not going to do it.'

Amelia said nothing.

'Try her again,' suggested Peter.

Not to be outdone by the other students, and wanting to show who was in charge, Amelia turned Tabitha around, and set off at a trot back towards the poles.

'Amelia, slow...' urged Peter.

But it was too late.

Where Tabitha stopped, Amelia carried on, clearing the first pole and landing in a sprawled heap on the other side.

The sprawl did not move, there was silence. But then the sprawl stood up and began to dust herself down.

'Well done, Amelia. You've cleared your first fence, but I think you're supposed to take the horse with you,' called an anonymous voice from among the students.

Even Peter began to laugh as he checked Amelia over, though he soon stopped when he saw the look on her face.

Not to be defeated, Amelia squared up to Tabitha and made it clear that they were both going to clear the poles even if it took all day.

It was a battle of wills. Four more times Amelia rode Tabitha to the pole, and four more times Tabitha refused. But on the fifth time, and for no apparent reason, Tabitha stepped over the poles without any hesitation.

Amelia smiled and patted Tabitha's neck as the others applauded.

And as the days passed, and the course progressed, confidence built. Poles were turned into fences, and the students moved from the indoor school to the outdoor arena.

By the end of the second week, Giles had the students riding bareback.

'It is all about your legs,' he said, 'steering the pony with your legs.'

At the end of the course there was to be a gymkhana, to which all of the students' families and friends were invited.

Amelia's father was there to watch. Giles had told him that Amelia showed real promise as a rider.

So it came to the jumping, the climax of the day. Seven fences, and who could clear in the fastest time. Amelia rose to the challenge. She knew she could do it.

She and Tabitha rose and landed as one. First fence cleared, then second, third, and fourth in quick succession. They flew over the double, fences five and six, to line up for the last, the highest fence, the seventh.

Everyone had but one thought, 'Would Tabitha refuse?'

Amelia pushed Tabitha on. No pony was going to get the better of her.

And with effortless grace, pony and rider cleared the fence with a foot to spare, to win.

The rosettes were awarded by Mrs Delaney. She stood next to a wooden table in the yard upon which they were laid out in neat rows.

Mr Delaney made a short speech, well short for Mr Delaney, and thanked everyone, and hoped that everyone had enjoyed themselves and would come back again. He asked Giles to say a few words. And Giles, after a few pleasantries said it was all about, "Posture, darlings, posture".

'And the overall winner of today's gymkhana, is... Amelia!' announced Giles.

Amelia beamed as she was presented with her big red rosette. First prize!

William couldn't have been prouder. He hugged Amelia. He just wished that Audrey could have been here too.

As William got into the car, Mr Delaney caught him by the arm.

'You know, you've got some little girl there,' he said. 'In all my years, I've not seen anyone so determined to succeed. She's going to do great things in life, William, mark my words.'

Jeremy: "As I read on from here, it struck me your father really had a cross to bear. How did he cope?"

Amelia: "As I said earlier, I just don't know how he coped, Jeremy, but he did, and he found comfort, like so many others, 'in the bottle'. I don't blame him, but it was so hard at the time and for years afterwards."

Decisions

In William's eyes, Amelia was now old enough to look after herself. He had decided she would stay at home. But Aisling, like Alex, was to go away to boarding school. That's what would be best for her. William could see that Aisling was finding it hard to cope at the local secondary school with what was happening at home. Her grades had slipped, and more and more frequently William was being called in to discuss her errant behaviour.

He didn't know what else to do. Audrey's mental health just seemed to worsen with time. And he didn't believe that postnatal depression could last for so many years.

Typically, after Audrey had been hospitalised for several months, the medical staff would manage to stabilise her condition. Her mood swings would lessen, the delusions would abate, she'd reconnect with the world around her. She would smile like her old self. And then she would come home, and for a while it would be happy families.

But then Audrey would stop taking her medication, she would decide that everything was fine and that she didn't need it. Then they would argue. He would drink. Amelia and Aisling would hide in their rooms, afraid.

It wouldn't take long for the illness to return, almost unnoticed to begin with. But something would happen, something always happened.

The problems at work didn't help either. How could half the livestock be stolen from Ballycapple Farm in one night and no one notice? Truth be known, he knew who and how, and he was sure that everyone else knew who and how, but no one was going to say or do anything.

William closed his eyes, and took another drink, trying to work his thoughts out.

He worried what Audrey might do next. The last time had been bad enough, he was sure everyone knew about it, but were too polite to say.

And Aunty Bea wasn't as young as she used to be. It was too much to ask for her to look after the children.

No, sending Aisling to boarding school was the best and only solution.

He was sure that Amelia would be all right. Her grades were good, unlike Aisling's. Anyway, ever since he'd bought Tabitha from the Delaneys, Amelia spent most of her spare time out at the farm with the pony, brushing her, talking to her, preparing her for the next competition. That was good, it took her mind off things, gave her something to concentrate on.

William poured another drink. That was how it was going to have to be.

Jeremy: "So, as a young teenager, I don't know how you coped with your siblings being away at boarding school, your mother ill, and your father drinking."
Amelia: "Well, Jeremy, I felt so lonely, but I had faith that I would overcome the situation somehow. I knew it would be alright in the end, and that has been the same throughout my whole life. I think my father gave me a huge sense of self-belief. And of course, don't forget I had my horses!"

Schooled

Amelia had decided that she was going to be successful in her life, and she was going to do it by herself. She was going to study hard and become a doctor. No one was going to stop her. Her thoughts had become clear, singular. It was as if she had awoken suddenly from her childhood. Everything seemed that much sharper, in focus, that much more real.

Amelia looked around the classroom.

Sat about her were Mary O'Farrell, Sara Jane Walsh, Edith O'Carroll, Susan Duffy and Christy Sheehan. They were all doctors' daughters. They were all clever and admired and confident, popular. Amelia couldn't help but feel envious, a little jealous. She knew she shouldn't, but she did.

Well, anyway, Amelia's mind was set, she was going to work hard and get one hundred percent in all of her exams and be top of the class, doctors' daughters or not. And she was going to be the best horse rider in the county, if not the country. She and Tabitha were going to win every competition.

Amelia knew that she had to stand by herself, what with Aisling and Alex off at boarding school, her mother sick, and her father spending more and more time away on business.

'Amelia Allen!'

Amelia blinked and looked up.

'Yes, Sister.' She smiled at the nun. She had learnt that if she smiled sweetly she was less likely to get a beating. She hated the beatings, she felt so ashamed and dirty.

'Pay attention,' barked the Sister.

'Yes, Sister, sorry Sister,' apologised Amelia. 'I was just thinking that I want to become a doctor.'

'Pardon?' queried the Sister.

'I've decided that I want to do medicine at university and become a doctor,' pronounced Amelia.

'Indeed,' said the Sister. 'Well, Amelia Allen, if you're going to become a doctor, you'll need to pay better attention in class. Of that you can be sure.'

Amelia could hear the silent gasps of her classmates. She could sense them staring at her, not directly, just a glance here and there, for no one else wanted to get caught not paying attention.

Amelia looked straight ahead, directly at the blackboard, eyes wide open, listening. With new focus, she knew she must not let her thoughts wander again in class or she would be in trouble and, more importantly, she wouldn't be able to become a doctor. Her pencil scratched the words the nun spoke into her notebook.

After lunch, in the playground, Sara Jane looked furtively about and then grabbed Amelia's arm.

'You were lucky to get away with that in class, Amelia Allen.' Sara Jane always used Amelia's full name when she thought Amelia had been in the wrong. 'You know it's what the nuns live for, any chance to catch you out, and "whack you" with the ruler.'

Sara Jane slapped Amelia's wrist, hard.

'Ow! What did you do that for?' asked Amelia.

'If you want to be a doctor you should pay more attention in class!' teased Sara Jane. 'Not that you've got any chance of becoming a doctor anyway.'

Sara Jane laughed as she backed away.

Amelia rubbed her wrist. She wasn't going to let Sara Jane get away with that, no way, even if she was her best friend, and chased after her.

'How you expect to become a doctor when neither of your parents are doctors, I do not know,' provoked Sara Jane as she turned and ran.

'Why you...' Amelia gave chase, dodging in and out of the playground's clustered groups of children.

'You need to pay attention more, Doctor Amelia Allen,' taunted Sara Jane, backpedalling fast.

'Don't you worry I will,' Amelia promised herself. 'Just you wait and see who's going to be top of the class.'

Jeremy: "Did you really think you found refuge in the horses?"
<Amelia smiles>

Riding

Spring had come, and Amelia was getting ready for her first major competition. Her father had turned over a few acres of Ballycapple Farm for her and Tabitha to use to practice. He had even had some multi-coloured fences built and painted from wooden poles and barrels.

The Delaneys had said that Tabitha would perform better with blinkers, she would be less distracted in the competition arena. So, today, Amelia was trying them out on Tabitha.

Her father had taken time off to come and watch. He stood across the field and waved. Amelia turned, looked down, and pushed Tabitha on. In an instant Tabitha's reluctance to move had been transformed as she surged across the ground, beating an ever faster pace.

Amelia's hair was tousled by the wind, her eyes watered, but in a bound Tabitha had cleared the first barrel. She patted Tabitha on the shoulder.

'Good girl, good girl,' encouraged Amelia, and then looked across at her father who cupped his hands and shouted.

'Try the double barrels, Amelia, the double barrels.' He then waved his arms towards them, urging Amelia on.

Amelia's heart pounded, she had never jumped a fence so high before.

'Daddy, why so high?' she called.

'Hush, just do it, don't think about it, Amelia,' her father urged. 'Drive Tabitha on, go on kick her, get her over it. Go on now, don't hesitate!'

Amelia obeyed, and away she and Tabitha went, full on towards the double barrels, but at the last second Tabitha dived to one side and Amelia went straight over her mane, crashing down.

Amelia screamed.

Amelia couldn't see. Tabitha had kicked her in the face as she had escaped down to the back end of the field.

Amelia lay still.

William ran over and pulled his daughter to him, wrapping her in his strong arms. Her face was bleeding. He took his handkerchief out of the inside pocket of his jacket. It fluttered in the breeze.

Amelia choked a little in the wash of tears and blood. She was in shock.

'There, you'll be fine. Just a cut and a few bruises,' he reassured as he wiped his daughter's face. 'Don't you worry now.'

William stood. Tabitha had returned to the site of the fall and was grazing without a care. William reached out and grabbed the reins. He then pulled Amelia up and handed them to her.

'Up you get,' he ordered. 'Get right back on that horse and jump that fence now.'

Amelia was in utter disbelief.

'After a fall always get straight back up on your horse,' he said.

And so Amelia did.

She turned Tabitha around twice, pulled her up and then drove her forward.

Stride followed stride, and then in a moment, horse and rider cleared the double barrels with air to spare.

William looked on.

'You know,' he said to himself, 'old Niall Delaney was right, I've sure got some little girl here!'

And then he called across to her.

'No jump is too high for you in this world, Amelia.'

<Jeremy waits for Amelia to open up>
Amelia: "Jeremy, for me the horses started out as my escape and comfort, and for the most part were a refuge. But as time passed, through my father's blind determination for me to succeed, they became a source of conflict. I felt so stressed, at times I couldn't even eat."

Head First

Amelia made sure to mark off each day on the kitchen calendar in the run-up to the competition. The event was to be held near Claremorris, west of the Shannon, fully the other side of the country. It would mean leaving on the Friday, straight after school, and staying over on the Friday night to be ready for the competition on the Saturday.

On that Friday morning, Amelia had a long chat with Tabitha while she was grooming her. Tabitha sparkled from head to toe

Amelia pressed her mouth to Tabitha's ear.

'Please, Tabitha, please, please, please, jump the fences,' she implored. 'My daddy is bringing me so far away, he really wants me to win. But if you refuse he'll be mad, then I'll get into trouble, so please can you, you know, jump the fences for me.'

Amelia dashed home from school.

Outside, on the drive, Tabitha was loaded in the horse box trailer, and the trailer was hitched to her father's white Peugeot 504. But where was her father?

Amelia went inside the house. There were raised voices coming from the kitchen.

'You can't be serious!' pleaded her mother. 'Surely you're not taking that child to Claremorris at this time of night. You won't get there until midnight. This horse riding business has been become an obsession for both of you.'

'I told you about this two weeks ago, Audrey,' explained William.

'So you say,' questioned Audrey.

'I did,' defended William.

There was silence for a moment and then Amelia could hear stamping and clattering from behind the kitchen door.

'No one tells me anything around here,' stated Audrey. 'You never involve me. You all talk about me behind my back.'

Amelia could tell that her mother was starting to get really frustrated.

'That's not true, Audrey. You know it's not true,' said William.

'Oh, yes it is!' she exclaimed.

'Come on, Audrey. Pull yourself together,' encouraged William. 'Please pull yourself together.'

There was a crash as something hit the floor.

'You've always been the same, keeping things from me. I know all about your little secrets,' accused Audrey.

'What secrets?' asked William, bewildered.

'Don't pretend you don't know,' insisted Audrey.

For a while there was a pause in the argument.

'Can't you see, Audrey, it's not you who's talking, it's the illness,' said William.

'What illness?' said Audrey. 'You've all just made that up to deceive me, to cover up your secrets.'

'Look, clam down, Audrey,' said William. 'I promised I'd take her. She's really been looking forward to this weekend.'

Audrey said nothing.

'Audrey, Amelia will be home any minute, so let's stop arguing,' suggested William.

At which, Amelia decided to push open the kitchen door.

Her mother stood with her back to her father, staring out into the garden. There was a pan lying in the middle of the floor.

'Amelia.' Her father looked at her, directly. 'Why don't you go and get changed and get your stuff. Could you just give your mother and I a moment. Could you, love, eh?'

'OK, Daddy. I'll see you outside, by the car,' said Amelia.

Amelia turned and closed the kitchen door behind her.

Audrey's face was as stone, her eyes lost in some distant place. Her body frozen, vacated. No tears escaped those eyes. No words passed her lips, only the shallowness of her breath.

William walked to her, and put his arms around her, to find her, to be with her.

They stood together, separated, William trying to hold on, forever.

William closed his eyes.

'Now listen, Audrey, I've got to go, otherwise we'll never get there. Do you want me to get someone to be with you?' he asked.

William waited for a response.

'Audrey, can you hear me? I've got to go,' he said again.

No response.

'Audrey?'

With the slightest flicker of her eyes, Audrey turned.

'William?' she said.

'Audrey, I've got to go. I've got to take Amelia to Claremorris for the horse riding competition.'

'Now?' she queried.

'Yes, now,' said William. 'Will you be alright?'

'Of course I'll be alright,' said Audrey. 'I'm fine. Why do you ask?'

William said nothing, and reached for his car keys on the hall table next to the red carnations he liked to give Audrey.

Audrey smiled.

'Have a lovely time,' she said.

William held his breath, and then sighed.

'We'll try. See you on Sunday. Love you, bye.'

And them William kissed her tenderly.

Outside, and Amelia was already sat in the car.

William leant down and opened the door.

'Amelia, you'd better go inside and say goodbye to your mother,' he said. 'Then we'll leave.'

William got into the car, closing the door. He checked for neutral, put the key in the ignition and turned it. And as the engine started he held the steering wheel in his hands. He waited.

Amelia reappeared, followed by Audrey.

Amelia sat back in the car.

'Did you say goodbye to your mother?' asked William.

'Yes,' replied Amelia.

William depressed the clutch, and put the car into gear. The engine note rose as he gently pushed down on the accelerator pedal. The car began to move.

'Bye, bye.' Amelia waved to her mother.

Audrey waved back from a distance.

William looked both ways as the car and trailer pulled out of the drive.

And as they turned up the road he could see Audrey standing in the front doorway, her arm raised, blowing kisses from the palm of her hand.

'Love you, Mummy,' shouted Amelia, craning out of the passenger window.

Audrey disappeared from view, and Amelia closed her window.

'OK, love?' asked William.

'OK, Daddy,' replied Amelia.

It took seven hours and many stops on the way, but by midnight, William, Amelia and Tabitha pulled into the bed and breakfast. It had been a journey where not much was said, but, perhaps a lot was understood.

Their late arrival caused much commotion. Almost the whole household had been awoken.

Tabitha had to be stabled, never an easy task in the middle of the night. But, with patience, Tabitha settled and all went to bed.

Amelia awoke to the homely smell of a cooked breakfast, though she wasn't sure she could eat it, she felt so nervous, so sick to her core. Food wasn't going to be of help today.

She sat next to her father at the breakfast table and picked at her plate.

'Eat up, Amelia,' said William. 'It'll do you the world of good. It'll give you the strength to get over those fences and be able to make that pony jump. She's got a great old pop in her, you know.'

Amelia smiled on the outside.

Tabitha gleamed in the sun, her coat brushed to perfection, though getting her to the arena hadn't been without incident. She was tired, she was cranky, and she'd tried to take a bite out of Amelia.

Amelia stood by her, as smart as she could be, holding her reins. They made quite a picture.

It was a massive show jumping event, much bigger than anything Amelia had been to before. The grass seemed a little overgrown, and the fences seemed huge. She had walked the ground with her father. He had been full of advice. "Come up at this angle... And kick her here... And if she doesn't go, give her a little bit of the whip... And get over that fence now, come on", he'd said.

Amelia was a bundle of nerves.

Her turn came.

She went to the start.

A nod from the official and she did a lap of the arena.

The bell went.

She prayed for a nice clear round.

Up came the first fence, a little cross with a bar behind it.

She whispered to Tabitha.

'Please jump over the fence, Tabitha, please jump.'

But in a juddering halt Tabitha's head went down, and Amelia tumbled to the ground.

In the silence of embarrassment, Amelia picked herself up and gathered Tabitha's reins. She pulled Tabitha, and walked across to approach the fence again. She looked to the crowd and she could see her father.

'Come on, get on that pony, and kick her, and...' he shouted, exasperated.

Amelia didn't hear the rest of what he said, his voice was lost in the wind that blew.

She remounted.

The bell rang again.

Up to the first fence again.

'Come on Tabitha, don't let me down.'

Again Tabitha dug her heels in.

Again Amelia flew over her head.

Tabitha started to run off, Amelia chased after her.

'For God's sake, can you not even jump the first fence,' shouted William. 'Get that pony over the bloody first fence, we've driven all this way.'

Amelia was mortified, she was going to be in so much trouble.

Tabitha had stopped running.

Amelia stretched up to Tabitha's ear.

'Tabitha, last chance now.'

For a third time the bell rang.

And for a third time Amelia rode Tabitha to the fence.

But Tabitha was clear about what Tabitha wanted to do.

This time Amelia managed to hang on as Tabitha pulled up and then darted to one side away from the fence.

'Miss Allen, three refusals, you're eliminated,' said the voice over the tannoy. 'Please take your pony out of the arena.'

Amelia streamed tears.

Her father clasped Tabitha's reins.

'What are you crying about now?' he yelled with exasperation. 'You couldn't ride a donkey.'

'I'm so sorry, Daddy. I'm so sorry.'

William said nothing more.

Jeremy: "So much seemed to happen in your life, and at times with unbelievable speed. But I'm still not sure what Amelia was really thinking and feeling."

Amelia: "Yes Jeremy, I suppose you could say that. Perhaps my emotions don't come across in the prose. But let me tell you, on the outside I was a normal young girl, but on the inside I was so fractured and I just couldn't bring the pieces of me together, so I fell apart."

Leaves Fall

For Amelia the joy of horse riding came with the time she would spend at Ballycapple Farm, just her and Tabitha. She would talk to her pony and her pony did not judge her, or scold her. Her pony loved her, and she loved her pony. Perfect harmony.

When she could, Amelia would ride Tabitha from the farm way out to the beach. Ten, fifteen, twenty miles at a time, through woods, across fields, galloping onto the sand, going up into the dunes. This world was alive, fun, carefree.

But what Amelia enjoyed most was just being with Tabitha. Often she would ride out to her favourite oak tree and lie beneath the leaves to read her book, to dream. These were the best times.

Of course Amelia enjoyed the competitions too, though it sometimes seemed that it was her father who wanted to win them more than she. He got so wound up by it all, one moment full of praise, the next, shouting and angry. It was if his whole world revolved around show jumping.

At events her father would frequently disappear for hours on end, talking to this person, chatting to that person. And more often than not, Mrs Hanlon would be there.

Amelia had noticed that her father always had a smile for Mrs Hanlon and she for him. It was, "Oh William, it's so lovely to see you...", or, "Fancy meeting you here...", or, "Kathleen, you look delightful..." and so on.

Amelia did like Mrs Hanlon. She was kind and helpful. She seemed to know everybody in the horse world and was always a good person to turn to for advice. And Amelia was sure that Mrs Hanlon liked her. In fact Mrs Hanlon was forever giving her presents.

One time, she'd given Amelia a beautiful handmade cuckoo clock. Amelia loved it, she'd put it up on a shelf in her bedroom and used to look at it, waiting for the little figures to come out when the time was right.

Though, Amelia wasn't sure that her mother liked Mrs Hanlon. On the rare occasions they met, pleasantries were short and her mother always had a reason to be going somewhere else. Amelia had even caught her mother arguing with her father about Mrs Hanlon.

Her mother had called Mrs Hanlon, "That Woman", and had wanted to know what her father had been up to. He'd said, "Nothing, don't be so paranoid". And that started a whole raging row. Amelia had hidden in her room. She just wanted it all to stop.

Amelia's mother never came to her horse riding events. It was her and her father's thing. Amelia would have liked her mother to come. It would have made her very happy to see her parents together, just like they used to be, devoted, in love. But Amelia had noticed that her mother rarely left the house these days, except to go to stay at the hospital.

And as the seasons passed on to each other, and school terms ended, Amelia withdrew more and more into her horse world.

In the past, she'd always been popular at school. She'd helped other children with their homework, but now her friends were more interested in socialising. Amelia's father wasn't keen on her socialising. Perhaps it was because of the things he'd seen, or because he wanted to protect her, or maybe he wanted to keep her just the way she was, his little girl. Whatever the reason, Amelia was not extended the same freedoms that her friends were. In fact Amelia's father took things even further. He was always checking the books she read. He didn't want his little girl corrupted. Compared to her friends, Amelia became left behind, naïve.

When Amelia wasn't with her pony, she fell into the leaves of her school books. Her desire to be a doctor led her to become the top student in her year, the top student in her school, destined to be head girl. She was so far in advance academically that she skipped a year, alienating her further from her classmates.

Her friends talked to her less and less. They gave up inviting her to parties, her father never let her go anyway. Amelia worried. She struggled to understand what was happening. She began to think it might be because she was too fat. She progressively ate less and less, and was very careful to keep her diet secret.

But then, as her weight started to tumble down, so did her life.

Ounce by ounce it fell, pound by pound until she was no more than skin and bones. At less than five stone, her hair started to fall out, she became weak.

She gave up riding. She couldn't ride, she didn't have the strength.

William couldn't believe his eyes. What had happened to his little girl? One moment healthy, full of life, the next... He could hardly bring himself to look at her.

He took Amelia to the doctor's, but nothing would work.

Her school had suggested that perhaps she should leave, she was having a bad impact, she was a poor role model.

Amelia had become histrionic.

William was confused.
William was distraught.
William was angry.
William lost his temper.
'You stupid child, what have you done?' he shouted.
Amelia looked scared, even her father didn't want to know her.
She began to cry.
'That's right cry, as if that'll make things better,' he scolded.
Amelia felt cornered.
She had stopped crying, her breathing was still erratic.
The last of the tears rolled down her sallow cheeks.
The tears kissed her lips.
William shook his head and started to walk away.
But as William went to leave the room, he turned.
'You know, you've become so ugly,' he said, 'no man will ever want you looking the way you are. You're a disgrace!'
'But Daddy...'
He slammed the door in frustration and was gone. He had had enough.
Amelia was lost.
She felt like she was the loneliest girl in the world.

A Way

"Sometimes there is a choice to be made, a choice that only you can make, others can't do it for you. Others might suggest a choice to you, they might try and tell you, shout at you, demand that you..." Amelia thought through these words the doctor had said to her. They played on her mind.

She hadn't seen her father for the last few days. Aunty Bea said that he had been called away on urgent business.

Her mother had taken to her bed, curtains drawn.

Earlier, after finishing the housework, Amelia had taken her a cup of tea. But now the tea sat cold on the bedside table, untouched. Her mother slept.

Amelia closed the bedroom door as quietly as she could.

She walked across the hall.

She stood in the bathroom.

She tried to not look in the mirror.

Amelia couldn't bare to see what she had done to herself.

She wanted to be loved.

How she hated her father.

How she loved her father.

She felt like she should scream and rage, but only silence came.

She felt like she should weep, but she had no more tears to cry.

And then, in a glance, she saw her reflection in the mirror.

Caught in her own gaze Amelia stared right back.

She decided to face up to what she had become.

If she was going to be the doctor she wished, she needed to overcome her anxieties.

Amelia baked a cake.

Cooking, and particularly baking, was something she'd always enjoyed, that is until recently. Over the years Aunty Bea had taught her this and that. Amelia had even gone to cookery classes with her mother, though that was sometime ago, before her mother had become ill again.

It was a simple sponge. She'd spread jam between the two halves. It was still warm.

She cut two slices and put them on plates on a tray. She made some fresh tea, and poured two cups. And with the tray laden, she climbed the stairs and pushed open her mother's bedroom door.

'Mummy, Mummy are you awake?' she asked. 'I've made some cake and a cup of tea.'

Her mother stirred, and with a little effort managed to sit up.

'Amelia?'

'Yes Mummy, it's me. I've made some tea and cake. Would you like a piece?'

'Pull the curtains, dear. Let me see.'

Amelia put the tray down on the end of the bed and opened the curtains.

Her mother sat up and blinked in the light.

'The cake looks lovely,' she said. 'It smells delicious.'

Amelia handed her mother a plate, and replaced the cold tea on the bedside table with fresh.

Her mother took a bite.

'This is wonderful, Amelia. Are you going to have some too?'

Amelia paused, and then she lifted her plate.

Her mother smiled.

Amelia ate some cake.

In fact, Amelia finished a whole slice of cake.

Jeremy: "Amelia, after you recovered from anorexia, I see you began to do the things that normal teenagers do."
Amelia: "Indeed, we all make our mistakes and have to learn our lessons, Jeremy!"
<Amelia smiles>

Smoke Lesson

Aisling was home from school and didn't Amelia know it. Amelia had to almost double- take when she saw how much Aisling had changed. No longer that quiet, awkward child. Now she was a young lady with a refined accent and a demeanour to match. She expected to be waited on hand and foot, "Amelia, be a dear, and fetch me a cup of tea", "Oh Amelia, I am sure you will not mind, I have left my laundry for you in the wash basket. If I could have it for tomorrow".

How Aisling played up to their father, with airs and graces, dropping names every chance she could get. Telling him tales of the well-to-do of Dublin. Aisling had the inside track, often the tales were tales that the well-to-do would not want to be told. Their father lapped it up. Nothing was too much trouble for his darling daughter Aisling. "Butter wouldn't melt" seemed to be the easiest way for Amelia to describe her sister.

But then one day, as Amelia made to leave the house, she couldn't believe what she saw. Aisling was there in the porch, her hand in their father's jacket pocket taking a cigarette from his packet.

Aisling looked up to see Amelia staring straight at her. It was too late to put the cigarette back, so she smiled nonchalantly at Amelia, and began to walk away.

'Not so fast, Aisling,' said Amelia. 'What do you think you're doing?'

'Going out for a moment,' replied Aisling.

'Does Daddy know you've taken one of his cigarettes?' inquired Amelia.

'Why do you want to know?' responded Aisling. 'Are you going to tell him?' Amelia thought for a moment. She wasn't going to tell their father.

'I didn't know you smoked,' she said. 'Aren't you a little young?'

'There's a lot you don't know about what I do,' replied Aisling with a sliver of a smile.

'Like what?' asked Amelia.

'Now that would be telling,' replied Aisling as she turned and walked back into the house.

Amelia stood and looked at her father's jacket.

Perhaps it was time to stop trying to be so good. She'd never smoked a cigarette, even though most of her friends had. No, she shouldn't, but then why not? Wasn't this what being a teenager was all about, a little rebellion.

Amelia had decided. She got a box of matches from the kitchen, put on her coat, and went for a walk.

She reached the end of her road and thought it would be best to head away from town. So she turned right.

When she was sure that no one could see, Amelia put the cigarette in her mouth, struck the match against the side of the matchbox, and held the flame to the end of the cigarette. The flame burnt and she sucked in.

The smoke rasped her throat. She couldn't breathe. She thought she was going to choke. She coughed and coughed.

Amelia thought she heard something.

Oh no, it was her father's car. She could recognise the noise of the engine anywhere.

He was the only person she knew who had a diesel car.

Amelia looked about. There was no where to hide.

Without a thought she hid the cigarette in her pocket, and tried to fan the smoke away.

The engine got louder and louder, the car drew closer and closer.

'If he passes me, I'll wave,' thought Amelia.

She kept on walking, there was smoke. It was coming from her pocket. The cigarette was still alight. She was on fire!

Amelia tried to pat it out, but it just fanned the flames. Smoke billowed out.

Amelia could hear the sound of the car's tyres rolling along the road, the tapping of the engine. She daren't look.

The car slowed.

Her father drew alongside.

'Are you alright there, Amelia. You seem to be on fire,' he commented.

Amelia stopped, and turned towards the car.

'By the way, Amelia,' he added. 'A word to the wise, most people put the cigarette in their mouth if they want to smoke it.'

And then he laughed, heartily.

Amelia could still hear him laughing as his car pulled away up the street.

She had never felt so stupid as she stared at the blackened hole in her jacket pocket.

Jeremy: "Oh, before I forget, I have something here for you, Amelia."
<Jeremy reaches underneath the table and presents Amelia with a slice of cake>
<Amelia opens her eyes wide>
Amelia: "Yum! Jeremy you see, even you know I like cake! My love of cake is ironic isn't it?"

Adam's Cake

Things had got better, much better. Though her father was away a lot, her mother had just returned from hospital. She was her old self, for the time being anyway. And Amelia was doing well. She was eating again. And despite Sara Jane's relentless jibes, her grades at school were just what she needed to apply for medicine. And, to top it all, Alex was home.

To celebrate, Amelia decided to bake a cake. She loved to bake. It was a joy, a rediscovered passion. It had helped her put weight back on. It had helped her rebuild relationships. And the smell. There was something about the smell that brought a homeliness back to the house. It evoked feelings of tradition, of family. It drew people together. Cake brought smiles.

By common consensus Amelia's lemon cake was her best, though her orange cake was something to be admired and tasted too. Amelia would turn the cake upside down, puncture it many times with a fork, and squeeze the juice from oranges into it. The juice would soak all the way down. It smelt wonderful, and tasted even better.

Amelia's cakes were certainly popular with her brother. Whenever he came home from boarding school, Amelia would bake him a cake to take back. It didn't take long for Amelia and her cakes to gain a reputation at Alex's school. Everyone wanted a slice.

Alex stood in the kitchen, plate in hand, cake in mouth.

'Mmm... This is truly delicious, Amelia,' he praised. 'You've outdone yourself, again.'

'Why thank you, Alex.' Amelia loved having Alex home. It was just like old times, when they were little children.

'Do know who would also like a slice of this cake?' asked Alex.

'No,' replied Amelia.

'Adam. He loves your cakes, Amelia, he can't get enough of them.' Alex took another bite, catching the crumbs with his plate. 'He particularly likes the orange cake, it's his favourite.'

'Really!' exclaimed Amelia.

'In fact, he asked me to ask you if you would bake him a cake,' said Alex.

'A cake for Adam? Not an extra cake for Alex then?' quizzed Amelia.

'No, he pleaded with me to ask you,' said Alex. 'He was literally on his knees begging.'

'I don't think I've even met this Adam,' responded Amelia.

'Oh, he's a great guy you'd like him,' described Alex. 'He's in the year above me, we row together for our house. In fact he's about the same age as you. Tall, good looking, blue eyes. All the girls are after him.'

Alex took another bite of the cake.

'After him you say,? questioned Amelia.

'Yes, they say he's a fine thing,' added Alex with a glint of mischief in his eye. 'You know, Amelia. He said to me that if you're half as beautiful as you bake, he wants to marry you! All I could say was that, though you were my sister, you were the most beautiful girl in all of Ireland.'

Amelia blushed with shyness. The subject of boys, let alone marriage proposals, was something she had no experience of.

The kitchen door opened. Their mother walked in.

'Who's the most beautiful girl in all of Ireland?' she inquired.

Alex coughed, and tried to ignore the question, but Audrey stood waiting for an answer.

'Amelia.' Alex squirmed.

Amelia had to laugh.

'Well that's very nice of you to say that about your sister, Alex,' commented Audrey. 'Though I don't know why she should find it so funny.'

'Mummy,' said Amelia. 'Alex is trying to marry me off.'

'Is he now.' Audrey was intrigued.

'Apparently, Adam, his school friend, likes my orange cake so much that he said he will marry me if I bake him a cake,' declared Amelia.

'You know what I would do, Amelia?' proposed Audrey.

'No,' said Amelia.

'If I were you I'd bake him a cake, but on one condition,' suggested Audrey.

'What's that?' replied Amelia, a little hesitant.

'That he takes you to your graduation ball at the school,' counselled Audrey, 'he gets the cake, and you get someone to take you to your ball.'

'But I don't even know Adam,' protested Amelia, both horrified and intrigued with the prospect.

'I'm sure he's very nice, after all he's very complimentary about your orange cake,' said Audrey. 'Alex, you wouldn't be having your sister on now, would you?'

'Oh no, Mummy,' replied Alex. 'Adam is positively infatuated with Amelia... Well with her cakes, anyway, I'm sure he'll like her when he meets her and takes her to her grad.'

It was Alex's turn to smile.

'That's that then,' concluded Audrey. 'Get baking Amelia, you've a young man to impress!'

Amelia was open-mouthed.

And so it came to pass that Amelia's orange cake was called "Adam's Cake".

When presented with the proposal, Adam was absolutely delighted and said that it would be his honour to take Amelia to her graduation ball.

So Adam had his cake and ate it!

Jeremy: "You have told us that while you yourself suffered pain growing up, every now and then we see examples when you were manipulative and hurtful to your own family and friends, and that honesty jarred me."
Amelia: "I feel guilty about being that way. But isn't it telling how teenagers can behave with loved ones, depending on how they are feeling inside themselves."

Telling Sara Jane

With the graduation ball, school had ended. It was a strange feeling. One day Amelia was a child, well a teenager, and was going to school, the next day she was not. No more teachers, no more lessons, no more exams. Well no more for the time being.

She had no doubt that when she got into medical school there would be no end of lectures, but for the moment it was nice to pretend that there would be no more schooling.

In the meantime, Amelia had got a part-time job in the local fish and chip shop to earn a little extra money. Amelia had never had a job before, she'd always been too busy studying, or riding her horse, or helping out about the house. It felt good. She felt she'd grown up, she was an adult, she had a job and she had her own money.

And best of all, her father could hardly disapprove, even though she knew that he wanted to. How could he? Amelia was choosing to work, taking some responsibility, earning a little money, contributing, while all of her friends were either idling around at home or off having a great time at their parents' expense.

Amelia felt happy.

And each day Amelia would wait for the post to arrive. She would hurry to the doormat after the letter box had clattered and check the mail. She was waiting for the letter of confirmation from the medical school.

Days formed into weeks, and weeks settled by.

She had grown used to her routine so much that she almost missed the letter when it arrived, and placed it, by mistake, onto her parents' pile of correspondence on the hallway dresser. As she made to leave for work, she noticed the Dublin postmark and underneath, "Miss A. Allen..."

Amelia held the letter. She knew whom it was from, indeed she was certain what it would say.

She opened it.

And there it was in typed text. She had been offered a place at the Royal College of Surgeons in Dublin, a prestigious medical school where all the doctors' sons and daughters would go. She'd already received her examination results some weeks before. She'd come fifth in the entrance exam. Fifth out of hundreds of applicants from all over Ireland and beyond. But this confirmation, this piece of paper, was what she'd been waiting for.

'Right,' Amelia said to herself.

She grabbed her coat, checked she had keys, and got into her mother's car.

There was only one place she was going.

The thought of all the times that Sara Jane had taunted her about not being able to go to Surgeons, because her mum and dad were not doctors, just kept playing over and over in her mind.

And she thought about the exclusion she'd felt, not being a doctor's daughter. Well, she could be a doctor now, and she could go to Surgeons.

Amelia arrived at Sara Jane's house, and with the piece of paper clutched in her hand knocked on the door.

'Hi, Amelia,' said Sara Jane.

'Look, Sara Jane, look,' said Amelia.

Amelia thrust the piece of paper in front of Sara Jane.

'I got in, I got into Surgeons,' she said.

And then, at that moment, the moment of Sara Jane's realisation, Amelia saw her closest friend as she truly was, humble, fragile, almost broken.

'Congratulations, Amelia,' said Sara Jane, 'you really deserve it.'

In the silence that followed, Amelia knew that she'd taken out the cruellest of revenge on Sara Jane. For Amelia had known that Sara Jane hadn't got into any medical school, let alone Surgeons.

How Amelia regretted what she had done.

YOUNG ADULT

Jeremy: "You must have been so relieved when you finally left home and went to medical school."

Amelia: "No Jeremy, not at all. You see part of my coping mechanism was to set myself goals to achieve and to get on with life. I wasn't feeling relieved to be leaving home, I was more looking forward to the adventure of starting medical school. I couldn't wait until the end of the summer."

The End of Summer

It was the end of summer, and Amelia had a boyfriend. It was something of a surprise to everyone, not least Amelia. Though a year younger, Donal Cormack was in all ways much more worldly wise. Tall, muscularly handsome, and from a good family, Donal had asked Amelia out after Mass.

The families had known each other over the years. And while Amelia's father was uncomfortable with the thought that his daughter had a boyfriend, there was little that he could object to. Though he did make it clear to Donal, in a private, one-to-one conversation, that his daughter's honour was sacrosanct.

Amelia and Donal played tennis, occasionally went for walks or cycled, and would frequently go to the cinema. He liked to watch action films, particularly the ones with Sylvester Stallone in them, of which there appeared to be a great many.

Donal's conversation was always polite, but short. For Donal, words were to be used sparingly, only when necessary. His true passion was rugby. When not playing, he was training, and when he was not training, he was watching rugby. Rugby was all.

Alex called him Rambo.

Amelia told Alex not to, but Alex persisted, and soon everyone called Donal, Rambo, though not to his face. Amelia knew that she shouldn't find it funny, but she did.

September, and the day she had been waiting for came, Amelia's first day at medical school.

The day before, her father had driven her and her belongings to the all girl hall of residence. Little had been said in the car, her father seemed to have other things on his mind. Her mother had waved her off from the house, in the shadow of the front porch. It was as if no one knew what to say other than, "Goodbye", "Good luck", "Don't forget to call".

After her father had left, Amelia had sat in her room, surrounded by all that she'd brought from home. She'd felt a surge of release. It was as if her whole being had become unburdened. It was just Amelia now, her choices, her future.

Amelia went to all her classes, all her practicals, and all her tutorials. The library became her second home. Amelia did what Amelia did best, she studied.

In many ways, university life came easily to her. She knew she was there to work, and she was ambitious to become a doctor. She found living in a hall of residence straightforward compared to her often solitary, disjointed existence back in Loch Garman. She did miss family life, but she'd missed family life at home too.

Amelia made friends quickly, but she did not get too involved. And though the temptation was always there, she did not go out partying, or drinking.

From time to time she would return home. Everyone was always pleased to see her. Occasionally she'd meet up with Donal, when he wasn't playing rugby. He was in his last year of school and planned to go straight into the Army.

Strangely enough, Amelia's best friend at university was a girl she'd known for almost all her life, a girl from Loch Garman. In the past, Amelia had never really got on with Sinead O'Keefe. They were opposites and their paths had rarely crossed back home. But here they were in the same hall of residence, in rooms that faced each other across the hallway.

Sinead was studying art. Though Amelia observed that Sinead was living life to the full rather more than studying. This intrigued Amelia.

Sinead had classic Celtic good looks and a temperament to match. She was never short of a boyfriend or something to do, though she did make time for Amelia.

Their friendship was complementary. Amelia would often cover for Sinead when she failed to return in the evening. And Sinead would try to get Amelia to come out of herself, but with little success.

Though their worlds were somewhat different, they would often talk late into the night and share their thoughts and feelings, which made it all the more of a shock when, without a word, Sinead did not return to university at the start of the summer term.

To begin with, Amelia could not understand why. She tried to contact Sinead, but was told that Sinead was not at home. She was told no more than this. She wrote to Sinead several times, but received no replies. Perhaps Sinead did not get her letters. Amelia asked around at university. She spoke to Sinead's friends, but no one knew.

It was only at the end of summer term, after her exams, that Amelia found out what had happened.

Sinead had become pregnant.

Jeremy: "How did you feel when suddenly your best friend Sinead got pregnant? That must have been a huge deal in Ireland in the eighties. I wanted to get some sense of what the young Amelia thought as I read that."

Amelia: "Jeremy, I was shocked because it was so sudden. I had no idea what had happened to her. And I was really sad that I had lost my best friend overnight. But also I was frightened for her and myself, because we all had the fear of God drummed into us by the nuns about not getting pregnant before marriage. And there was I in the thrust of my first love with Donal, it made me even more reticent sexually in case I ended up the same way as Sinead. Jeremy, please understand that if you got pregnant before marriage in Ireland in the eighties your life was ruined."

Jeremy: "But let me challenge you a little bit here now Amelia. We see you weren't afraid to use your charm and flirt to get what you wanted."

Amelia: "But flirting wasn't a crime then, Jeremy. It is now apparently."

Breaking Bones

There was a chance to work in London during the summer holidays. Amelia took it. She had never been to London before, in fact Amelia had never been out of Ireland before. Though the work was menial, it paid.

Amelia had been working for about a week. While it was wonderful to experience life in the city, her job was living up to everything she suspected it might be, unfortunately.

The Norlandic Hotel, which was situated on the edge of Hyde Park, was an impressive building. Constructed at the height of empire, amid some of the most prestigious hotels in the city, it boasted rooms that few could afford to stay in.

Being a chambermaid was hard graft, which Amelia didn't mind, but the way she was treated was just awful. No wonder the British Empire collapsed.

The housekeeper, a Mrs Forsythe, simply didn't like female medical students with their "better than everyone else attitude". And if there was one thing worse than female medical students, it was Irish female medical students. They turned up, if you were lucky, for a few weeks in the summer and thought the world of themselves and that it owed them a living. And if that wasn't enough, by the time she managed to get them to be of some use, they'd be off. Students, useless, she hated them.

Amelia was late, she abhorred being late, not least because of the grief Mrs Forsythe would give her. She thought it best to run.

It was raining. Amelia slipped and hit her arm hard against a bollard. It hurt like hell. But she picked herself up and hurried on.

With moments to spare, Amelia clocked in.

Mrs Forsythe allocated the day's rooms in her usual prejudiced manner, particularly after Amelia said that she'd hurt arm and that it might be broken.

'You Irish, you're all the same,' declared Mrs Forsythe. 'You're all lazy. As a special favour I've given you ten extra rooms today, Amelia.'

Mrs Forsythe chuckled to herself in a way that only she found funny.

'So you'd better get on with it if you're going to finish on time,' she added. 'And furthermore, I want you to clean behind the beds and up in the corners of the ceilings. I don't want to find any spiders' webs. Got it? Now be off with you.'

As ever, Mrs Forsythe did a pre-inspection of the rooms before allocating them.

Amelia suspected that this "pre-inspection" was merely a ruse concocted by Mrs Forsythe to steal any tips that had been left for the chambermaids.

Amelia's arm really hurt. In her first room, she could barely lift the telephone, let alone the mop and bucket, but she persevered. However, after five rooms the pain had become too much. She went to find Mrs Forsythe.

'Look, I'm in a lot of pain here,' explained Amelia. 'My arm is very sore, I think I've broken it.'

'You get on and clean those rooms,' demanded an unsympathetic Mrs Forsythe. 'Stop complaining or I'll give you five more rooms. Go on, get on with it.'

Amelia was already behind. Five more rooms would be terrible.

Mrs Forsythe swung both her arms in a gesture to make Amelia get a move on.

Amelia turned and went into her next room. Mrs Forsythe followed, and stood in the doorway, watching her every action.

'That's it, you are just another lazy Paddy!' she exclaimed. 'See those cobwebs up there, you need to get rid of them. What will our guests think?'

'I can't reach the ceiling, it's too high,' replied Amelia.

'Come on, use your initiative,' ordered Mrs Forsythe. 'Stand up on the bath and reach the ceiling like all the other chambermaids.'

Amelia stood up on the bath.

The bath was wet.

She slipped.

Amelia howled as her arm hit the floor. The pain was excruciating. Her elbow began to swell up.

Amelia tried to calm herself. She closed her eyes and took slow, deep breaths.

Mrs Forsythe stood frozen to the spot, clearly unsure about what to say.

Amelia managed to stand. Mrs Forsythe did nothing to help.

'Right now, that's it,' declared Amelia. 'I'm a medical student and my arm is definitely broken. So I'm going to the hospital. I don't care whether you let me or not, I'm going down to the hospital. And I'm going to tell the Manager.'

The hotel manager, Mr Barrington, was a man who liked everything to plan, and everything just so. He ran the hotel on military lines. There was a chain of command, and procedures for all eventualities. Unless staff were there to help guests with their immediate needs, they were not to be seen.

So it was something of a surprise when a young chambermaid burst into his office, clutching her arm and ranting. Experience told him to just sit at his desk and listen.

'That woman! Never in my life have I been so badly treated,' raged Amelia. 'Oh my God, that woman, she hates me. She's always been the same since I started working here. She's been hell-bent on making my life miserable. She's got no consideration for others. She thinks we're worse than the lowest of the low. And this morning, to cap it all, she's been making my work unbearable. I told her I'd hurt my arm, but she made me stand up in the bath, and now I think I've broken it, so I'm going to the hospital for an x-ray.'

Mr Barrington waited until he thought the young chambermaid had quite finished.

'And you are?' he inquired.

This question appeared to catch Amelia off balance.

'Your name, girl. Your name,' he pressed.

'Amelia, Amelia Allen,' replied Amelia.

The immaculate Mr Barrington stood and walked around his immaculately ordered desk.

'May I?' he asked.

He looked at Amelia's arm and swollen elbow. Clearly something was very wrong. 'It's policy to send an employee's supervisor with them in the event of a visit to a medical facility outside of the hotel,' recounted Mr Barrington.

'If you think I'm going to hospital with that woman, you've got another thing coming,' said Amelia. 'I'm going by myself.'

'Well, um...' But before Mr Barrington could add anything else to what had been a somewhat one-sided conversation, Amelia had exited his office, slamming the door in her wake.

'Broken?' queried Amelia.

'Fractured,' said the accident and emergency doctor.

'Oh,' said Amelia.

'And something of a complex fracture,' concluded the doctor as he examined the x-ray more closely. 'It'll need a cast for eight or so weeks.'

'Oh,' repeated Amelia.

'And no heavy lifting,' instructed the doctor.

'But, my job...' argued Amelia.

'You'll have to ask them for something a little more desk-bound I'm afraid,' advised the doctor.

'Oh.' What else could Amelia say?

A little later in the afternoon, Amelia returned to the hotel. Now that she couldn't do her job, she felt sure she'd have to return to Ireland and stay with her parents.

For the second time in one day Amelia found herself in Mr Barrington's office. This time her arm had a cast and was in a sling.

She stood somewhat uncomfortably beside a rather subdued Mrs Forsythe.

Glances were not exchanged.

'Miss Allen,' said Mr Barrington, standing as he addressed her directly, 'in light of the incident that occurred this morning, the hotel feels it is only fit and proper that we put you on sick leave as you are unfit for work.'

'Sick leave?' questioned Amelia.

'Yes, sick leave,' replied Mr Barrington. 'You will not, of course, be able to work in the hotel while on sick leave, but you will receive sick pay at full salary.'

'Paid sick leave?' queried Amelia.

'Yes,' said Mr Barrington. 'And to ensure that you have all the time necessary to complete a full recovery, we propose to put you on sick leave for the full duration of your contract until the end of summer. We do not expect you to return to the hotel.'

Mrs Forsythe coughed.

Amelia couldn't believe her luck. She fully expected to be dismissed there and then.

'Paid up until the end of the summer?' Amelia wanted to confirm what she'd been told.

'Yes,' repeated Mr Barrington.

'No need to come back to work?' continued Amelia.

'No need at all,' replied Mr Barrington.

'OK!' Amelia was delighted.

'On behalf of the hotel,' said Mr Barrington, 'we would like to thank you for the work you have done, and your consideration in resolving this matter in a discrete and satisfactory manner,' concluded Mr Barrington.

Mr Barrington made to shake hands, but rapidly realised that Amelia's broken arm prevented him from doing so. Instead he nodded, and passed her the relevant disclaimer to sign, on which, without thought, Amelia duly scribbled her signature.

'Mrs Forsythe will help you collect your things,' added Mr Barrington, 'and if you stop by the accounts department, I've instructed them to give you a cheque for your sick pay in its entirety.'

'Thank you, that's so kind of you, Mr Barrington,' replied Amelia.

Mr Barrington sat down and continued with his paperwork. The meeting was over.

Mrs Forsythe opened the door. Amelia stepped through and smiled. Mrs Forsythe said nothing, she just glared.

It turned out to be a glorious summer. And while her friends were having a dismal time as chambermaids under the ever angry Mrs Forsythe, Amelia was having a wonderful time, though she realised after a few weeks, there was only so much sightseeing to be done, particularly by oneself. Amelia had to be busy, always.

Then, in a rather bizarre turn of events, opportunity struck. Amelia managed to land a job as a park police officer, purely by chance.

Her friend, Matthew, who had failed his first year exams and had to return to Ireland, had said to Amelia, "You could do this job. You should apply".

Amelia pondered how to approach the interview. She' had heard from Matthew that the park police inspector had an eye for the ladies, and so chose to wear her favourite figure-hugging red dress. She got the job.

Being a park police officer essentially consisted of opening and closing the park gates, and enforcing the park rules, which, given her broken arm, she struggled to do.

But it was in the last two weeks of summer that Amelia came into her own, The Bolshoi Ballet were performing in the park and the now cast-less Amelia was given the job of minding the lead ballerina, a job she would have paid to do for she absolutely loved ballet.

As far as Amelia could work out, "minding the lead ballerina" consisted of being a general dogsbody sent wherever, whenever, to do whatever was asked of her. Amelia didn't mind. It was a job she really enjoyed, and despite the obvious language difficulties, she seemed to be quite successful at. Indeed, the cast of the Ballet took to her so much that they tried to adopt her, and on the last night the lead ballerina took off her shoes and threw them to Amelia. Amelia looked inside, and the ballerina had signed them.

'From hotel chambermaid to *member* of the Bolshoi Ballet in one summer,' thought Amelia. 'Not bad, not bad at all!'

Amelia had landed on her feet again.

Jeremy: "You are such a contradiction, so in control when you wanted to be, but losing that instantly when a man comes along..."
< Amelia shrugs, and throws her hands up in the air>
Amelia: "Me and men!"

Men!

It didn't seem possible, but Amelia's second year at university was passing faster than her first. Her desire to succeed did not relent. If anything, it grew stronger, though she did try and balance her work with some pleasure. She mixed a little more at university, and even allowed herself the odd party. And though Donal had joined the army as a trainee officer, she spent as much time with him as she could.

Donal had invited her to the cadet officers' annual ball. Amelia agreed to go, but on condition that Donal booked separate rooms in the hotel where the function was to be held.

Perhaps it was a genuine mistake, but Amelia was not impressed when she arrived at the hotel to find that Donal had booked a twin room and not two singles.

They rowed.

The evening was not a great success, and despite Donal's pleading, Amelia returned to university. She had work to do, she always had work to do.

Amelia did remember to return home to Loch Garman from time to time. And she did think about her family on occasion. Generally her visits were greeted with a warm welcome, but not this weekend.

Though her mother was always glad to see her, her father was positively frosty and glowered at her. All her mother would say was, "Don't worry, dear, I'm sure he'll get over it".

It wasn't a pleasant weekend. In fact Amelia considered going back to University early, but she knew that her mother, who seemed to be on the up at the moment, would be very disappointed.

When dinner came, her father, who was normally full of chat and the things that were going on, said nothing. He just looked to his food.

Amelia decided to break the ice.

'What's wrong, Daddy?' she asked. 'You've hardly said a word to me all weekend.'

Her father looked up, stared at her, and then returned to his food. It was if she was a ghost.

Silence persisted.

And then, suddenly, it was broken as her father placed his cutlery back onto his plate and turned to her.

'You know what's wrong, Amelia,' he said. 'And I'm ashamed to be sitting here eating at the same table as you.'

Amelia was bewildered. She just looked at him and shrugged.

Her mother closed her eyes. She knew what was coming.

Her father pushed himself back from the table and made to leave. He turned on Amelia.

'As well you might shrug at me, my girl,' he shouted. 'You know damn well what I'm talking about!'

'I have no idea what you're talking about,' replied Amelia.

'Don't deny it,' he argued. 'I know that you think everyone must be at it at university, but I brought you up to be better than that. I brought you up to wait until your wedding night! You'll hardly be able to walk the aisle in white now, will you! What colour do think will suit? Cream, beige... red!'

And then it clicked.

'You think I've been sleeping around, don't you,' said Amelia.

'I don't think, I know,' retorted her father.

'Well, let me tell you, I haven't,' asserted Amelia. 'I don't know where you could have got such an idea from.'

'Do you want me to tell you?' Her father stared directly at her.

'Go on, tell me whatever pack of lies you've been told about me,' replied an indignant Amelia.

'No one told me anything,' stated her father. 'I found things out for myself.'

'You did now, did you?' Amelia was enraged.

'I did.'

Father and daughter faced off, neither willing to back down, both certain of the truth.

Unnoticed, Amelia's mother slipped away from the dining table and returned to the kitchen.

'Well, what is it that you think you found out?' questioned Amelia.

'I'll tell you what I found out, my girl,' countered her father. 'When you went to Donal's annual ball and you stayed in that hotel, it wasn't your own room that you slept in, it was his!'

'What?' Amelia was outraged.

'That's right, you and he slept together!' accused her father.

'I did not, that's just not true,' defended Amelia.

'But it is, I know,' said her father. 'I rang the hotel to speak to you and they told me that you and he had booked a room together. Why would they lie, eh, tell me that. Why would they lie?'

Her father stood back and crossed his arms. In his eyes the case for the prosecution was made, and it based on rock solid evidence.

'I didn't sleep with Donal, believe me. It was simply a hotel booking mistake.' Amelia's eyes began to water.

'Damn right it was a mistake!' ranted her father. 'A mistake that you were ever my daughter.'

'Donal booked the wrong type of room, was all,' sobbed Amelia.

Her father pointed directly at her.

'You are no longer a member of this family,' declared her father. 'I want you gone by the time I get back.'

At which he stormed out of the house, doors slamming behind him.

Amelia burst into tears. She went to the kitchen to find her mother hunched on a kitchen chair, rocking back and forth.

'I didn't do anything, Mum. Believe me,' she pleaded.

But her mother just kept rocking back and forth, looking to the ground, saying nothing.

Tears turned to anger.

Amelia grabbed her stuff, and without another word, strode out of the house, like her father.

'If he wants me to go, I'll go, but I won't come back.' And with that thought Amelia left.

Jeremy: "But we see you were completely naïve at times when it comes to men."
Amelia: "Yes, when I look back, I know I should have been more in control of my own destiny, Jeremy, and I don't know why I wasn't more worldly-wise."

Miss Naive

Amelia refused to go home despite her mother's best efforts to broker the peace. She had long since ended her relationship with Donal, but her father was just as stubborn as he always was and refused to listen to reason, even though everyone had told him nothing had happened at the hotel.

So Amelia decided to go to London again to work for the summer. It was suitably far away from Ireland. It was a chance to earn some money and have a little fun after a hard year's studying.

This time she had found a position as a waitress at the Embassy Square Hotel. And though her training consisted of the manager taking her to a table, picking up a glass, wiping it five times, and saying, "That's how you waitress!", Amelia took to the job straight away. She much preferred it to being a chambermaid.

The trickiest part of the job was carrying the customers' plates on a massive tray above her head, but with confidence and a few near misses, Amelia became adept.

When it came to communicating with the customers, Amelia was a natural. Her flawless smile and easy-going, naive charm made her an instant hit. She was always engaging, listened to everything said, even when the customers were clearly drunk, which they often were.

On a very busy Saturday evening, one particular table, table seventeen, was being particularly demanding. Everything they asked for was different from the menu and had to be checked with chef. Undaunted, Amelia, who was always willing to oblige, scurried back and forth, attending their every need. And as the customers on table seventeen consumed more and more wine, their banter became evermore raucous.

It didn't help that one of them came from Dublin. He had black hair and a small moustache, and he viewed Amelia as a long lost cousin whom he demanded tell tall tales of his fondly remembered place of birth. Amelia duly did, much to the amusement of the rest of the table.

Just as Amelia had taken their order for desserts, the man tapped her on the elbow. 'Will it be the nicest dessert I'm ever going to have in my whole life. Amelia?' he asked.

'Oh, it will be,' replied Amelia. 'It's going to be a lovely dessert. I've tasted it today and it's delicious.'

'Is it big?' he queried.

'Oh, yes,' said Amelia. 'It'll be a lovely portion. I'll ask the chef for an extra big serving for you.'

He smiled, and Amelia smiled back.

After the desserts had been prepared, Amelia put them on her tray. She lifted the large tray above her head, her body dwarfed under its shadow, and negotiated her way to table seventeen.

She put the desserts down before each of them, saving the Dublin man's dessert for last.

Just as she made to leave, he turned round and tapped her on the elbow.

'May I have a microscope, please?' he requested in an over-loud voice.

'Oh yes, I'll run off and see if I can get you one,' responded Amelia robotically, not noticing the stifled laughter coming from the table.

She hurried to the bar, she was already late in taking the order from the couple sat at table forty-three.

'Oh, my God,' panted Amelia. 'That bloke wants a microscope now. He's been driving me crazy all night. Where in the name of God am I going to get a microscope for him now?

'Oh, for goodness sake, Amelia. You are so naive!' chuckled the barman.

She sighed and looked on.

After the customers on table seventeen had left, Amelia found they had left an enormous tip for her troubles.

Amelia smiled, God how she needed a holiday!

Jeremy: "Ah, you might say you wanted to be in control of your own destiny with men, but you couldn't stop flirting with them to get what you wanted, could you, Amelia?"

Amelia: "I admit I occasionally flirted to get what I wanted and still do. But why not?"

Jeremy: "But why did you let them walk all over you?"

Amelia: "I couldn't help myself, I loved being with men, I needed to be with them, and somehow I was prepared to give up my independence because of that when I was in a relationship. But I still knew how to have fun with them."

<Amelia bursts into a smile>

A Wing and a Prayer

'The Lake District,' repeated Amelia.

'Yes, the Lake District,' confirmed Miriam, a fellow medical student and party girl.

'Fantastic idea,' approved Amelia, never one to say no to fun. 'I haven't been camping for years. I used to go with my family every year in Ireland. We went to Kerry, and Barleycove, and Bettystown. I love camping!'

And so, with plans made, that is to say they'd agreed a destination, backpacks packed, and some sixty pounds in cash between them, Amelia and Miriam set off for the weekend.

The bus arrived in Windermere, deposited Amelia and Miriam by the side of the road, and pulled away in a faint-blue haze of exhaust smoke.

The girls stood and admired the picture-postcard, stone buildings.

'So,' said Amelia, 'let's go camping.'

'Amelia, we've no tent!' explained Miriam.

'Sure, we'll just borrow one,' replied Amelia.

'OK, so we'll borrow a tent.' Miriam wasn't convinced.

The camp site was a short, scenic walk from the town.

Upon arrival, the girls found a patch of grass in the sun and sat down. They observed their fellow campers. Amelia nudged Miriam, indicating towards two young men who had just finished putting up their tent. She got up and went over to them. Miriam followed.

'Look, em, is there anyway we could rent your tent off you for the night?' flirted Amelia. 'It's a gorgeous warm day, you'll be fine for this evening sleeping under the stars.'

'Rent our tent?' questioned the young men. They stared at the two pretty girls, and then looked at each other.

'Yeah,' answered Amelia. 'We want to go camping, but we don't have a tent, so we'd like to rent your tent.'

The young men seemed a little perplexed, until the taller of the two had an idea. His face brightened.

'But where will we sleep?' he asked.

His friend's face now beamed too, sharing similar thoughts.

'Well, we'll rent your tent off you, and you can sleep outside the door of the tent,' clarified Amelia.

Amelia and Miriam nodded to each other in agreement. The young men pondered the proposition.

"OK, so we'll rent our tent to you for twenty-five pounds for the night,' offered the tall young man, enchanted by Amelia, how could he say no to those brown-flecked eyes.

'Brilliant.' Amelia was clearly pleased with the offer, and started to put her hand forward to shake on the deal, only to have her arm tugged back by Miriam.

'But that's almost all of our money!' exclaimed Miriam through her teeth, trying to both whisper and shout at the same time.

'Don't worry, we've got a tent for the night haven't we,' reassured Amelia.

And with a blank-faced Miriam appearing to be persuaded, Amelia shook on the deal.

'So, will you come out and have a drink with us, girls?' suggested the tall young man.

'We would, but we've very little money left,' admitted Amelia.

'Ah, don't worry, we'll buy you a drink,' he offered.

Introductions followed.

And at this everyone smiled, though Miriam felt events may have overtaken her. 'Would you like something to eat?' asked John, the taller of the young men, keen not to let opportunity slip away. 'How do you fancy a slap-up dinner of baked beans on toast?'

The evening had passed boisterously. And with last orders called, they ambled their way back to the tent, full of drink and playful banter.

However, the warm summer's day had turned decidedly cool beneath the night sky.

'How about we all sleep in the tent, to keep warm?' ventured John.

'Now that's a thought,' replied Amelia.

For a while she appeared to give consideration to John's proposal.

'No, we've paid you our money,' said Amelia. 'We'll sleep in the tent, and you'll sleep outside.'

'But, it's our tent,' argued John.

'But, we've paid you the money,' countered Amelia.

Amelia folded her arms, and Miriam stood alongside.

Realising that the girls were not open to John's idea, the young men gathered their things, and prepared for a colder than expected night under the stars.

With morning's first light, Miriam peered out from the tent.

Ian and John's sleeping bags were there, but the young men were not to be seen. 'They must have gone to get washed or something,' she thought.

She turned to the dozing Amelia, and prodded her.

'Anyway, what are we going to do today?' asked Miriam.

'Well, there's no way we can rent the tent for a second night,' said Amelia. 'We've no money left. In fact we've not the money to catch the bus.'

'Oh,' replied Miriam.

'I think we'll have to say our goodbyes, and try and hitch home,' sighed Amelia.

And so it was that Amelia and Miriam's camping weekend ended after just one day. 'We needed to plan more,' reflected Miriam.

'We needed more money,' concluded Amelia.

Jeremy: "So another core theme in your book is mental illness, and specifically your mother's. When did it really hit home for you?"

Amelia: "Well, on one occasion, when I returned home from university and realised that everybody else knew what was going on, it forced me to face up to things. It gave me permission to acknowledge the reality that my beloved mother was very ill."

In Sickness and in Health

It took until the end of autumn term before Amelia resolved to return home, despite what her father had said. She was going to be the better person and hold out the hand of reconciliation. And if he refused, well that would be his problem. Amelia hadn't heard from her mother in months, but she knew her mother would never give up on trying to bring them back together.

Loch Garman had changed little since she'd been at university. If anything the town was a little smaller, a little more claustrophobic. The people hadn't changed. Same faces, same places.

Amelia stopped at the grocery shop to look for some carnations for her mother. The bell rang as she pushed open the glass-panelled door. As ever, Mr Healy was chatting to one of his customers. She was sure that the only reason many of the old people came in was for the conversation. She found a bunch of red carnations, her mother's favourite. She remembered well that bittersweet scent, and took them to the counter.

Mr Healy broke off his conversation and turned to Amelia.

'Why if it isn't young Amelia Allen,' he said. 'Haven't seen you in a while. I heard you were off at university studying to be a doctor.'

Amelia nodded.

Mr Healy took the carnations and proceeded to wrap them.

'For your mother?' he asked.

'Yes,' replied Amelia.

'We were all shocked when we heard what happened,' he commented. 'People didn't know what to say... Well, you know, what can you say. I do hope she gets better soon, you know, recovers.'

'Sorry, Mr Healy, what happened?' queried Amelia.

Mr Healy was all of a stutter.

'Um... You don't know?'

'Know what?' questioned Amelia.

'Um... I'm not sure I should rightly say.' Mr Healy busied himself taping the wrapping paper, hoping it would be distraction enough so that he wouldn't have to answer.

But Amelia was clearly waiting for him to respond.

Mrs Haughey, Mr Healy's customer, prodded him with her walking stick.

'You can't not tell the girl now you've started the conversation, can you, Darragh? It wouldn't be right.'

'Well, what happened?' demanded Amelia.

'Um... I know your mother's not been well over the years, and no one thinks any the less of her for it,' he mumbled. 'She's a fine woman. Always such a lady, and done the best she can for you children...'

'Darragh!' Mrs Haughey prodded him again.

'It must have been a month or so ago,' he continued, reluctantly. 'She had to be taken home by the police.'

'Taken home by the police,' repeated Amelia. 'Why?'

'She'd, um, got lost in town,' answered Mr Healy.

'You really are hopeless sometimes, Darragh,' commented Mrs Haughey. 'Tell the girl straight or I will.'

Mr Healy looked to the floor and passed the wrapped bunch of flowers over the counter to Amelia.

'It was just that, just that she had forgotten to put on any clothes.' Mr Healy rushed the words out as quickly as he could, somehow hoping that they wouldn't be noticed.

A moment passed.

'Oh,' said an unflustered Amelia. 'I hope people didn't take offence. You know she just isn't herself sometimes. Anyway must go. Thank you for the flowers. Goodbye.'

Amelia pulled the door open. The bell rang, quietly.

'Goodbye, Amelia,' replied Mr Healy, clearly embarrassed. 'I hope your mother gets better soon.'

Darragh Healy felt like he'd been saying that for all of Amelia's life.

Amelia rang the door bell, though she didn't need to, she had a key.

No one answered. She turned the handle, it wasn't locked.

'Anyone home?' she asked. 'It's me, Amelia. Hello?'

She could hear clattering coming from inside. She stepped across the threshold, and headed for the kitchen. It was Aunty Bea.

'Hello, Aunty Bea,' greeted Amelia. 'It's lovely to see you. How are you?'

Aunty Bea jumped, literally.

'Amelia, honey,' she replied. 'I haven't seen you in an age. Come here and give your favourite aunt a hug. Have you lost weight?'

'Really, do you think so?' said Amelia, secretly pleased, not that Amelia needed to lose even a pound.

'I'm afraid your mother and father aren't here,' said Aunty Bea. 'They've just popped out for a moment. I thought I'd help out in the kitchen.'

'Aunty Bea, you should be taking it easy,' said Amelia who thought Aunty Bea looked frail and worn out. 'Why don't you let others look after you?'

'I'm too set in my ways for all of that,' sighed Aunty Bea. 'If I stop, I'm worried I'll just drop down dead.'

'Don't say that, Aunty Bea,' exclaimed Amelia. 'You'll outlive us all, mark my words.'

Aunty Bea shook her head and put the kettle on.

'Tea?' she asked.

'Yes please,' responded Amelia. 'I bought some flowers.'

'My, aren't they pretty,' commented Aunty Bea. 'I'll put them in a vase.'

Aunty Bea busied herself with the flowers and making the tea. She put some biscuits on a plate, and placed the vase of flowers on the kitchen table.

After the tea had brewed in the pot, Aunty Bea gestured to the table, and she and Amelia sat.

'Is this a new table, Aunty Bea?' asked Amelia.

'Yes it is, my child,' replied Aunty Bea, as she sipped her tea. 'Your parents have bought a lot of new furniture recently.'

Amelia looked at the new table. She thought the old one to have been much more tasteful.

'Why have they bought a new table?' she queried

With both hands Aunty Bea carefully placed her cup in its saucer and looked across at Amelia, steeling herself.

'Must have been a few months ago now,' she explained, pausing to hold back her own feelings. 'Your poor father came home from one of his business trips to find that your mother had sold all the furniture, every single stick of furniture that's been in our family for generations, all sold to one of those unscrupulous antiques dealers for half nothing.'

Aunty Bea dropped the weight of her head into her hands.

Amelia didn't know what to say.

Aunty Bea drew breath and continued slowly.

'William tried, but the rogue dealer wouldn't sell the furniture back, and so your father went out and bought all new furniture. Bless him. The man's a saint.'

'What did he say to Mum?' interjected Amelia.

'Ah, honey, sure your poor mother didn't know what she was doing, God love her.'

Aunty Bea shook her head and lifted her cup to take another sip of tea.

Amelia stared at flowers on the table.

Aunty Bea put her cup down.

'Honey, your mother's got a lot worse recently,' she said. 'I'm storming heaven every day for all of you. I just hope that the Good Lord will answer my prayers.'

Numb, Amelia reached to Aunty Bea. Her emotions were locked inside and wouldn't escape.

For some time, Amelia and Aunty Bea sat quietly in each others company, alone with their thoughts.

Suddenly Amelia started, she heard the familiar sound of the key turning in the lock. It must be her parents returning from wherever it was they'd been. She felt Aunty Bea squeeze her hand and they both stood up.

'That must be your parents,' announced Aunty Bea.

Amelia swung round as Audrey entered the kitchen.

'Amelia! We didn't know you were coming,' proclaimed Audrey, as she threw her arms around Amelia, delighted. 'Oh, it's so wonderful to see you. How have you been? I've missed you so much, darling.'

William stood in the doorway. He said nothing.

'I brought red carnations,' said Amelia. 'Aunty Bea's put them in a vase on the table. I hope you like them.'

'Oh, they're lovely, Amelia.' Audrey grinned with delight. 'Look, William, Amelia's brought some beautiful deep red carnations, my favourite.'

Amelia looked at her father, trying to sense his mood. His face was hard to read.

'Have you brought just yourself?' he asked.

'I have, Dad,' replied Amelia. 'Donal and I split up quite some time ago. He wasn't the right one for me.'

'Oh, right,' he said.

Amelia walked to her father and pushed her face to his chest. She looked up, straight into his eyes, and saw the strength and support of the father she knew and loved.

He raised his arms and folded them around her.

Jeremy: "As you re-establish your relationship with your father, we see you deciding to flirt your way around the world again, young Amelia."

Amelia: "Oh now, Jeremy, don't be telling the world about all my little secrets!"

\<Amelia winks at Jeremy, Jeremy blushes>

Don't Tell Your Mom

America for the summer.

Amelia could scarcely believe it, she was in America!

Now, admittedly it wasn't Boston or New York, where all her friends had gone, but it was Chicago. And Chicago looked like it could be a lot of fun.

She and her friend, Fiona O'Bannion, were staying with the Mcleans, old acquaintances of her parents.

George and Marissa Mclean lived in Chicago's leafy suburbs with their son, Mitchell. Amelia guessed that Mitchell was pretty much her age. Amelia also noticed that Mitchell had an eye for her.

If she was honest, she hadn't really wanted to spend the summer with Fiona, but her mother had insisted, saying, "Fiona's a nice, sensible girl. You can rely on Fiona. She'll keep you from getting into any trouble".

Fiona had been the quietest girl in Amelia's class. She'd never been anywhere before, let alone America. In Amelia's eyes, Fiona was a good-natured, kind and dependable friend, but she was way too straight. Not that Amelia would ever share her thoughts about Fiona with anyone, least of all tell Fiona. Perhaps she was being a little unkind, for Amelia would readily admit that she was hardly worldly-wise herself.

Anyway, Amelia was determined to make the most of her summer. She was determined to have fun. She had been told that you had to be twenty-one to drink alcohol in America, and that most everybody had fake IDs so that they could drink. Amelia decided that getting a fake ID would be her mission, not that she drank alcohol.

Mitchell was only too keen to help, and drove Amelia and Fiona to his father's office on the pretext of showing them his father's place of work. Amelia and Fiona set about doctoring and photocopying their birth certificates, while Mitchell engaged his father in conversation. And within an hour the girls were sat in Mitchell's car, clutching their own fake IDs.

'Will we get into trouble for this?' asked an uncertain Fiona.

'Oh, no, no, no, no,' replied Amelia.

Mitchell looked back at Fiona in the rear-view mirror, and then winked across towards Amelia sat beside him in the front.

'Well, you know, if anybody finds out it's fake, Fiona, you'll go to prison,' teased Mitchell.

'What, what, my God, that's terrible!' exclaimed Fiona.

'Ah, don't worry about it,' comforted Amelia. 'I'll come and bail you out. I'm gonna' get loads of tips as a cocktail waitress.'

The fake IDs led to work at a local bar, Amelia as a cocktail waitress, and Fiona mixing drinks. Fiona's parents owned a pub back in Loch Garman, and as a such she was able to put her extensive knowledge to use.

The first day on the job was interesting, but not lucrative. In fact even when Amelia and Fiona pooled their tips there was less than two dollars and some change. Subsequent days were little better. Amelia began to wonder if Fiona was right about how to dress for bar work. Amelia had always been told to dress to impress.

Mitchell had the answer.

'Have you taken a look at yourselves?' he suggested.

'What do you mean?' queried Fiona, slightly taken aback by Mitchell's rather direct observation. Fiona had always considered herself to be quite attractive and well- presented, she dressed as she had always dressed for bar work.

Amelia caught Mitchell's eye, and then looked across at Fiona, smartly dressed, clean, tidy just like her. Skirts a respectable length, below their knees, and their tops were not too revealing. It was clothing that the nuns would have approved of, sensible clothing for bar work. Amelia understood.

'I see,' said Amelia.

'Finally,' said Mitchell.

Amelia pulled up her skirt to her knees.

'Like this?' she teased.

Mitchell motioned upwards with his hand.

The skirt rose a little further, to reveal all of her knees and tanned shapely legs.

'Well, that's a start,' winked Mitchell, and as he left room he added, 'see how you get on. Oh, and you might wanna' try a bit of makeup.'

Amelia wasted no time in reducing the length of her skirt with scissors, needle and thread.

Fiona said it was demeaning, and folded her arms.

Thirty-five dollars in tips! That was more than Amelia was paid in wages.

Amelia was delighted, the plan had worked brilliantly she mused to herself.

Fiona looked at her own pitiful handful of change.

The proof was indeed in the tipping.

It was obvious, and the results repeated themselves each night for the rest of the week.

Amelia decided to experiment further, and shortened her skirt to the middle of her thighs.

Fifty-nine dollars! That was more than Amelia and Fiona earned together in wages.

Amelia looked at Fiona, and Fiona shook her head.

'Oh no you don't, Amelia Allen!' protested Fiona.

'Give me that granny skirt of yours, Fiona O'Bannion,' demanded Amelia. Amelia cut four inches off the hemline.

They laughed, and their friendship was forged.

One hundred and twelve dollars in one night! Amelia was sat in the middle of her bed surrounded by dollar bills.

Fiona beamed, and took a photograph.

Jeremy: "But Amelia, why didn't you stay mad at the men in your life when they were treating you so badly?"
Amelia: "Because, Jeremy, I was taught always to forgive and forget."

A Lesson in Forgiveness

Amelia's course was becoming increasingly hands-on and hospital based. There seemed less and less time for socialising, work had taken over the vast majority of her life, she hardly saw her parents these days.

Often she had to catch a break when she could. Whatever timetable she thought she was on soon changed as the day and the needs of the patients unfolded. But Amelia loved it, no day was the same, and there were always new people to meet and get to know, even if it was for the shortest of times.

'Amelia, Amelia Allen?' said a voice.

Amelia looked up. She couldn't believe it.

'Shane O'Farrell,' she declared. 'Well what a surprise. I didn't know you worked here.'

'I don't,' he replied. 'I'm here following up on an elective with one of the consultants. May I?'

'Of course.' Amelia put her book down.

Shane pulled up a chair.

'And you?' he asked.

'I'm also doing an elective for three months, you know,' replied Amelia trying not to stare. Shane O'Farrell! She'd always thought Mary O'Farrell's older brother to be a fine thing, ever since she had known him from her school days, but now he was that much older he seemed to have developed film star good looks.

'I almost didn't recognise you,' he said. 'Last time I saw you were at my sister's birthday party.'

He thought for a moment.

'Fifteenth?' he ventured.

'That's right,' replied Amelia. 'My you've a good memory, Shane.'

'Oh, I never forget a pretty face,' he charmed.

He looked to his watch.

'Look, I've got to go,' he said. 'How about I give you call and we go for a drink, catch up on old times?'

'That sounds great,' said Amelia.

He asked for her number.

Amelia wrote it on the scrap of paper she found in her bag.

'See you then,' he said, stuffing the paper into his pocket. 'Bye,' said Amelia, as she smiled and waved.

True to his word, a few days later, Shane O'Farrell called, and they arranged to meet at the Crown Bar in town.

He was so interesting, captivating. And his smile, Amelia thought she would die for his smile.

He said he was off to Dublin for the weekend to visit his cousin, and would she like to come?

Amelia didn't quite know what to say. Since Donal, she'd positively stayed away from dates of any sort, not that she'd been asked by anyone.

'Come on, you'll love it,' he encouraged. 'It'll get you away from here. A chance to enjoy yourself. My cousin's got plenty of room.'

Amelia wavered, unsure.

'And I promise to be on my best behaviour,' he added, flashing his white smile.

'OK, so I give in,' agreed Amelia.

Shane's cousin turned out to be on call. He apologised, but said that there was nothing he could do about it. So he gave Shane and Amelia a set of keys to his flat and told them to come and go as they pleased.

Amelia had never experienced Dublin's nightlife before, and Shane was keen to show her a good time. Bar followed bar, and then they went onto a nightclub. Shane seemed to know people everywhere. In fact he knew too many people! Much to his embarrassment, they had to make a hasty retreat from the first nightclub they went to, something about an ex-girlfriend who'd become a "bunny boiler".

Amelia had a wonderful time. Shane couldn't have been any more charming.

Amelia was entranced.

The following weekend, Shane took Amelia sailing out of Loch Garman Boat Club, down the River Slaney. She knew he was a brilliant sailor, he had sailed all his life. And in the evening they sat on the beach around a fire, toasting marshmallows, and laughing.

And then he leant across and stole a kiss.

Spring turned to summer, and Shane had become the centre of Amelia's world. She hardly saw her family, let alone her friends.

It was either the urban whirl of Dublin, or the coastal charms of Rosslare. Amelia started living life, and she loved it.

At the end of the summer, Amelia went on holiday to Greece for three weeks with her friends Miriam, Fiona and Mary, Shane's sister. This had been arranged long before Amelia and Shane had started going out with each other. But all Amelia could think of was Shane, she longed to be back on the River Slaney.

Amelia was overjoyed, there he was to collect them at the airport. She couldn't stop talking.

That evening, Shane just wanted to stay in. Amelia didn't mind.

They had a Chinese takeaway.

'Amelia, I have to tell you something,' he said.

'What?' asked Amelia absentmindedly, while watching TV.

'I've met someone else,' he explained.

His words fell like a stone.

Amelia turned and looked at him.

'What?' she asked in disbelief.

'I've met another girl,' repeated Shane. 'I'm sorry, Amelia. She was here, and you weren't.'

Amelia was silent, in total shock.

Her heart broke, absolutely.

She could say nothing, she struggled to breathe.

'Look, I'd better be going,' said Shane. 'Take care I'll see you around.'

And with just those words he upped and left.

Amelia knew who the other girl was, the girl who'd stolen her love. She couldn't believe it. For two days she paced, anger brewed inside her.

She wanted to tell the other girl what she really thought, but as time passed, and she spoke to her friends, they told her what Shane was really like. How he flitted from one girl to the next, and kept as many as he could on the go.

Everyone knew, except Amelia it seemed. No one had wanted to tell her.

She felt so foolish and angry, miserable, and cross with herself that she was still mad about Shane.

Amelia schemed.

She decided she would go and see the other girl.

She knocked on the door.

Sheila Maloney looked shocked to see Amelia.

Sheila Maloney was Mary O'Farrell's best friend from secondary school. She stood there, startled.

Amelia could see Sheila looked afraid.

'Sheila, I'm not here to be angry with you, I'm here to forgive you,' announced Amelia.

Sheila didn't know what to say, it was not what she had expected.

After some thought, Sheila decided to invite Amelia in.

'Amelia,' she ventured finally, feeling guilty and uncomfortable. 'I, I...

thought you'd be so angry, and here you are wanting to forgive me?'

'I was angry, Sheila,' said Amelia, 'but I can't bear having bad feelings with anyone. You can have him.'

'OK, um...' stuttered Sheila, 'thank you. Would you like to stay for a cup of tea?'

'No, thank you, Sheila, I will go now.'

And with a smile, Amelia left.

Shane called later that day.

He told Amelia he'd made a terrible mistake, he wanted her back, he didn't love Sheila.

Amelia's plan had worked, but she knew that Shane would never change his ways.

SINGLE WORKING WOMAN

Jeremy: "Look, there was a bit of a disconnect for me between your focus, intelligence and dedication to your career, and the 'craziness' that followed you around."

<Amelia raises her eyebrows>

Amelia: "Well, you know what, Jeremy, my father always used to call me 'the absent-minded Professor'. But to me, I was always just me. I don't define myself by what I do, and I certainly didn't define myself then as being a doctor, or a mother, or a wife. I was always just me. I basically acted from my heart. My heart ruled my head a lot of the time, and it often got me into trouble."

Christie's Presents

Amelia's first Christmas working as an intern was on geriatrics rotation. Christmas was always going to be a busy time and never more so than on the geriatric ward, for winter was no respecter of the old.

She hung onto the trolley in the corridor wishing she had more hands as she shuffled through her pile of patient notes. They never seemed to be in the right order, no matter how often she rearranged them. A loose-leaf folder tumbled to the floor, paper scattered everywhere.

Amelia swore.

'Patience, Dr Allen, patience,' remarked Dr James as he leant forward and helped her collect her notes. As ever, he winked and smiled his way down the corridor.

'Thank you, Dr James,' replied Amelia somewhat belatedly as he disappeared behind the next set of doors.

Dr James, the Head of Geriatrics, was a lovely man. Amelia noticed he had a smile in his eye that put those around him at ease, and a confidence that gave certainty in an uncertain world. As a trainee doctor, Amelia could wish for no better boss, and best of all, she got on really well with him, they just clicked.

The ward was bulging and the hospital staff busied themselves between the beds, drawing and opening the privacy curtains, checking temperatures and blood pressures, all to be noted on the clipboards at the end of the beds. Medicines were dispensed, cups of tea offered, but most of all it was conversation that the patients valued, a little time, some reassurance.

And as Amelia did her rounds, she checked each clipboard against the patient's file. She would make a point of passing the time of day. She would introduce herself and explain what she was doing. She would ask them how they were, and listen to what they had to say.

Mr Keating told of his aches and pains and said he was looking forward to his son visiting later that day.

Mr O'Slattery, who preferred to be called Seamus, was not short of conversation, however Amelia's lack of knowledge about "the form" did make it somewhat one-sided.

Mr Dawley wanted to know when his operation was going to take place, Amelia said she'd check for him.

And then there was Christie, Mr O'Dempsey, though Amelia was not allowed to call him Mr O'Dempsey, she had to call him Christie, everyone called him Christie.

Christie always asked after her, he wanted to know everything about her, and would not take no for answer. Over the weeks and months since Christie's operations, he'd had his legs amputated because of his diabetes, they had gotten to know each other well.

Christie was never short of advice for Amelia, particularly when it came to finding her a suitable husband. He'd made it quite clear that Amelia should not be spending her time with the decrepit old men to be found on the geriatric ward. She should be courted, wined and dined.

Had he been a few years younger, and not married Mrs O'Dempsey, Christie insisted he'd have swept Amelia off her feet, and they'd would have been married within the year and would soon be expecting their firstborn. But he thought that Amelia needed to put on a little weight if she was going to be able to bear him the ten children he wanted.

Two weeks before Christmas Amelia learnt that Christie was going to be sent to a nursing home. She felt terrible. Christmas was a time for family, and she knew he'd be really lonely.

'Why is he being sent just before Christmas?' demanded Amelia.

'Amelia, it's just the way of the world,' explained Dr James. 'His wife isn't going to be able to cope with his needs at home. It's as simple as that I'm afraid.'

Amelia stared at Dr James as he sat burrowing through the paperwork on his desk.

He looked up.

'Be careful, you can't get too involved,' he advised. 'I know it's not the best of outcomes, but in the circumstances it's the best that can be done, Amelia.'

Dr James returned to his paperwork.

Amelia assumed that was the end of the conversation. She turned and stepped out of his office. However, she heard the shuffling of paper stop momentarily as she left.

As the days counted down to Christmas, work got busier and busier. Staff were stretched thin due to the holidays, but the patients kept being admitted. Amelia was not going home, she was working over the festive period.

With Christmas Eve just five days away, came the realisation that she hadn't finished her Christmas shopping. And Amelia kept thinking about Christie alone in the nursing home without his family.

She called up Dr James.

'Dr James, which nursing home has Mr O'Dempsey been sent to?' she asked.

'Why do you want to know, Amelia?' queried Dr James.

'I thought I'd send him a card,' explained Amelia.

There was a pause at the other end of the telephone line.

'A card?' repeated Dr James.

'Yes, a Christmas card,' stated Amelia.

Dr James relented and told Amelia the name of the nursing home. He hoped that she would remember his advice and not get too involved, but suspected that wasn't going to be the case, being Amelia.

'Thank you, Dr James,' said Amelia.

Amelia struggled to think of the right presents to get people. The stores thronged with shoppers all trying to find that last minute, perfect gift. Her mind was blank, and she had spent the last hour searching, but not finding.

She imagined Ballinora Nursing Home to be a cold, uninviting place, probably Victorian with Victorian attitudes to care.

'What should she buy Christie?' she wondered.

Time pressed.

Something traditional, thoughtful, something useful. It didn't have to be amazing, just something considered.

Victorian nursing home. Cold. Cold sheets. Socks, the gift that every man gets for Christmas. So she'd buy him a really good pair, long socks that go above the knees, socks that would keep him warm, seasonal socks. Amelia decided to also buy a box of chocolates to sweeten the nurses in the nursing home in case they might not let her see Christie.

With her presents purchased, together with suitable festive paper, Amelia returned home, wrote Christie a card and wrapped the presents.

The final days running up to Christmas were frantic. Amelia found herself rushed from one patient to the next, with never enough time. She did manage to get some sleep, but often forgot to eat.

All too soon it was Christmas Eve, and Amelia realised she needed to give Christie his present because she would have no time on Christmas Day. She decided to go and visit him straight after her day had ended.

To begin with Amelia was lost. She couldn't find the nursing home, it was outside of town in some back-of-beyond rural location, but eventually by driving down what seemed like every road in the vicinity, she stumbled upon it.

The nursing home was as she had imagined.

Her footsteps crunched on the gravel driveway. She climbed the stone steps and eased open the arched wooden door.

Beyond the entrance way, a uniformed nurse sat in the shadow of a lamp at the front desk.

'And how may I help you, madam?' The nurse did not look up as she said this.

'I'm here to see Mr O'Dempsey,' said Amelia.

'Your name?' The nurse began to open a large book marked "Visitors".

'Dr Allen,' replied Amelia.

The nurse looked up.

'Is this a professional visit?' she asked. 'Because if it is I have not been made aware, you are not on the pre-registered visitors' list for this evening.'

'No, it's not professional, it's personal,' clarified Amelia.

'Oh,' responded the nurse and returned to the visitor's book. She leafed through to today's page, and turned the book to face Amelia.

'If you could fill in your details here.' The nurse indicated to the next empty line in the book, and passed a pen to Amelia.

Amelia duly completed her details.

'If you could just wait a moment, Dr Allen, over in the visitors' area,' requested the nurse, 'I will send for someone to show you the way.' At which point the nurse picked up the telephone receiver and spoke in hushed tones.

Amelia sat.

A wide stone staircase wound its way up to the next floor. Above, where there may have been a large chandelier in former times, there was now just a painted-over ceiling rose.

'Follow me,' said a voice.

Amelia glanced up and smiled at the orderly. The orderly did not smile back. He looked decidedly put out at having to come and collect a visitor.

Amelia and the orderly ascended the cold stone stairs, and then followed a warren of corridors. They stopped at a door.

'In here,' he said gruffly.

Amelia pushed open the door.

'I'll wait outside,' added the orderly and sat on a chair by the door.

It was the smell that struck Amelia first. It was vile, a composite of over-cooked food and industrial cleaning products trying to mask something worse.

Christie was sat up in bed, looking to the window, even though the curtains were drawn.

Amelia walked across to him.

'Hello, Christie,' she said. 'It's Dr Allen.'

'Oh, doctor, doctor. How are you?' asked Christie.

'I've missed you.' Amelia could see moisture forming in his eyes.

'I am very well, thank you,' replied Amelia. 'And you, how are you, Christie?'

Christie thought for a moment.

'As well as I can be, Amelia.' He managed a smile.

'Well, happy Christmas,' said Amelia. 'I didn't know if Santa was coming to you here, so I thought I'd bring you a present.'

Amelia gave him his parcel.

'You can open it, Christie,' she offered, hoping he would.

Christie carefully unwrapped the parcel and looked at the woollen socks. He started crying.

'Christie, Christie, Christie. What's wrong with you?' asked Amelia.

'Have you not forgotten, Doctor? I've no legs,' he said.

Amelia swore at herself. How could she be so stupid. How could she forget he no longer had legs. That was the reason why he was in the nursing home. He was in a wheel chair. That's why his wife had sent him here.

In that moment of panic, Amelia was lost for words. Then they came to her...

'Sorry, Christie,' she apologised. 'I've given you the wrong present. How stupid of me. That was for the next patient. Sorry about that, Christie. Yes, of course I know you've no legs.'

Amelia rummaged in her bag and took out the box of chocolates she thought she might have had to bribe the nurses with.

'Here's your present,' she said.

She handed it to Christie.

He unwrapped it.

'A box of chocolates.' He paused and tears started to flow from his eyes again. 'Doctor, have you forgotten? I'm diabetic.'

Amelia closed her eyes. It could not be worse.

What could she say?

And then Christie started to laugh, and laugh, and laugh.

He laughed so hard he started to cry again.

He laughed so hard he struggled to breathe.

'And to think,' he gasped, 'I was going to sweep you off your feet.'

Jeremy: "A consistent theme in your story is that you always managed to find the wrong man, and then you listened to him."

Amelia: "Yes, unfortunately I did manage to do that. Or perhaps they found me, and stupidly I did listen to them."

Jeremy: "So why do you think that was?"

Amelia: "Who knows? Perhaps I was working out some very deep-seated father issues."

Get on your Bike, Amelia

Amelia was single again. True to form, Shane had cheated once more, but this time she let him go.

For fun, she went out for a drink in the Montgomery Vaults with Kate Buchanan, who was a trainee doctor at the hospital, when in strode Rory, Kate's cousin. Rory was quite a lot older, he was a surgeon at the hospital. And Rory was extremely good looking. "More good looking than he deserved to be" was how Kate described him.

Rory spotted Kate and her friend, asked what they'd like to drink, and after going to the bar, returned with all three drinks held in his hands. He sat down and passed the drinks around.

'Well, aren't you going to introduce me, Kate?' He positively beamed at Amelia, who tried not to blush.

'Amelia, this is my cousin, Rory,' she said flatly. 'Rory, this is my friend, Amelia.'

Rory offered his hand, which Amelia took. His grip was firm, his handshake emphatic.

'Do you work at the Hospital too?' he asked.

'Yes. I'm an intern with Kate,' replied Amelia, trying not to stare. 'I'm doing Geriatrics at the moment.'

'Then you must work for Dr James,' commented Rory.

'Yes, Dr James,' said Amelia.

'Good man, Dr James, very good with people,' added Rory. 'Bet he likes you.'

Amelia blushed.

Rory stood up, clutching his empty glass.

'Another drink, anyone?' he offered.

Kate and Amelia hadn't touched the first drink he'd bought them.

'We're fine, Rory, thanks,' answered Kate.

Rory went to the bar and engaged in conversation with the barman.

'Well?'' said Amelia.

'Well what?' replied Kate.

'You never told me about your cousin,' said Amelia.

'What's to tell?' responded Kate.

'Single?' queried Amelia.

'Yes,' answered Kate.

'Handsome!' declared Amelia.

'So I'm told,' sighed Kate.

'Surgeon!' added Amelia.

'Yes,' groaned Kate. Rory tended to have this kind of effect on women.

Rory returned from the bar, and while he never excluded Kate from the conversation, it was clear that Amelia was the centre of his focus.

And so it was by the end of the evening that Amelia had agreed to go on a date. Kate did her best to not shake her head or roll her eyes.

Soon, date followed date, and within a matter of weeks it was Rory and Amelia, a couple. Even Amelia's appearance had begun to change. She transformed from smart to casual, from elegant party dresses to jeans and big chunky jumpers. Amelia even learnt to drink, though she was not in the same league as Rory. In fact Rory was in a league of his own when it came to drinking.

Perhaps Amelia was too close, too starry-eyed, to realise that he was an alcoholic.

And weeks passed to months.

The partying was nonstop. Often Rory would drink himself comatose, but he would always be up and ready the next day.

Amelia tried to understand the drinking. Once, in a rare departure from his usual secretive ways, Rory spoke of his first girlfriend and how she had committed suicide.

Perhaps Amelia mistook Rory's morose character for that of a brooding intellectual, Rory certainly was extremely intelligent.

And while Rory was handsome, and did have a distinct attraction, he was not generally liked, certainly not among his peers.

Yet Rory's family were very warm and welcoming, open and supportive. Amelia felt at home with them.

Somehow the whole relationship with Rory seemed to give her the things that were previously missing in her life, and though they had few common interests, she just wanted to make it work, she always wanted to impress him.

One night, when Amelia was feeling lonely and Rory was on call. She decided she would cook chicken, potato and broccoli bake. It was delicious, her speciality, but took hours to make.

And when it was cooked, she placed the hot dish in the centre of the kitchen table and stared at it. Dinner for one. Well, she'd actually cooked enough for many more.

She decided that if Rory couldn't come home for dinner, she would take dinner to Rory. She wrapped the dish in kitchen foil, insulated it with tea towels, and placed it in a plastic bag, adding knives, forks and dishes.

The bag steamed in the drizzle-filled evening air as she unlocked her bicycle. With a push, she was astride and began peddling along the pavement. She peddled harder, it really was cold.

Amelia dodged a tree, and bumped down onto the road, only just remembering to check for traffic coming up behind.

It took some fifteen minutes to get to the hospital.

Soaking wet, she dismounted from the bicycle and leant it against a concrete bollard near the rear entrance to the main building.

With her plastic bag in hand, she slipped in through the open doorway, showing her pass to the porter who happened to be waiting there.

Amelia found a phone, and "bleeped" Rory.

No answer.

She tried again.

Not knowing where he was, she wasn't sure what to do.

She asked the porter if he'd seen Dr Buchanan. She told the porter that she had Dr Buchanan's dinner ready for him.

'Smells delicious, Miss, he's a lucky guy,' said the porter leaning over the bag. 'I'll tell you what, Miss, I'll bleep him.'

And so the porter bleeped him.

Rory answered immediately.

'Oh, Dr Buchanan,' said the porter, 'your girlfriend's here, at the rear entrance.'

Amelia couldn't hear Rory's reply, but a moment later the porter spoke again.

'Well, I think you should talk to her,' he said down the telephone. 'She's here, and she's made your dinner.'

The porter passed the phone to Amelia.

'Oh, hi, Rory,' said Amelia. 'I'm here and I've got some dinner for you.'

'I've already eaten, I'm not hungry,' muttered Rory, clearly distracted.

'Oh...' Amelia felt deflated.

'Got to go,' said Rory. And with that the line went dead.

Amelia's face turned red, but she didn't cry, she was too cold. She just stood there.

'You know what, Miss, I'm hungry,' remarked the porter, feeling sorry for Amelia.

Amelia turned.

'Well, he's not coming down,' she said. 'He doesn't want to see me. Would you like it?'

'I'd love it,' beamed the porter, 'and I'll bring it around to all the lads.'

And so the porter ate the chicken, potato and broccoli bake.

He leant across to Amelia.

'Miss, you're better than that,' he said. 'Don't worry, and don't go making him anymore dinners.'

'Thank you, you're too kind,' replied Amelia.

'No, thank you, Miss,' said the porter.

Amelia got on her bike, and in the cold drizzle, cycled home, no chicken, potato and broccoli bake, no Rory. And she vowed to herself that she would never make chicken, potato and broccoli bake again.

Jeremy: "But on the other hand you had me in stitches reading about your antics running around in circles because of men."
<Amelia flashes a smile at Jeremy>
<Jeremy leans forward, refills her glass, and just brushes her hand with his>

Round and Round We Go

It was just what Amelia needed, a holiday. Given that things weren't getting any easier with Rory, Amelia had decided to take Aisling with her on her road trip to Edinburgh. But it was Rory who dominated the conversation.

Aisling had only met him once and thought he was just wonderful.

'You should try living with him,' commented Amelia. 'If things aren't done his way then things aren't done at all. Sometimes I think he sees me as just some kind of pet, some kind of plaything to have around when the mood suits him.'

'Oh,' said Aisling.

'And the drinking,' continued Amelia. 'I thought Dad could drink, but he's a positive teetotaller by comparison. Do you know what?'

'No, what?' asked Aisling.

'Sometimes he gets so drunk that he passes out and I have to literally drag him home,' complained Amelia. 'You know, it's no way for a surgeon to behave.'

'Oh,' was all Aisling could think of to add to the conversation.

'And, you know,' persisted Amelia, 'it would be good if we did something that didn't involve alcohol for a change, like going to the opera or the theatre, or even the cinema. And would it hurt him to smarten up once in a while? From what I can tell he's got the one pair of jeans and that's about it.'

Aisling decided to listen patiently, Amelia had much to say on the subject of Rory, and mostly it wasn't good.

'Did I tell you...'

'...JESUS CHRIST!'

Their car swerved, violently, scattering grass and bits of bush all over the roof as it skidded off the road and tipped into a hedge.

Aisling pulled herself back into her seat and shook her head.

Amelia kept staring in front of her, gripping the steering wheel.

122

There was silence.

The engine had stopped running.

'My God, you're an eejit!' shouted Aisling with her eyes still firmly shut.

'Don't worry, don't worry,' assured Amelia, 'I was aiming for the back of him.'

'What were you doing aiming for the back of him for?' Aisling had opened her eyes.

'Well, it was going to be really hard to swerve out of the way totally,' explained Amelia. 'So I thought if I aimed for the back of him, I wouldn't hurt him too badly.'

'Oh, my God!' exclaimed Aisling 'You're a lunatic.'

'Are you alright?' asked Amelia.

'I think so. And you?' replied Aisling.

'A little shaken,' said Amelia.

They got out of the car.

Surprisingly, not much damage seemed to have been done, just a few dents and scratches. And with a little effort, they managed to pull the car back from the hedge and onto the verge.

The car started after a fashion, and Amelia and Aisling continued on their journey north to the ferry port, though a little more attention was paid to the road.

Even with the sun shining, the wind that blew across the Irish Sea was cold. Amelia tried to climb as high and as far forward as she could on the ferry. And if she could she would have stood at the very bow of the boat, full on to the wind, but she had to make do with a small, partly covered deck about halfway along the boat's side.

Aisling had gone inside to warm-up, but Amelia just wanted to sense the sea. There was something so real about it, something so entrancing about the way the waves swelled, the smell, the taste. And when she looked to the horizon, she saw nothing but water. She was adrift in its expanse. She felt a true sense of perspective, and all her troubles didn't seem to matter much now.

Scotland.

The ferry had docked, and Amelia and Aisling had disembarked. They checked their map and worked out the route they should take to Edinburgh.

The sun held in the sky, though the traffic was heavy.

'Do you love him?' asked Aisling.

Amelia wasn't quite sure what to say, which in itself almost answered her sister's question.

'Or is it just some kind of infatuation?' pressed Aisling.

Amelia thought.

'Or, perhaps,' continued her sister, 'and more to the point, do you think he really loves you?'

'You know, I'm torn about him,' mused Amelia, 'his family are great. I really like his mum and dad. They're so normal. But, my intuition tells me that it won't last.'

Aisling looked at Amelia, and thought round and round we go!

With that thought the traffic came to a sudden halt.

Amelia struggled to see ahead from behind the articulated truck sat in front of her. Then with a rumble of exhaust smoke, the truck pulled away. Amelia was left at what she assumed to be a T-junction, though all of the traffic seemed to be coming from the right.

'Which way, Aisling?' she asked.

Aisling rustled her map, and without looking up, pointed to the right.

'Right it is then,' said Amelia, spotting a gap in the traffic and pulling out.

Cars started flashing her, trucks and buses beeped their horns. The road went round to the left, and continued turning to the left, Amelia followed the road.

Aisling glanced up, dropped her map, and almost leapt into the back seat as a car came straight towards them.

'Amelia,' she yelled, 'I think we've gone the wrong way.'

'What do you mean?' queried Amelia. 'I turned right just like you said.'

'Amelia!' shouted Aisling.

'What, can't you see I'm concentrating?' replied Amelia. 'They all drive like lunatics in Scotland. Why are they all beeping at me?'

'I know,' said Aisling. 'That's because you're going the wrong way around the bloody roundabout!'

'Roundabout, how could that have happened?' exclaimed Amelia. 'Oh my God, my God, I am! How do I get off it?'

A massive double decker bus was driving towards them, flashing its lights and sounding its horn. Instinctively, Amelia yanked at the steering wheel, and the car veered sharply to the left and mounted the central island of the roundabout, where it came to a halt amid some flower beds.

Aisling sighed with relief, and then turned on her sister.

'You are positively the worst driver I have ever had the misfortune to travel with,' she said. 'Are you trying to get us killed? You're the total raving lunatic, not the Scots.'

Amelia could only laugh. And eventually, Aisling laughed too.

It took over an hour for Amelia and Aisling to be rescued from the roundabout.

There was a tap at the driver's side window.

Amelia wound it down.

'Good morning, ladies,' said the police officer.

'Good morning, officer,' smiled Amelia and Aisling in unison.

'And might I inquire as to what you are doing in the middle of the roundabout?' he asked.

Amelia thought how polite the police officers seemed to be in Scotland.

'We drove onto it, officer,' flirted Amelia, without a hint of sarcasm.

'Indeed you did,' remarked the police officer, opening his notebook, and making ready his pen.

'May I see you driving license, Miss?' he requested.

Amelia reached across, found her bag, and got out her driving license. She handed it to the police officer, who then noted her details.

'Well, well, Dr Allen,' he said. 'You are aware that not only is it dangerous, but it is also an offence to park on a roundabout.'

Amelia wasn't quite sure what to say. She'd never had to deal with a roundabout before, nor did she know what she should and shouldn't do with one. She figured the that telling the truth was always best.

'I'm sorry, officer,' she repented innocently, 'but I've never seen a roundabout, we don't have them in Ireland. I think I must have turned the wrong way by mistake.'

'On that last point, Dr Allen,' replied the police officer, 'I think we can all agree.'

Amelia's car had to be towed off the roundabout. The traffic had to be stopped, it caused miles of tailbacks.

After due consideration, and even a smile or two, the police officer let Amelia off with a warning. He then pointed the girls in the direction of Edinburgh, escorting them until they were out of his jurisdiction.

Aisling and Amelia agreed not to talk about, mention, nor refer to Rory for the rest of the holiday. They were in no doubt that to even say his name would be a jinx.

A 'Death Cert'

With Rory a distant memory, another Monday dawned. It was late, there was never enough time. And if the state of Dr James' desk was anything to go by, there never would be. Paperwork, lots and lots of paperwork. Too much paperwork. Amelia sighed. However, she'd made a promise, and she was going to keep her promise. Her boss needed his holiday too, and she had offered to clear the backlog. And so Amelia set to it.

Blood test results checked, cross-referenced and filed. Junk mail binned. Memos read, responded to and archived. Invoices signed and passed back to accounts. Letters of referral verified and appointments booked. And last, but not least, a death certificate requiring completion. As ever, the accompanying notes and charts were incomplete. Amelia checked the admission documentation, "suspected heart attack", and added this to the death certificate, which she signed and put in the post.

As midnight approached, there before Amelia was something she hadn't seen before in Dr James' office, a clear desk! He would be thrilled with her.

Time for bed.

Morning came all too quickly, and Amelia dressed in haste, had no breakfast, and hopped out of her apartment while trying to put on her remaining shoe, only to return to retrieve her bag and keys.

She reached the bus stop to find that the bus had left without her, and would not return, no matter how much she shouted and swore after it. Amelia checked her watch, twenty minutes before the next bus, she'd have to walk.

And so Amelia arrived at work, hungry, breathless and dishevelled. Not the best of starts to the day.

She bleeped the on call house officer for the handover. Luckily there were no concerns. She checked with the ward sister, and made her way to her office via the coffee machine.

Tuesday proved to be busy, but not frantic. Amelia even had time to check and deal with Dr James' newly-arrived post. And she managed to leave before eight.

Wednesday was pretty much a repeat of Tuesday, except Amelia had some breakfast before she left, though again, she missed the bus and had to walk.

Thursday was busier.

On Friday things just didn't stop.

Saturday morning, and Amelia decided she would check that everything was alright on the ward. She quite enjoyed the fact that Dr James was away. She warmed to the increased responsibility and autonomy. Even though she had to put in the hours, she didn't mind at all. And as she left, the ward staff said there was no need to come in tomorrow. They reassured her that she could stay at home, they'd call if she was needed.

Monday came around again. Dr James was back from his holiday, and smiled as he passed through the ward. Amelia was pleased that she's managed so well while he'd been away.

So it came as something of a surprise when the tannoy rang out.

'Will Dr Allen please report to Dr James' office immediately. Dr Allen to Dr James' office immediately.'

'That's me,' Amelia told the patient she was talking to. 'You'll have to excuse me, there must be an emergency, I have to go.'

'Dr James is everything OK?' she asked as she entered his office.

He was sat at his desk staring at a letter.

'Is there some kind of emergency?' she questioned.

'Emergency? No,' he said.

Dr James continued to gaze at the letter, and then shook his head.

Amelia was puzzled. What could all this be about? She'd completed all his paperwork.

Dr James leaned forward, gesturing to Amelia to sit.

'Dr Allen, would you read this letter to me, please,' he asked.

And Dr James passed the letter across to Amelia.

Amelia cleared her throat.

'Dear Dr James, thank you very much for sending the death certificate for Michael. Please be aware that Michael is not dead. Michael is sitting beside me having a cup of tea. Why are you sending a death certificate to me? Because Michael's not dead...'

Amelia hung her head and closed her eyes. How could she have made such a mistake.

'Dr Allen,' said Dr James, 'it appears that in your enthusiasm to clear my paperwork, you've completed and signed a death certificate for a man who's very much alive.'

Amelia raised her head, and opened her eyes. She looked directly at Dr

James, deciding that it was best to face the consequences of her actions, and wondered quite what was going to happen next.

Amelia bit her lip.

Dr James looked directly back at her.

And then he burst out laughing.

'You know, Amelia,' he mused, 'God loves a trier, and heaven knows you tried to do your best. I can't remember the last time I saw my desk, so I thank you. Just try and be a bit more careful next time, eh?'

Jeremy: "I just couldn't keep up with all these men in your life."
<Jeremy smiles and shakes his head>

Anyone for Toast!

It was a beautiful house, it belonged to a friend of Helen's who had taken a sabbatical to go travelling. Amelia was delighted to have moved to Dublin to begin her new job.

It was a fresh start, a fresh start that she really needed. She even had a new boyfriend, Luke. He was a few years younger than she was, and though they'd only gone out on a few dates, she definitely felt an attraction.

Gone were the thoughts of settling down in a country practice and having a large family. She had decided on a full-on medical career in hospital medicine. Family would have to come later, if she ever found the right man.

Amelia knew Helen from medical school, where Helen had been a dental student. They were great friends, who had become separated by distance and all-too-busy lives, but now they were reunited and sharing this beautiful house in the heart of Dublin.

Helen was full of life, perhaps a little too full if the bathroom scales were to be believed, but she was just the sort of person to bring balance to Amelia's rather too work- centred existence.

'I'm gonna' go on a diet, I need to lose weight,' announced Helen at breakfast as she flipped through the pages of a glossy magazine.

Amelia looked up from her toast.

'A diet?' she asked. Amelia realised she hadn't worried about her own weight for a long time.

'"Guaranteed to lose weight", that's what it says here.'

Helen showed Amelia the page in the magazine, and then continued to read aloud, '"Shed pounds in days, eat and drink all you want", now that's my kind of diet.'

Helen pushed her plate away.

'And the catch is?' queried Amelia.

'No catch,' said Helen. 'From what I read here it's a boiled chicken and tea diet.'

'Chicken and tea?' chuckled Amelia.

'Yep, no dairy, no sauces, no vegetables, no alcohol, nothing, just boiled chicken and tea for ten days, oh and water,' replied Helen.

'Let's do it,' acquiesced Amelia.

'Well, that's settled then,' said Helen, snatching Amelia's buttered toast from her hand and tossing it in the bin.

And so Amelia and Helen went on the diet, chicken and tea for ten days, every day, for every meal.

They had to come home to cook the chicken, taking it in turns to do so. But they managed, though after the ten days, they were, literally, starving.

Helen was pleased and proud of herself. She'd managed to lose many pounds, and not a drop of alcohol had passed her lips, an achievement in itself.

Amelia had become little more than skin and bones herself, but she was also very pleased with the results.

'We need to celebrate,' said Helen. 'My father's got tickets to the rugby on Saturday, and we can have a drink or two. After all this detoxification, we need to re-toxify!'

'Brilliant idea,' agreed Amelia.

Amelia was engrossed by the rugby match. It was full of energy and aggression, speed and impact. She clapped her hands and cheered, the sounds solid in the autumnal air.

After the match they went to O'Flannigan's.

Helen's father, who insisted Amelia called him "John", jostled his way back from the bar with a tray bearing three pints.

Amelia had never drunk a pint in her life, and was, in her own words, "Completely three sheets to the wind within minutes", but she was having a great time.

They talked of rugby, what was and what could have been, and John entertained Amelia with tales of Helen's childhood, much to Helen's embarrassment. But he told them with humour and the pride that only a devoted father can.

Amelia was having fun.

People came across to say hello, some to chat for a while. There didn't seem a person in the bar that John or Helen didn't know.

One man who walked over to them and chatted was particularly funny and engaging.

She called him "Boylie". He had a bit of a belly, but all in all Amelia thought he was attractive, she liked the macho rugby player look.

'Who's that chap?' she asked, after the man had walked away.

'That's Boylie,' said Helen.

'He's nice,' remarked Amelia.

'Do you fancy him?' quizzed Helen.

'Well, I'm not sure,' replied Amelia. 'He seems attractive.'

So Amelia and Helen worked their way to the bar.

'I'll go and get Boylie over,' said Helen.

'Oh no, please don't,' begged Amelia.

'I am, I am, you fancy him,' urged Helen.

'I don't know if I fancy him or not,' said Amelia.

Helen went across and got Boylie to come over and chat anyway.

Suddenly Amelia realised that she was meant to be meeting Luke in town.

'No, no, stay,' insisted Helen.

'I said to him I'd ring him later,' explained Amelia. 'I feel really bad, I have to go into town.'

'Oh no, no, no. Stay, stay, stay,' pleaded Helen.

Amelia decided she'd have just one more drink and then go.

Helen and Boylie were delighted, and of course "just one more drink" became two, then three, until eventually, "just one more drink" became "one drink too many".

And so, worse for drink, Helen and Amelia ended up going off to a nightclub with Boylie. And in the stupor of the evening, Boylie tried to kiss Amelia, and Amelia ended up kissing him back.

Amelia felt awful. What about Luke?

She'd had loads to drink. She felt confused. How could she be attracted to Boylie?

The three of them ended up going back to the house.

'I'd like toast,' demanded Boylie.

So Amelia went to make it for him.

After putting bread in the toaster, Amelia suddenly thought, 'Oh my God, what about Luke?' So she checked the telephone voicemail, and there were about seven messages saying, "Where are you? We're supposed to be going to the movies".

Feeling guilty, Amelia went out the back door to visit Luke.

She walked a mile up the road.

She knocked on his door. It must have been two o'clock in the morning.

The door opened.

'It's you,' he said, standing in the doorway, wearing pyjamas. 'Where were you? I called by your house, and I went to all the movie theatres to see if I could find you, but you weren't there.'

'Can I come in?' asked Amelia.

'Well, if you want to, come on in,' said Luke.

He lifted his arm and ushered Amelia in.

Then, between one thing and the next, and before Amelia knew it, they were kissing and more. But almost as quickly as the passion had started, it was all over.

Amelia couldn't believe what had just happened.

She got up, put on her clothes.

'I've got to go, Luke,' she said. 'I've got to go.'

Luke rolled over.

'Won't you stay?' he asked Amelia, but she was gone, already out of the bedroom and down the stairs. He heard the front door close.

Amelia must have been gone for over two hours. As she came in through the kitchen door, as quietly as she could, she could hear voices from the living room. It was four in the morning, and Helen and Boylie were still up.

Boylie was giving Helen a foot rub for some reason or other when Amelia entered the living room with the cold, burnt toast.

'Where the hell have you been?' asked Helen giggling.

'I was just making the toast... It took a while,' replied Amelia in all seriousness, and then she sat down.

Helen just looked at Amelia as if she was mad, and then continued to banter with Boylie.

After about half an hour, Amelia felt tired. She stood.

'Look, I'm going to bed,' she said, and so she did.

She collapsed onto her lovely, big bed, and looked at the ceiling.

'Oh my God!' she whispered to herself, and then fell asleep.

It seemed like moments later, but several hours must have passed, the sun was up.

Amelia awoke. Her mouth was dry, so she stumbled downstairs to the kitchen in search of a glass of water.

She looked at the kitchen clock, eleven o'clock in the morning. She could hear snoring coming from the living room. Boylie was asleep on the couch, mostly naked, half-draped in a blanket.

She walked across and shook him to wake him up.

'What are you doing here?' she asked.

'Don't you remember last night?' he replied. 'You gave me a blanket, and said I could sleepover?'

'Oh, that's fine then,' remarked Amelia.

Boylie yawned, and then sat up.

'Right, how about a fresh slice of toast and then I'll go,' he suggested. 'Perhaps a little fresher than last night. Oh, and a cup of freshly brewed coffee, if it's not too much trouble.'

He said it all with a wink.

Amelia went back into the kitchen, made proper toast and some coffee. She then returned to the living room.

She put down the coffee, and handed the toast to Boylie, who promptly took a large mouthful.

'Mmmm, nice toast, brown not black,' he said. 'Your cooking's really improved. This toast is edible, just the way I like it.'

He grinned and half-hid behind his cup of coffee.

Amelia glared, but then glanced to the window. Someone was about to come to the front door.

Luke!

She slid down in the seat, trying not to be seen.

'Why are you going like that in the seat?' asked Boylie.

There was a knock at the door, firm and loud.

Amelia jumped up, dashed through the kitchen and then up the stairs. She ran into Helen's bedroom.

'Helen, Helen, Helen, Helen!' she yelled. 'I'm going to bed. Please answer the door because I think it's Luke, and Boylie is down on the couch in his boxer shorts. It's going to look really bad if I answer the door in my nightie.'

There was another, more insistent knock at the front door.

At which Amelia turned and scurried off to her bedroom, slamming the door behind her. She jumped into bed, and pulled up the covers like a naughty child trying to hide.

The knocking at the front door was relentless.

'This is ridiculous!' announced Helen from the landing, loud enough for Amelia to hear.

Helen descended the stairs trailing her glamorous, flowing nightgown, and opened the front door.

'Oh, Luke, it's you,' she said. 'How are you?'

'Is Amelia in?' asked Luke.

'I think so,' replied Helen. 'Why don't you come on in.'

She gestured for Luke to enter with a graceful sweep of her arm.

'Do you know Boylie?' she asked, as they passed the living room on their way to the kitchen.

'Uh, yeah, I think so,' answered Luke, 'from a while back, at the rugby.'

'Oh yeah, that's right,' said Boylie, as he stood in his blanket in the living room doorway and shook Luke's hand, 'Good to see you.'

At which the blanket tumbled to the floor.

Luke was speechless.

Helen directed Luke to the kitchen table.

'I'll stick the kettle on for you, feel free to make yourself some tea,' she said, 'and I'll go and see if Amelia's up.'

Amelia was cowering under the bedclothes, her eyes shut, hoping that it might all go away when Helen burst into her bedroom.

'Right, it's like this,' she said. 'Luke's in the kitchen, Boylie's in the living room. Take your pick. I'm going back to bed now, it's your problem.'

'Oh my God, oh my God, what am I going to do?' stammered Amelia.

Helen shrugged in amusement, and good to her word, floated back to bed.

Amelia decided to brave it, and went downstairs to the kitchen and Luke.

She didn't know what to say to him.

'Hello, Luke, how are you? Have you been to Mass?' was all she could think of.

'Yes,' he replied, staring straight into her eyes, 'though it looks like you should be the one going to Mass.'

'No, no, no,' answered Amelia. 'Nothing happened between myself and Boylie. He's just had toast, and I'm chatting to you in the middle of his toast.'

Luke sighed.

'Anyway,' he continued, 'I think we've reached a point here where we shouldn't be going out anymore.'

Amelia thought about what he'd said. In her heart she knew he was right, and their relationship was pretty much over.

'I think you're right,' she replied. 'We'll call it a day. Thank you so much for coming round. It was really nice of you.'

And that was that.

Amelia let Luke out.

When she returned to the living room, she found that Boylie had gone too.

Amelia trooped slowly upstairs to Helen, and entered her bedroom.

Helen was awake, laughing herself sick.

'Oh my God, what are you like?' she said. 'One minute, two men, the next, none.'

<Amelia puts her head in her hands>
<Jeremy picks up her book and starts to read>

Party On

Amelia was not in the mood for party planning. News from Loch Garman wasn't so good. Her mother was having another unwell phase, and Amelia had been told that her father was lonely, fed up and drinking heavily again.

With Alex occupied starting up his business, and Aisling away, travelling the world, she felt that she should be there. But though she'd healed the rift with her father, she'd been so busy, everyone had just drifted apart.

'I know what will cheer you up, Amelia,' suggested Helen.

'I don't want a Christmas party,' spelt out Amelia.

'Yo, ho, ho, you do!' said Helen.

'I don't,' stated Amelia.

'Well, whether you do, or you don't, I've decided we're going to have a Christmas party,' continued Helen. 'It'll be good for us, just what the doctor ordered. Now, who shall we invite?'

Helen feigned thinking by resting her chin in the palm of her hand, and then answered her own question.

'I know,' she said, 'Men.'

Amelia closed her eyes and shook her head, but Helen was insistent.

'I'm going to invite Boylie,' declared Helen. 'He's a right *craic* and he'll bring loads of his rugby mates.'

'Please don't invite him,' pleaded Amelia.

'Why?' asked Helen.

'There's something about him,' replied Amelia. 'I don't know, I think he's trouble.'

'Well, that didn't stop you before at the nightclub,' responded Helen, 'when you had your tongues down each others' throats.'

'I was drunk, so drunk,' sighed Amelia.

'Don't tell me you didn't fancy him that night,' remarked Helen.

'Oh God.' Amelia dropped her head into her hands. She could remember every moment of that weekend in all-too-vivid detail.

'See, I know you fancy him,' teased Helen.

'Go on, invite him and his rugby mates if you must,' relented Amelia, but somewhere a voice was telling her she should stay well away from him.

As parties went, it was a great party. The house was alive with people and drink and music and food, trimmed with every Christmas decoration imaginable, all thanks to Helen. It just worked. Smiles, and conversation and joy flowed.

Boylie proved to be charm itself, though this perception was perhaps aided by Amelia having a drink or two too many.

'Oh, he's lovely,' she mused, he reminded her a little of her father. A notion she supported by a somewhat convoluted thought process. Whenever she went out with someone she really liked, where she was more keen on them than they were on her, it didn't work out. So why not try going out with someone who is more keen on her than she is on him. What better candidate than Boylie! What harm could it do? Given everything that was happening back in Loch Garman, she needed some fun in her life.

And so, much to Amelia's surprise, and Boylie's delight, they got together that night.

Kieran and Amelia, a couple. It took a while for Amelia to get used to calling Boylie, "Kieran". She had only ever known him as Boylie. But a couple they were, living the life in Dublin.

In social groups Kieran was nothing but entertaining. He had the gift. He could warm to anybody, and everybody warmed to him. However, Amelia found that, when they were alone together, he could become moody, with a tendency to anger on occasion.

Kieran's mother, Niamh, really liked Amelia, and Amelia loved being in Niamh's company. Niamh had a wisdom about her that so reassured Amelia. Where Kieran offered amusement and distraction from the rigours of life, Niamh gave Amelia emotional support, particularly with her own mother's ongoing illness.

Sometimes, when she was out with Kieran, Amelia would think about Luke. She knew that Luke was too young for her, and that her dalliance with Kieran, on that fateful weekend, put any chance of a future with Luke out of the question, but, even so, she still felt an attraction for him.

And though Niamh never said, Amelia soon realised that Niamh was keen to marry Kieran off, to tame his errant ways. She wanted grandchildren. But strangely Niamh never pressed Kieran or Amelia on the point. Perhaps she didn't want to interfere, or perhaps she thought that now wasn't the right time. Amelia couldn't quite work it out.

As days and weeks and months passed, Kieran started to take Amelia for granted. He started to do more of his own things without mentioning it to her. Arguments followed. Amelia thought about ending the relationship, the bad times seemed to be outweighing the good.

And then, on Valentine's day, Kieran proposed.

Amelia was taken completely by surprise. She hesitated, but then she said yes.

For a while their relationship improved, but old ways die hard and Amelia seriously considered returning the ring.

Kieran had gone on a golfing trip the very week that his mother had to go into hospital for a routine operation. It was Amelia who accompanied Niamh to the hospital. It was Amelia that sat by her side, reassuring her that all would be fine.

Then, just as Amelia made to leave, Niamh beckoned her to her bedside.

'I know he's my son, and I love him so, he's a dear boy and I want him to be happy,' she said, 'but I have come see you as my daughter, and I want what's best for you too. So what I have to say has to be said, I cannot keep my peace any longer. Kieran...'

Niamh reached out and squeezed Amelia's hand.

'Kieran's not the right one for you my dear,' she said. 'It won't work, trust me.'

Amelia didn't know what to say. Niamh's words were a complete surprise, a shock. What could she say? She looked quizzically at Niamh, but all she saw was absolute clarity in her eyes.

'Amelia,' continued Niamh, 'I just ask that you listen to me and think about what I've said and what you're about to do.'

'OK,' was all Amelia could manage.

'Thank you,' said Niamh.

'I'll... I'll see you later, after the operation,' said Amelia, as she leant over and kissed Niamh goodbye.

'See you later, dear,' replied Niamh.

As a doctor, Amelia thought she should be able to cope, be able to deal with the most difficult of circumstances, after all that's what doctors are trained to do, but when the phone call came, Amelia just slipped slowly to the floor and cried.

At three-thirty that afternoon, despite the best efforts of the operating theatre team, Mrs Niamh Boyle had died, unexpectedly.

MARRIED

The Red Hot Hen Night!

On the day of his mother's funeral, Kieran said to Amelia that he just couldn't lose both of the women in his life. In grief, Amelia reaffirmed her commitment to him.

What else could she say?

They set a date for the wedding.

From death comes life.

Michelle Edwards, a paediatrician friend, organised Amelia's hen night in Dublin. Aisling had returned from wherever she had been travelling. Both the other bridesmaids, Miriam and Helen, came, as did Amelia's oldest school friend, Sarah Jane from Loch Garman.

The plan was to stay in the Merilee Hotel and then go out for dinner, drinks and onto a nightclub.

Amelia dressed in her best party clothes with high-heeled shoes. She wore a really bright red lipstick, the type that stayed on for twenty-four hours. Amelia thought that this would save her from having to re-apply it, particularly if she'd had a drink or two.

As she sat facing the mirror, she remembered that her father had always said to her, "Make sure you wear a nice lipstick".

The hen night party-goers met in the hotel's foyer. Some had been in the bar, others had just come down from their rooms. Amelia was the last to descend the stairs, and immediately became the centre of attention. All were smiles and kisses.

Outside, the evening wasn't cold, and the hen party walked the short distance to the restaurant for dinner. The food was good, and with a few drinks inside them, the party- goers began to tell tales of Amelia. There were many tales to tell.

How about the time Amelia managed to crash her car straight after it had been repaired, much to the amusement of the mechanics who'd just fixed it. Or when Amelia did the homily at the school retreat, only to have it said again by Father Rafferty, much to the annoyance of the rest of the school. Or when a customer at that London restaurant asked her for a microscope. Or when she'd bought a pair of socks as a Christmas present for a man who'd just had his legs amputated.

Helen said she knew a great pub, just round the corner, O'Flannigan's. A place that would be forever in Amelia's memory, the place where she first set eyes on the love of her life.

'Of course, at the time, Kieran wasn't the only love interest in Amelia's life,' added Helen.

Everyone wanted to know more. Amelia had long since tried to forget that particular weekend of re-toxification. Not her finest hour.

And the more they drank, the more they laughed, though by now one or two of the party-goers had had one or two drinks too many. But onto the nightclub they went.

Pounding music, pressing bodies and hot lights made a heady mix. Almost everyone was up for a dance. It was a great *craic*, though Miriam was now slumped in a booth, her head on the table with the drinks.

Helen said it was time to take Miriam back to her hotel room.

Miriam was presented at the glass doors of the Merilee Hotel, propped between Helen and Amelia, but the duty manager shook his head.

'No, we are not letting you in,' came the muffled response to the rigorous banging on the doors.

'This is ridiculous, we're doctors,' argued Helen.

'You don't look like doctors,' said the duty manager. 'You've had too much to drink. Ladies. Go away, you are not coming into this hotel.'

'But we're staying here,' protested Helen. 'We've paid money, and all our clothes and everything are upstairs.'

And so the stand-off continued.

Miriam, who looked the wrong shade of pale, was phasing in and out of consciousness.

'This is crazy,' thought Amelia. 'I'm going to have to do something to get Miriam to her bed.' So she went round the corner with Helen, leaving Miriam to be tended to by the others, and rang the hotel. She asked to speak to the duty manager, and pretended to be a garda síochána from Stall Street.

'This is Sergeant Maguire speaking...' said Amelia from the rather dubious smelling telephone box.

Helen, who'd managed to crush inside with Amelia, cracked up laughing.

'Are you sure you know what you're doing? whispered Helen.

'I'm only going to play a joke,' explained Amelia, her hand over the receiver.

She then continued her conversation with the duty manager.

'I believe you have three doctors outside,' she said, 'and one is very seriously ill and you won't admit them.'

'That's not true,' replied the duty manager.

'Oh is that so?' questioned Amelia. 'One of my boys has told me it is so, because he saw them outside your hotel. Would you like me to come round in person and investigate the problem further?'

There was a moment's silence.

'If there's been a problem,' explained the duty manager, 'rest assured, the problem is no longer.'

Amelia put down the phone, and ran back to the front of the hotel, a giggling Helen in tow.

The duty manager appeared behind the glass doors, fumbled with his keys, and then opened them.

'Doctor, I'm so sorry,' he apologised, 'I didn't realise you were a doctor. Is there a problem? Is this lady sick?'

'She's very, very sick,' replied Amelia, looking at the limp form of Miriam, who was one breath away from throwing up.

The party-goers made their way to the elevator.

The duty manager followed.

'Let me accompany you to you room, ladies,' he said and ushered the ladies into the elevator.

As they ascended, Amelia leant across and spoke to the duty manager.

'You haven't heard the end of this, you know,' she said. 'My brother is a senior council. The way you treated my friend has been simply atrocious. You'll be lucky to keep your job after this.'

The duty manager was shaking visibly. He kept apologising for any inconvenience caused, but his ingratiating attempts to seek forgiveness were simply met by a bedroom door slammed in his face.

Miriam was helped to the bathroom where she clung to the toilet bowl.

Amelia and Helen sat on the side of the bath and watched.

'Never could hold her drink,' commented Helen.

'No,' agreed Amelia.

Amelia looked to the mirror above the basin. Her red lipstick was still on.

'I'm surprised you didn't ask Father Rafferty to perform your wedding ceremony,' remarked Helen, changing the subject.

'As it happens, I tried,' said Amelia, 'but it turns out he's no longer a priest. He left the priesthood some ten years ago to get married. By all accounts, he's got a family now.'

'Well there you go,' reflected Helen. 'Who'd've thought it, a Father has become a father.'

At which Miriam threw up.

Amelia knelt down beside her.

'There, there,' she reassured, 'you'll feel much better now. Would you like some water to drink, Miriam?'

'No, no thanks,' groaned Miriam, and proceeded to be sick again.

Fireworks

Amelia was a little disappointed.

No, in truth, Amelia was more than a little disappointed, she felt completely let down. How could her own father not speak about how kind, and gentle, and loving she was. Amelia had always idolised her father.

And as for, "...and Amelia is a very determined young lady, a point perhaps best demonstrated by the fact that, against tradition, she's chosen to keep her family name", well, what a thing to say. How could he! She felt as if she was ten, and was being scolded for not doing as she was told. This was her wedding day, and it was meant to be the best day of her life.

Thus, a very disappointed Amelia sat with her arms folded, looking less than happy as the proceedings continued.

Kieran stood up, and surveyed the gathered family and friends. The chatter in the room dropped to a muted hush. Kieran delivering his bridegroom's speech was always going to be something worth listening to.

Amelia did not know what Kieran was going to say, but she hoped that he, at least, would tell everyone how wonderful, and beautiful, and gorgeous she was, and how much he loved her. Not that she was in any way vain, or self-centred, or craved attention, she reminded herself quickly.

'Amelia said that I should mention her as often as I could while I'm doing the speech,' stated Kieran.

'Well, that's a good start,' thought Amelia.

'On behalf of Amelia and myself, I'd like to thank everybody who helped make today the best day of our lives.'

This was met with polite applause.

'In particular I'd like to thank Amelia personally.'

He paused and turned to Amelia with a broad smile. He then continued.

'For without Amelia, and Amelia's parents, William and Audrey, and Amelia's sister, Aisling, and Amelia's brother, Alex, and Amelia's aunt, Aunty Bea, and Amelia's friends, Michelle, Kate and Sarah Jane, and Amelia's wedding co-ordinator, Janet Harding, and of course, anyone else I've forgotten to mention, Amelia's wedding would not be what it is today.'

The polite applause was interspersed with the odd chuckle.

Kieran turned to the bridesmaids, and with a grin and a wink raised his glass. 'Amelia and I toast Amelia's bridesmaids, Aisling, Helen and Miriam, a job well done!'

He lifted his glass.

'Amelia's bridesmaids, Aisling, Helen and Miriam,' responded those in the room. Kieran waited for the noise to die down and looked to his family.

'Amelia and I would also like to say a special thank you to Amelia's mother-in-law, Niamh, may she rest in peace, and Amelia's father-in-law, John, without whom Amelia would not have a groom to marry. A special thanks to Amelia's parents-in-law!'

'Amelia's parents-in-law,' laughed everyone.

'In addition, Amelia and I would like to thank Amelia's best man, David, for managing to get Amelia's groom to Amelia's wedding on time, and I might add, for managing to get Amelia's groom to Amelia's wedding sober, well, mostly sober!'

'To Amelia's best man,' toasted Kieran.

'Amelia's best man,' roared the captivated audience.

'So, in conclusion, Amelia and I, cannot express how grateful we are to all of you for making today, Amelia's wedding day, so wonderful.'

He paused, the room was quiet, expectant.

'To Amelia's wedding day,' he declared and raised his glass once more. 'Amelia's wedding day,' cheered the wedding guests as they rose to their feet.

Amelia knew that Kieran's speech had been very funny, but she really wanted him to say that he loved her, or that she was fun, or she was kind.

'Well, maybe I'm none of those things,' she worried. 'Maybe I'm not fun, maybe I'm not kind, maybe he doesn't love me, because he never said anything like that.

And then Amelia thought, 'Neither did my father.'

Behind her smile, Amelia felt as if she was floating, like a little bird, high up above the people sat at the tables.

'I don't really feel I'm part of this,' she thought. 'I feel I shouldn't be here.'

So as Kieran sat down, Amelia decided to stand up.

'I'd like to say a few words,' she said.

The wedding guests became quiet, regarding Amelia with interest.

'I'd like to say a big welcome to everybody here,' she announced. 'I hope you have a wonderful night, and I open my arms to my new family, and I thank you all very much for coming.'

For the briefest of moments there was silence, and then the wedding guests applauded.

Dazed and confused, Amelia sat down. The proceedings continued.

After the speeches had ended, and dinner had been eaten, the cake was cut, the bouquet tossed, and the dancing started, though not without incident.

Aisling had decided to invite Gerald to Amelia's wedding, essentially on a blind date, after Brendan, her latest boyfriend, had dumped her unceremoniously the week before.

However, Brendan arrived unexpectedly at the wedding reception uninvited, dressed in a white tuxedo. Aisling allowed herself to be wooed away. Gerald just shook his head, and made for the bar.

Amelia had seen the events transpire from across the room, and became enraged. She lost control.

'This guy's dumped Aisling, and now Aisling is dumping Gerald,' she thought as she crossed the room to confront Aisling.

'What the hell are you doing?' she said.

Everyone turned to see Amelia facing up to Aisling and Brendan.

'And you, you maggot,' she continued, 'you leave my sister alone.'

Janet, the wedding co-ordinator, quickly recognised that this wasn't in the script for a well executed wedding, and stepped to the fore.

'Well, everyone, it's time for the fireworks now,' she said, as she tried usher the wedding guests outside.

'I'll give you fireworks,' shouted Amelia, gesturing at Brendan. 'You get this jerk away from my wedding, he dumped my sister, and is not welcome here.'

Now, even the band had stopped playing. There was nothing like a family squabble to add interest to an otherwise dull evening of playing the same old tunes over and over again.

Kieran gesticulated to them to carry on, hoping the music might drown out the fracas on the dance floor. He ran across to Amelia.

'Let's dance, honey,' he said, and grabbed Amelia before she could say any more.

It was then that Amelia realised she was letting herself down, badly, and allowed Kieran to lead her away. And as Janet managed to persuade Brendan to leave, so the wedding guests returned to their celebrations.

'Have I said that I think your dress is beautiful, like you,' whispered Kieran as the newlyweds spun round and round to the music. Amelia melted.

'What a fool she'd been,' she thought, and she smiled as she'd meant to smile all day.

Of course the irony was that Amelia really didn't like her wedding dress. Her mother hadn't been able to come and help her pick it out, and Amelia had ended up choosing a wedding dress, that on reflection she didn't like. A stupid gold coloured dress, by a very expensive French designer. Something to be different. Typical.

And as her wedding day came to an end, Amelia looked to the night sky, and watched the closing firework display. She thought it was amazing. She and Kieran had gone up the avenue, to the top of the castle, to see the display from the master bedroom.

'They're fantastic,' said Amelia, transfixed, 'well worth it.'

'Amelia, you know, I wouldn't expect any less from you,' remarked Kieran. 'You just blew up our last five hundred pounds in smoke and fireworks. No expense spared, it's the wedding of the year!'

Learning How to Scuba Dive

It was the day after the wedding, and Amelia knew she'd done the wrong thing, she'd made the wrong decision, she'd married the wrong man. She wondered how many other newlyweds had thought the same on the morning after their wedding.

She knew it wasn't the right thought to have at thirty thousand feet, en route to their Caribbean honeymoon.

Kieran had the window seat and was dozing off.

She looked at his placid face, his half-turned up smile.

Or perhaps she had made the right decision.

No, she knew, to be even thinking these thoughts meant she'd made the wrong choice.

What was she going to do? Divorce? She an Irish catholic! She would be excommunicated by church, state, family and friends without a second thought. Even if she could get a divorce, she could hardly do it after being married for one day. And anyway what grounds did she have? A feeling that she had chosen the wrong man.

Oh God, what had she done?

Amelia sighed and asked the flight attendant for another glass of wine. All she could do was wait, make the most of it, and see how things were going to play out.

Well, at least she got to choose the honeymoon destination, though that was only because Kieran had no money and couldn't be bothered to organise it himself.

No matter, she'd be able lie in the sun and relax for a week. She'd have massages and treatments every day in the health spa, be waited on hand and foot, and eat and drink until she could eat and drink no more.

Despite the beauty of the location, the grandness of the accommodation, and the sun- filled weather, and Amelia's company, Kieran was clearly bored.

When they went for their daily massage, Amelia could hear him chatting to the masseuse in the room next door.

When they went down for dinner, Kieran would make a beeline for the bar, and engage in conversation with whomever happened to be propping it up.

After a day or so, he managed to find someone to play golf with. Amelia was not interested in golf, and spent her time by the pool, reading.

Then, out of the blue, Kieran said he wanted to go scuba diving, it was something he'd never done. He insisted that Amelia came along. After an half hour introduction in the pool, the instructor said that they were now ready to try their first dive.

Amelia blinked. What? She'd barely been paying attention to what had been said. She had been more interested in ensuring that her tan was even, as they had swam around the pool, than doing this and doing that with a bunch of heavy scuba gear.

As she sat on the boat heading out into the bay she was at least a little reassured because there were other couples for whom scuba diving was clearly a new experience.

She traced her arm over the edge of the boat, her hand cutting into the blue-green water, and looked back to the shoreline and the Pitons that touched the sky.

The boat slowed, turned and dropped anchor. They were asked to kit up. Some minutes later, after a brief safety review, they were sat on the boat's edge.

Kieran raised his thumbs, and the next moment he was gone, tumbling backwards into the water.

'Oh my God,' were the only words that Amelia could manage as the instructor pushed her off the boat. She hadn't even put her thumbs up.

Amelia thought she was going to die. She couldn't breathe, she didn't know how to use the equipment, she didn't know what the equipment did.

Kieran bobbed back up to the surface and swam across to her.

'This is fantastic,' he said.

Amelia sputtered water everywhere, struggling to stay afloat.

'What's wrong with you?' he asked.

'I'm gonna' drown!' shouted Amelia.

Kieran clearly wasn't listening, or if he was, his intentions were less than kind. He put his hand on top of Amelia's head and pushed her down under the water.

'Come on, stop being stupid,' he joked. 'It's easy, just dive down. It's wonderful all the things you can see.'

Down went Amelia. She tried, but just couldn't get the breathing. She resurfaced, gasping for air, at which point one of the instructors also pushed her head down.

Amelia freaked, and in a few moments she'd discarded her gear and was swimming for shore.

She left them to it.

She was never going to go scuba diving again. It was the most frightening thing she had ever done. She felt she was totally out of control.

And worst of all, nobody seemed to care about her.

Talk about sink or swim!

Kieran loved it, and couldn't see what all the fuss was about. He'd thought that Amelia had over-reacted.

After that, Amelia refused to leave the poolside and her books.

Kieran had to make his own entertainment.

Newly Weds

Amelia, Kieran and their luggage had returned from the honeymoon mostly in one piece. It was a honeymoon which they had each enjoyed, but in their own way. In fact having to go with each other was the only detraction from an otherwise perfect holiday.

As they stepped through the door of Amelia's Dublin apartment, which was now their home, it was clear that each had their own way of doing things.

Kieran had picked up the phone to arrange to go out for a drink, while Amelia began unpacking, though she soon became distracted opening the letters that had arrived during the time they had been away. She decided to make some tea.

'Tea, Kieran?' she asked.

'No, I prefer coffee,' he replied. 'OK.'

The letters were mostly bills and circulars, except for a handwritten letter from Canada, redirected from her parents' address. Who did she know in Canada?

The kettle had boiled. She put the Canadian letter to one side and made the drinks. Kieran almost spat his out.

'No sugar!' he exclaimed.

'Sorry, I forgot. One?' she replied.

'Two sugars,' instructed Kieran, passing back the coffee.

Amelia duly went and put sugar in Kieran's coffee.

'You're gonna' have to be do better than that if you want to be my housewife,' he said, taking back the coffee.

Amelia looked at him. Housewife, indeed.

Kieran just smiled that mischievous smile of his, the smile he thought made everything better. He walked off into the living room, and turned on the TV. And in an instant he was lost in the rugby.

The letter was from Ross Byrne, she found herself pleasantly surprised. She'd been to medical school with Ross, and even though she'd always quite liked Ross, she'd lost touch over the years. He'd got a job in Toronto, that was probably why she'd lost touch. He was well, had got married and they were expecting their second child. Good old Ross! He asked how she was, and how were her parents, and if she was ever out his way, to look him up.

There was a shout from the living room. Someone had scored in the rugby.

Amelia put the letter down. She'd have to reply. As she opened the rest of the post, she heard more shouting from the living room. Kieran clearly liked his rugby.

Then, with Monday just a day away, Amelia decided to get everything ready for work. She went to the bedroom and finished unpacking her bag. There was a lot of laundry to be done. She'd have to do the washing.

'Anything for the wash, Kieran?' she shouted across the hall.

No reply.

She tutted and walked to the living room.

'Anything for the wash?' she repeated.

'What? Can't you see I'm busy watching the rugby,' replied Kieran, eyes fixed on the TV.

'I'm going to do the laundry now, do you want anything washed?' she said again.

There was a pause in play. Kieran looked round.

'Yeah,' he said. 'When you unpack my bag you'll find the dirty stuff in the bottom. Don't get the coloureds mixed with the whites, will you, they'll run.'

There was a whistle, and Kieran returned to the match.

This wasn't quite what Amelia imagined wedded bliss to be. Though she shouldn't really be surprised.

Amelia and Kieran hadn't discussed any of the practicalities of being married. Each had just assumed how the other would behave. They hadn't talked about it at all. How Amelia regretted skipping the weekend marriage guidance course the church had offered. She had thought she was going to get an understanding husband, happy to support her professional career. Kieran clearly thought he now had a housewife to be at his beck and call.

Dutifully, Amelia returned to the bedroom and unpacked Kieran's bag. She added his washing to hers, making sure not to mix the colours.

She didn't know whether to laugh or cry. It was like something out of the last century. In retrospect she was surprised that Kieran hadn't asked her father if she came with a dowry.

Well, the laundry wouldn't wash itself. There was nothing to be done but get on with it.

Barely had she finished loading the machine, when she heard Kieran ask for more coffee.

'And don't forget the sugar this time, two spoons, honey!'

Opportunities

Kieran expected his meal to be on the table when he came from work in the evening, but after four nights of complaining about Amelia's cooking, Amelia refused to cook anymore. He could do it himself from now on.

And so the pattern was set. Kieran would cook, drink and fall asleep in front of the TV, and Amelia would clear up the mess.

She knew he didn't enjoy his job much. He'd taken what was available and it caused him stress, not that he'd say. Impression and image was all to Kieran. It's what made him such good company when socialising. He was always up for making people laugh and smile, no matter how he felt about things at work or at home. It was all about having a good time. People didn't see the other side of Kieran, what he was truly like.

A month on from their wedding and Amelia didn't sleep much. Often she would just lie awake thinking about this and that, about work, but mostly about her marriage.

It was clear to her that what Kieran wanted most was to be in control. If he wasn't in control, he'd become obstructive, argumentative. He'd take it out on her.

She was trapped in an incompatible marriage, but what could she do? She'd tried talking to Kieran. She'd even told him that she didn't love him, but he'd said it wasn't important, she'd grow to love him. And before she even thought about mentioning it, there was no way he was going to give her a divorce. That was that, marriage was forever.

After six months or so, Amelia began to realise that Kieran liked to have and spend money. He would never be seen by his friends not to have enough money to do what he wanted to do, whether it was a golf trip or some other flimsy excuse for getting drunk and having a wild time away from home. He wanted Amelia to be a housewife, but in reality he knew that Amelia had to work to earn the money for the lifestyle he wished to live. And therein lay his problem. Amelia earnt more than he did. Her career was on the rise, his was going nowhere. He was not in control.

Amelia decided to throw herself at her job.

It didn't take long for Amelia's career to go from strength to strength. If you showed a willingness and capacity for work it was surprising how quickly opportunities came. And Amelia was good at spotting opportunities.

After a couple of months, Amelia had been appointed to a committee and two working groups. She'd even gained an assistant. These new, additional responsibilities involved travel, mostly around Europe, and they gave Amelia a much higher profile.

And not spending time with each other certainly improved their relationship. Amelia felt less stifled, and Kieran pretty much had the freedom to come and go as he pleased. Though not happy, Amelia felt she was making the most of things.

It was just before their first wedding anniversary that another letter arrived from Canada, but this one wasn't handwritten, it was typed on official headed notepaper, it was from Dr Ross Byrne. Would she be interested in setting up a clinic with him in Toronto, a partnership. He'd heard great things about her over the last year, and believed that her specialisations were exactly what the clinic needed.

She thought it would be a chance to experience another culture, a chance to develop her career, a chance to have a much better lifestyle, the pay was a multiple of her current salary.

She hadn't finished reading the letter, and was already sold on the idea. What would Kieran think?

Well, for a man who liked to be in control, Kieran didn't take much convincing. He said that it was a great opportunity, which Amelia knew meant more money in his eyes, and he would be willing to forego his career for the time being, as long as they returned to Ireland in a couple of years.

Amelia almost laughed, "forego his career", indeed! He hated his dead-end job and this would be the prefect opportunity to get out of it.

Interviews followed and Amelia got the job.

She was not looking forward to telling her parents. Well, her mother in particular. Her mother, though experiencing a positive phase in the cycle of her illness, had come to rely more and more on Amelia, and she on her.

Strangely enough, it was her father who came to her aid. Her announcement, at Sunday lunch in the Loch Garman family home, brought a broad-beamed smile to his face, something she hadn't seen in years. Could he be so pleased that she was emigrating?

As she helped her mother clear away the plates, she noticed her father put his arm around Kieran and walk him into his study. They must have been gone for at least two hours. Amelia spent most of that time holding her mother's hand and reassuring her that she'd only be a phone call away if she needed her.

Eventually, after much muffled laughter, her father and Kieran emerged from the study, smiles all round.

'That's settled then,' concluded her father, shaking Kieran's hand.

'Absolutely,' replied Kieran.

'Typical,' thought Amelia. Today was supposed to be all about her, her new career in Canada, and making sure her mother would be alright. Instead, it's ended up as a drinking session behind closed doors between Kieran and her father, where decisions were being made without her.

'What's settled then?' queried Amelia, somewhat aggrieved at having to ask.

'Your future, Amelia,' replied her father, clearly delighted over something.

Kieran reached across and grabbed Amelia's hands between his.

'You father and I are going into business together,' he announced. 'Isn't it wonderful?'

Amelia didn't know what to say. She was sure it would end in disaster, but what could she do.

'I've always wanted to expand the business internationally,' explained her father, 'and with you and Kieran moving to Canada, what better opportunity to develop my feed supply distribution business. My knowledge of the Irish market, combined with access to Canadian feed prices. Well, we can't fail.'

He poured four drinks, and handed them out.

He raised his glass.

'To Canada!' he toasted.

'To Canada!' they replied.

The Promised Land

Amelia arrived in Toronto some six weeks before Kieran, he had work commitments in Dublin. She fell in love with the place almost as soon as she had stepped off the plane. It was so bright and big and fresh. It had a sense of the future about it, somewhere where she could make things happen.

And six weeks without Kieran opened Amelia's eyes to what life could offer. She was happier than she'd been in years. The work in the clinic was hard but rewarding, and though she didn't have much free time, what little she had, she spent exploring the city and its surrounds.

Ross Byrne and his family were wonderful hosts, and helped Amelia find a beautiful, quiet family home in the suburbs just a few blocks from where they lived. She hoped Kieran would like it, they'd discussed the house on the telephone and he'd agreed that she should go ahead with it, though he seemed more interested in complaining about the fact that all his clothes had been shipped out and he had nothing to wear except one shirt with a sleeve missing.

She loved the house, with its steep-sided roof, set in a wood-lined avenue. It had space, a lawn and a drive. It was perfect, a family home.

For the first time since their wedding day Amelia felt that she and Kieran were sharing their lives. Coming to Canada had brought them closer, and even though Amelia was very busy with the clinic, they'd started doing things together. They joined a local private ski club, skied all winter, and sailed big boats together on Lake Ontario all summer.

Could they have a future?

One thing that didn't appear to have a future was Kieran's joint venture with her father. Kieran simply wasn't a businessman. He tried, how he tried, but nothing would go right. When he attempted to purchase product, he didn't have the cash transferred to the bank account in time. When the product was finally delivered, it was the wrong grade and had to be exchanged, incurring additional costs. And then when he went to ship the product, he didn't have the right license or indeed any license. He'd tried to do everything himself when the key to being a successful businessman was to know the right people and persuade or employ them to do it for you.

Though, strangely, Amelia hadn't seen Kieran happier. She reasoned that it was probably because he was in complete control of his work and wife.

However, with Kieran's business faltering, Amelia's father flew over to try and help straighten things out, but the damage was done. Contacts were no longer interested, exchange rates had shifted, and legislation was about to change. He said that another aspect of being a good businessman was knowing when to cut and run.

Eventually Kieran managed to get a regular job through an acquaintance of Ross which proved to be very timely, they were going to need all the money they could get.

Amelia was pregnant.

Amelia wanted to make the marriage work.

She loved being pregnant. For once everything felt right. She was happy, Kieran was happy, they had a future, they were going to be a family.

On the seventh of June, a Wednesday, Amelia Alice Dorothy Allen gave birth to a healthy baby boy. The hands of the clock on the wall had turned to a quarter past the hour, and the time was duly noted. Kieran was overjoyed, a son, Victor Patrick Boyle.

Dine and Dash

Miriam had come to stay on a stopover for a couple of days, and as much as she loved seeing baby Victor, all Miriam wanted to do was party every night. This particular evening they'd just finished what was a late dinner. It was perhaps eleven o'clock.

Amelia was thinking of her bed.

'Now it's time to go out,' announced Miriam.

'It's a little...' Amelia didn't get a chance to finish her sentence.

'You'll babysit won't you,' Miriam nodded to Kieran.

Kieran yawned and nodded. He was off to bed whatever. As far as he was concerned, Miriam was Amelia's friend and it was up to Amelia to keep her friend entertained.

The night was warm, the air still. Amelia suggested they go to Toronto's premier rooftop bar. Set amid the skyscrapers of the commercial centre, it was gorgeous, and the views were just wonderful. It was Amelia's favourite place to go.

From their table you could see the city's lights scatter out across Lake Ontario.

Miriam ordered a bottle of wine.

They reminisced, and soon the wine was finished.

'Let's get out of here,' suggested Miriam. 'This is way too quiet.'

She called for the bill, but the bill didn't come.

Miriam called for it again, and again it didn't come.

'This is hopeless,' she said and went up to the bar.

When she returned she did not look happy.

'Are all the barmen in Toronto so rude?' she asked.

'Um...' mumbled Amelia.

'Do you know what he said to me?' asked Miriam, rhetorically, '"Sit down, madam, and we will bring it over to you". I said to him, "I'm not in school, you know". And he said, "Sit down and your waitress will be over to see you soon enough". I'm surprised they get any custom at all with an attitude like that.'

'They're not like this normally,' said Amelia.

'Well, we've been waiting for half an hour,' stated Miriam, 'I want to go somewhere else.'

Meanwhile the barman kept chatting to the waitress. There was nobody in the bar, nobody to serve, just Miriam and Amelia.

Miriam put up her arm and waved.

'Please,' she requested, 'may we have the bill.'

The barman just nodded and kept on chatting.

After a few more minutes, Miriam raised her arm again, and again the barman just nodded.

'Right that's it,' she said to Amelia. 'Just watch this. Get up, and make to walk out. They'll bring the bill over soon enough if they think we're trying to leave without paying.'

As they got up and started towards the elevator, there was an immediate flurry among the staff.

The barman vaulted over the bar.

'Stop, thieves, stop,' he shouted.

At which, two security guards promptly emerged from around the corner.

Miriam and Amelia stopped.

'What do you mean, thieves?' said Miriam. 'We've asked for the bill half a dozen times, and you haven't been bothered to bring it over to us.'

Amelia was mortified by the confrontation, and worried that someone might recognise her.

'You're thieves,' accused the barman, 'you went to leave without paying.'

'Don't be ridiculous,' said Miriam. 'We're professional women, doctors, and getting up seemed to be the only way to attract your attention from whatever the salacious, all-engrossing conversation you were having with our waitress was.'

'Professional thieves more like!' responded the barman.

Amelia could see that Miriam was on the verge of exploding with rage at this point.

'Perhaps you could bring us the bill now?' asked Amelia, trying to calm the situation down.

Hurriedly, the waitress returned with the bill and gave it to Miriam.

Miriam checked it.

'We only had one bottle of wine,' she said. 'You've charged us for two. Look at our table, there's only one bottle of wine. I'm not paying this. You're the thieves, not us.'

At which Miriam crossed her arms in a show of defiance.

There was now silence from all parties, a standoff.

Amelia cringed with embarrassment.

Eventually the bill was changed, and the bill was paid.

'Can you let us go now?' asked Miriam. 'We want to go.'

'You'll be escorted out of the building,' replied the barman, 'and you must never come back again, ever.'

'Don't worry,' retorted Miriam, 'I'll never come back here again in a million years.

This is the worst I have ever been treated, your customer service is atrocious. We'll be making an official complaint about this.'

The security guards did indeed escort them out of the building. They stood and stared in the elevator, and followed Miriam and Amelia until they had walked out into the street.

Amelia turned to Miriam.

'Miriam, that was my favourite bar,' she said.

'We didn't do anything wrong,' replied Miriam.

'But we did try to leave without paying the bill,' said Amelia.

'Only to attract their attention,' explained Miriam, 'so that we could pay the bill.

And then the bastards tried to overcharge us.'

Kieran laughed. He thought it was funny.

'Dine and dash,' he said, pointing at Miriam and Amelia. 'Dine and dash, that's what I'll call the pair of you from now on.'

Pulling Teeth

With Victor starting to grow, Kieran was keen for the family to move back to Ireland. And though Canada offered a good life, he missed his friends, his sport, he missed *the craic*. He insisted Amelia apply for a consultant post back in Ireland.

Amelia didn't want to move. Life was great in Toronto.

To placate Kieran, Amelia applied for a prestigious consultant post in Bath, a role she really wasn't that experienced for. She was sure she wouldn't get it, not just because she felt under-qualified, but also because she was Irish and the job was in England. After all, hadn't she always been taught in school that the English hated the Irish.

She was offered the job.

Kieran got his way, almost. It would be a lot easier to get to Dublin for the weekend from Bath, than from Toronto.

They were all moving to Bath.

On the day Amelia was due to leave, she had an appointment with a dental surgeon. She'd wanted her teeth sorted, and needed to have extractions before the orthodontist could fit braces.

She was all dressed up in her beautiful red business suit, with its black faux-fur collar, and matching chiffon blouse, ready for her last ever afternoon clinic in Toronto.

'Would you mind if you take off your jacket, Dr Allen?' asked Dr Gagnon, the dentist.

'I'm not sure about that,' said Amelia, realising that her blouse was somewhat see- through, and she had nothing on underneath.

'Well, there may be some blood,' he explained. 'And even though your jacket's red, it'll show the blood.'

So Amelia took off the jacket, and was left wearing her see-through top.

Dr Gagnon stared.

The dental assistant hurriedly put a bib over Amelia.

'Now, I won't put you to sleep,' advised Dr Gagnon. ' I'll just do the normal, local anaesthetic.'

A couple of minutes after the injections, he returned and tested to check that her mouth was sufficiently numb.

'OK, ready for the first extraction?' he asked.

Amelia nodded, warily.

Dr Gagnon pressed firmly on her shoulder to get purchase, and began to pull the first tooth.

'Ahhhh!' exclaimed Amelia, as her body writhed from side to side in the dentist's chair.

'What's wrong?' he asked.

'I'm very frightened,' confessed Amelia.

'There's no need to be frightened,' comforted Dr Gagnon. 'It'll be over momentarily.'

Amelia could see that he had nodded to his dental assistant to come across and help.

She felt two hands firmly rest on her shoulders. 'Open wide.'

Eventually, after much pulling, tugging and yanking, all four wisdom teeth come out.

'There you go,' said Dr Gagnon, smiling. 'Now that's a big fang!'

He held one of the teeth up for Amelia to see.

In Amelia's eyes it was enormous, the roots were like the roots on a carrot, no wonder it had taken so much effort to extract it.

Dr Gagnon put some cotton wool buds in Amelia's mouth to help stop all the bleeding.

'You're done,' he said. 'Now take it easy, rest. Shall we call you a cab?'

'No, I'll take the subway,' replied Amelia with a muffled voice.

'You're going to take the subway?' questioned Dr Gagnon. 'Are you sure?'

'I've got to get to my clinic,' explained Amelia, 'I can't let my patients down.'

It it was the tenth of January. It was minus twenty outside, and the wind chill pushed the temperature down further.

Amelia's clothing hardly suited, though she barely noticed such was the pain in her mouth. But, as ever, Amelia was determined to making it to the clinic.

The clinic was full. Amelia had never seen it so full.

Every mother and son she had ever consulted with seemed to be there to see her on her last day. It was both touching and daunting. She pressed on as best she could, she didn't have much time. She knew there was going to be a surprise party for her at three o'clock.

'I never would have thought it,' commented one patient.

'You would never have thought what?' asked Amelia.

'No, it's not right to say,' retracted the patient.

'Say what?' insisted Amelia.

'Well, that you'd be chewing gum while you're seeing patients,' replied the patient, reluctantly.

'No, I'm not chewing gum,' explained Amelia. 'It's cotton wool, I've just had my wisdom teeth taken out.'

'How many wisdom teeth have you had taken out?' inquired the patient in disbelief.

'Four,' said Amelia, her mouth throbbing.

'Jesus, what are doing here?' exclaimed the patient.

'It's my last day at the clinic,' replied Amelia. 'It's really busy, and I wanted to make sure I saw all the patients who need to see me before I leave.'

The end of the day came, finally, and the last patient said their farewell. Amelia slumped back into her chair, sighed for a moment, and then gathered her things.

The surprise party, which wasn't a surprise, was held in a local hotel.

In anticipation of Amelia's future in England, someone had thought it would be a great idea to do that most English of things, and have afternoon tea. The food looked delicious, stacked high on silver trays, but Amelia dared not eat a thing.

Amelia's emotions were in turmoil, clearly exacerbated by the loss of her wisdom teeth. However, she managed to hold it together, no tears flowed.

Did she really want to leave these wonderful people and this great life? Was her career so important to her? The truth was more that Kieran wanted to get back to Ireland and this was a compromise towards his desire. Amelia wanted her marriage to work.

They had a family now.

CAREER
WOMAN

The Life

The apartment was beautiful, elegant, part of a grade one listed Georgian townhouse in one of Bath's most desirable of locations. Amelia just had to have it. Kieran said it was too expensive. However, Amelia persisted, telling Kieran how happy they would be, how impressed their families would be, and how much she loved him. Eventually, she won him over, and he changed his mind. It was more than they could afford, but she reasoned life was to be lived.

With the need for money in mind, Kieran had set up a property development business, and projected that it would make a great profit. Amelia was sceptical, his attempt in Canada had ended badly. The numbers were all too tempting, the problem was neither of them had a head for business.

Bath was proving to be an ideal location for Kieran. He'd reconnected with all his friends in Ireland and London, and soon his social life was full of rugby, pubs, golf, and ski trips. Kieran was happy.

Victor was in nursery full-time and had settled well.

His grandmother doted on him whenever she got the chance. Somehow, having a grandchild had helped Audrey focus on staying well and sustain what was proving to be a long phase of good health. However, the effects of being in an institution did show, she lived in something of a bubble. Mass everyday, but not socialising. Still elegant. Routine was key to her life.

With both Amelia's brother and sister now settled in Loch Garman, Aisling having recently got married to Gerald, and Alex and his wife expecting their first child, her parents had the family support they needed close at hand.

Amelia was consumed by her work. Beyond the consultant post, she had started doing a lot of academic research in her spare time, and continued to manage the clinic in Canada. She spoke at seminars across Europe and the rest of the world. It was nonstop.

Had she stopped and been honest with herself, Amelia would have realised, that though she was achieving in her career, what she was really doing was running away from her marriage. Underneath it all, despite all that she'd tried, she was unhappy.

There seemed to be nothing between her and Kieran except convenience, and even then it wasn't that convenient. She was working twice as hard for half the money, with no social life, or time for Victor.

However, the reality was that Amelia had no time for reflection, she had no time to sit and discuss things with her family or friends. She was leading her life at such a pace that if it didn't make it on to the to-do list, or wasn't documented on her next meeting's agenda, or wasn't scheduled in her diary, then it simply didn't happen.

Pregnant.
It was as simple as that, Amelia was pregnant again.
Kieran was delighted, Amelia started to make plans.
Amelia wanted their baby to be born in Canada, Kieran did not. They argued. Amelia felt that Canada was the future, and she wanted their baby to benefit from Canadian healthcare and citizenship, like Victor. Kieran wanted the family to stay where they were.
Amelia pressed ahead despite Kieran's disagreement, and combined her monthly trips to the clinic in Canada with her antenatal care.
Disagreement turned to fracture.
Amelia started to resent Kieran for not providing for the family while she was working extremely hard. His business was not generating any cash. He wasn't looking for a job that might help bridge the gap between her income and their lifestyle. Amelia secretly harboured her aspiration that Kieran would become the main provider, and she would stay at home and look after the five children they were going to have. But underneath his macho persona, Kieran felt inadequate. He was never going to be as successful as she was and he struggled being a house husband. It just wasn't Kieran, no matter how hard he tried. Amelia knew he would not be the main provider.

'Kieran, great news, I've spoken to my boss, who's best friends with the owner of CoCon Construction,' said Amelia, from the living room doorway. 'And he says he can sort you out a job.'
'You did what?' barked Kieran from in front of the television.
'I've lined up a job interview for you,' persisted Amelia, feeling pleased with herself.
'I don't need your help to get a job, Amelia,' snapped Kieran as he flicked through the channels. Stop interfering.'
'I'm not interfering,' retorted Amelia.
'Yes you are!' shouted Kieran, becoming angrier. 'You're an interfering, conniving little bitch. Stick to what you know best, and stay out of my business.'
'But it is my business, Kieran,' she goaded, her temper rising. 'You need a job, I want you to have a job, a proper job.'
'You want me to have a proper job,' mocked Kieran. 'How dare you put me down like that. It's all about you Amelia, It's always all about you and what you want.'
'You're a pathetic excuse of a man,' she scolded. 'Every other man provides for his family, you don't! You just sit and watch TV, bet and pretend

166

to be busy. You're a waste- of-space.'

'And you're a can of piss,' he spat back. 'You're a crazy cow, just like your mother, and I'll have you sent to the loony bin!'

Amelia felt trapped between wanting to have a career, and wanting to be a mother. These two visions of her future seemed to be directly at odds, whatever she did to try and be one of them was harmful to being the other. Not only was she at war with Kieran, she was at war with herself.

Six weeks before their baby's due date, Amelia started to get labour pains on a return flight from Toronto. When she landed, she went straight to hospital. She called Kieran.

She was sat in the waiting room when he tumbled through the double doors, a confusion of anger and concern. She wasn't sure whether he wanted to hug her or shout at her, but before he got to utter a word, she was called.

They were escorted to the cubicle and offered a seat. The nurse performed some preliminary checks, and they were told a doctor would be with them soon.

It was more like a counselling session that anything else.

Kieran said how stupid Amelia was for trying to have their baby in Canada against his wishes and all good sense.

Amelia said Kieran's refusal to be supportive of her wishes had made things much worse than they needed to be.

And on it went.

In the end the doctor made it clear, Amelia needed rest and that travelling back and forth to Canada at this late stage of the pregnancy presented a risk, given the labour pains she had just experienced.

And so that was that. The baby was going to be born in England.

The Birth of Jaws

Amelia's waters had broken, and she went into hospital. She was calm, she knew what to expect after the birth of Victor. Everyone said the birth of your second child was that much easier.

'I'm in labour,' she informed the maternity staff.

The nurse measured the contractions.

'Oh no, you're not really in labour, my dear,' she declared. 'Go home and come back to us later.'

Amelia went home. She was in agony.

After a couple of hours, the pain became too much. Amelia began to cry. She screamed, and then clattered around the apartment, making so much noise that the neighbours underneath kept banging on their ceiling.

'What's going on up there? What's all the noise'?' they yelled.

'It's because I'm in labour,' Amelia yelled back.

'So go into hospital if you are in labour,' they suggested.

So Amelia went to the hospital again.

The nurse measured the contractions.

'Oh no, not yet. You're not fully in labour,' she said. 'Go home and come back to us.'

Amelia went home, again.

Fifteen hours later Amelia returned to hospital for the third time, Kieran drove.

'I can't move,' explained Amelia. 'I'm so exhausted, and the pain is so severe I'll have to have pethidine.'

Amelia knew that they'd have to admit her then.

The maternity team relented, gave her pethidine, and kept her in.

To Amelia, the pethidine was marvellous stuff, the pain just sailed away.

'This is nice!' said Amelia to no one in particular, 'I could get used to this.'

It was some six hours later before the maternity team decided to take Amelia to the delivery suite, though Amelia had no sense of the baby coming.

Amelia's phone rang, it was Cordelia, her research coordinator, she wanted to know about the renewal of her contract.

'Cordelia, I'm in the maternity ward,' stressed Amelia, 'and I'm in labour. Speak to the office about it.'

Amelia was about to put the phone down, but Cordelia clearly hadn't finished talking. Amelia sighed, waiting for the conversation to end.

'No, Cordelia,' she said, 'I can't speak to the office for you, I'm just about to give birth!'

At this, Kieran protectively grabbed Amelia's phone and told Cordelia what she should do in no uncertain terms. He turned the phone off.

'I'll tell you what,' said Amelia, 'that girl is worse than useless. Do you remember I offered her a room in our apartment for few days, while she sorted out hers. She stayed for six weeks. She only left after I went out and bought furniture for her and set it up in her apartment.'

Kieran nodded. Who could forget Cordelia, lovely girl but absolutely incapable of doing anything for herself. Another one of Amelia's stray dogs she'd picked up along the way who'd caused chaos in their life.

Amelia was clearly still pent up over Cordelia's phone call.

The maternity team thought the baby was in distress.

'Amelia, just focus on the baby,' advised Kieran.

'Yes. Yes, you're right. Just focus on the baby,' echoed Amelia.

This phrase now became Amelia's mantra, a mantra she would repeat every few seconds, but the baby remained in a distressed state.

'We're going to have to take you into theatre, Dr Allen,' said one of the maternity team. 'You have to have an emergency caesarian section because your baby is in distress.'

The team began to ready Amelia to rush her to theatre.

Just then one of the team shouted.

'No, no, no, no. Stop, something's happening.'

And almost in an instant, the baby was born.

Kristine Mary Boyle had arrived, the result of twenty-six hours of labour.

The Beginning of the End

Amelia had been working extremely hard for the last few months, but as ever they had no money. Where did it all go?

She'd started back to work, full-time, twelve weeks after Kristine's birth. It wasn't the maternity leave she'd dreamed of, particularly as Kristine was awake every night, and she'd had the Cordelia issue to deal with.

'You know, the older they get, the harder it is,' stated Amelia to one of her work colleagues. 'I haven't had a good night's sleep in... Well, since Kristine was born. She just doesn't sleep through the night at all.'

'I thought you were looking a little worn out round the edges,' remarked her colleague, 'with those panda eyes and that sallow complexion.'

'Thanks, Justin,' replied Amelia. 'I knew I could count on you.'

'Just telling you how it is,' he said. 'You wouldn't want it any other way.'

Justin smiled, Amelia glared back.

It was perhaps a week or so later that Amelia happened to bump into Nigel Carter in the corridor. They had started at the hospital on the same day. He worked in A&E, and Amelia liked him, he had an engaging confidence. They exchanged pleasantries.

'Is you daughter better now?' he asked.

'Better?' queried Amelia.

'Kieran brought her in the other day,' said Nigel. 'She'd been crying. I examined her, but could find nothing specific.'

Amelia remembered, how could she have forgotten.

'She's OK, thanks,' said Amelia.

Kieran needed money.

As yet, his property development business hadn't generated a single penny. All it seemed to do was suck cash up. This required doing, that wanted fixing, so and so had to be paid. It was relentless. And the annual golf trip was coming up.

The maternity leave that Amelia had taken, had created a big black hole in their finances, or more to the point, her choosing to buy those three John Kingerlees paintings, just before Kristine was born, had created the black hole.

When would she ever learn to stop spending money they didn't have? He took out an overdraft, he just needed Amelia's signature.

He took the bank papers into Amelia's work. He put the pen in her hand, grasped it and tried to make her sign. She refused. Kieran was livid. How dare she?

Then, unexpectedly, Amelia received a cheque in the post from Canada, a bonus payment from the clinic. Fantastic news! It was enough to clear their existing overdraft.

Amelia paid the cheque in. It was a great relief. She then closed the overdraft facility so that they could no longer overspend.

Three days later, Kieran called Amelia at work. He was in a blinding rage.

'You're a liar and a cheat!' he accused. 'How could you put that money in the bank account and not ask me first? I really needed that money.'

'What do you mean?' defended Amelia. 'I've paid off the overdraft. It was the right thing to do.'

There was silence at the other end of the line. Amelia could feel Kieran's anger.

'Kieran?' she said.

'I will never trust you again,' he declared. 'Our marriage is over!'

The line went dead.

Later that afternoon, Kieran reappeared at Amelia's desk with the overdraft request papers, and started shouting at her. He wasn't going to leave until he got what he wanted, and so it was, through sheer force of will that he broke Amelia.

Amelia signed.

Amelia was so angry. What had Kieran done with the overdraft? He'd gone on his golf trip to Ireland with his friends. Here she was, left at home with the kids, working really hard and trying to balance everything. How could he spend thousands of pounds on a golf trip?

Amelia decided she was going to go to Ireland too. She was going to take the kids and visit her family in Loch Garman. Kieran could come down after his golf trip and pick her and the children up on his way back to England.

Kristine still wasn't sleeping, and Amelia had noticed that her daughter seemed to have sweaty hands all the time. She decided she'd make an appointment to see Michelle Edwards, her paediatrician friend, while they were over in Ireland.

It was wonderful to be back in Loch Garman.

Amelia's family was delighted to see her and the children. Her mother, who was clearly better than Amelia had seen her in years, fussed around them.

That evening, Amelia fell asleep in the chair. She woke up in bed the next day. She couldn't remember how she'd got there, she must have been exhausted.

Kristine's appointment was at eleven, she'd have to hurry if she was to be on time. She left Victor with her parents.

Michelle greeted Amelia with one long, massive hug. How long had it been? And wasn't baby Kristine adorable. It took a while for the conversation to pass before they spoke of Kristine's health.

Michelle asked questions, Amelia answered.

Michelle examined Kristine for several minutes.

'Well, as far as I can tell, she's fine,' concluded Michelle.

'Are you sure?' asked Amelia.

'Yes. There's no need to worry,' assured Michelle. 'They're all different you know, children. Some sleep well, others don't. Some cry, some smile. It's just how they are. In any given week I might see a hundred of them, and I'm always surprised by how unique each one is.'

Amelia smiled, relieved. That was one less thing to worry about.

Amelia began to unwind. She laughed her way through the family dinner that evening. After everyone had excused themselves to go to bed, she found herself sat with Leah, her sister-in-law, and a bottle of wine.

Leah listened.

Amelia unloaded.

She talked about her work, commuting back and forth to Toronto to earn a little extra to keep her family going, staying there for a week at a time, working full-time at the hospital in Bath, doing all her research afterwards until ten, eleven, twelve o'clock at night.

She told Leah it was just getting too much. She never got to spend time with Kristine and Victor, never really got time to be a mother to them.

She confided in how bad things had got with Kieran, the fact that he said he longer trusted her and that he said their marriage was over.

'Life isn't fun,' she concluded. 'I'm just not really enjoying anything at the moment, it's all very, very stressful.'

'My God,' said Leah, 'you've three jobs, two of them in England, and one of them in another continent. Two young children, and marriage on the verge of complete breakdown. All you need to do now is go off and have an affair or something, and that would just top your life!'

Leah had tried to make Amelia laugh with that last joking comment. Amelia forced a smile.

'Let me go and get another bottle of wine,' said Leah, heading to the kitchen.

'That's it,' thought Amelia. 'I have no love in my life. I'm working like a slave.

Kieran calls me his "cash cow". That's it, I must do that. I must go off, have an affair and see if that makes me happy, because what I'm doing at the moment certainly isn't.'

The next day, Kieran arrived to collect everyone.

He was clearly hungover from what must have been a week's worth of drinking.

Amelia was still exhausted, and was no mood to be with Kieran, not that Kieran was in any mood to be with her.

Amelia decided to stay on in Loch Garman for an extra day or two. She told Kieran, he was absolutely furious. He started yelling and shouting at her. Amelia thought he was so angry because he'd hoped she would look after the kids on the ferry so he could have a sleep.

Amelia refused to go.

'Well, our marriage is over anyway,' he said. 'And if you don't come on this boat, that's it. You are never seeing me or your kids again.'

'Fine. Maybe that's the right thing to do,' retorted Amelia.

After they'd left, Amelia spent the whole day in bed, thinking.

'Right, something major is going to have to change in my life because otherwise there is no way I can keep going.' she said to herself.

When she flew home, Kieran didn't speak to her for a week.

She then flew out to Toronto on her monthly business trip.

On the Tuesday, Kieran was called into the nursery. Kristine had been biting people again.

'Well, she's only bitten two people today,' said Evie, Kristine's nursery nurse, as she handed Kieran the forms to sign.

'Only two today, Jaws,' joked Kieran, as he tickled Kristine.

On her return from Canada, Amelia arranged to see a marriage guidance counsellor without Kieran. They said, based on what she had told them, the probable outcome of the relationship would be separation.

Crossing the Line - No Way Back

After the high emotion of Ireland, each was waiting for the other to make the next statement about their relationship.

'Clare and Russell Markham are separating,' said Kieran, looking directly at Amelia.

Clare and Russell's children went to the same school as Victor and Kristine. In the time Amelia and Kieran had been in Bath, they had all become close friends. There was a good rapport between them all, Russell and Kieran particularly. Russell, though not Irish, had spent a lot of time in Ireland.

'Oh,' replied Amelia. She was surprised, she thought Clare and Russell were happy together. 'Why?'

'She's been having an affair.' Kieran spat out the words, he was angry for Russell.

'Oh,' said Amelia. Over the last few weeks she had continued her guidance counselling. She planned to leave Kieran when she returned from her next trip to Toronto. Amelia had decided that she was done after the awful rows they'd been having and Kieran saying, "their marriage was over", and that he had, "no trust".

Amelia was waiting in Schiphol Airport for her flight to Toronto when she got a text from Ross Byrne.

'I've split up from Abigail. Are you free? Do you want me to collect you from Pearson Airport?'

Amelia knew things weren't working out for Ross with Abigail, it had been like it for the last year or so. Amelia and Ross had often confided in each other at work.

She replied to the text. She was free, but she didn't need to picked up from the airport. Perhaps a drink, later?

Ross suggested the Mission Bar.

'Great, eight-thirty,' she typed.

'Looking forward to it,' he replied.

Amelia checked into the Tour Blanc Hotel in Toronto's commercial district. She often stayed there, she liked the views. She showered and changed into something she thought suitable for the evening. The dress was well-fitting, if a little short. It wasn't the usual type of clothing she packed for her business trips to Toronto, she'd consciously decided to bring it. She was glad she had, she wondered if Ross would like her in it.

Karl, the duty manager winked a smile at her when she stepped past the front desk.

She smiled back as she pushed through the rotating glass doors.

The Mission Bar was just a block away.

Ross was dressed casually, sat at a table, relaxed. He stood tall as Amelia approached. He held her arms, they exchanged kisses to the cheeks, she could smell the scent of aftershave.

They ordered drinks and chatted.

He told her what had happened with Abigail.

She told him what had happened with Kieran.

They drank more, the conversation drifted.

He smiled, and Amelia rubbed her hand on his arm.

They went back to Amelia's hotel. He asked Amelia if she was sure.

'It can't be undone once it's done,' he said.

Amelia said she was sure.

She opened her hotel room door and they stepped inside. That was it.

It was done.

Amelia awoke. She was facing away, towards the window. She could see dark rain clouds in the sky. She felt immensely uncomfortable. She knew she'd done something really bad, she felt that she'd failed in some way. She lay still.

Ross rolled towards her and held her close.

'So what now?' she asked. 'Do we have an affair or something?'

'Yes,' he said.

Amelia knew it was all wrong.

In her mind she'd finished with her marriage, but there was too much pain, too much hurt. She was in no state to have another relationship. She realised that this was not the best way out of her marriage. In her soul she just knew it.

She got dressed and sat on the couch. She said nothing.

Ross had to go, he was doing the school run.

He leant down and kissed her on the cheek.

'See you later,' he said.

Amelia smiled goodbye.

Her first surgery at the clinic wasn't until late morning.

She decided to go for a walk.

The cold air smacked her face.

She wondered if the rest of world was aware of what she had done.

She thought Karl, the duty manager, had winked at her again on her way out, this time knowingly.

175

'What the hell, it's my life,' she reasoned with herself, unconvincingly. But the truth was she was troubled, really troubled. It was the first time she had gone against her principles and she regretted it. She was sure that God would punish her.

She tried to distract herself, but couldn't focus.

Eventually, she bought a watch for Ross. She's seen his beside the bed, it looked shabby. She hoped the gift would make up for that fact that she could be no more than friends. She felt she'd let him down.

She gave him the watch when she left for England.

He'd given her a lift to the airport.

'You know,' he said, 'after I dropped the kids off that morning I went for coffee and the guy behind the counter, who I see most every day, said to me, "You must have got laid last night by the looks of that smile you have on your face". What could I say?'

She told him it just wouldn't work out between them, it just wasn't the right thing for her to do now.

He said they would be friends, always.

Amelia pressed the gift-wrapped box into his hand.

'For me?' he asked.

'For you,' she said.

'What is it?' He opened the box.

'You really shouldn't...' he said, but then added, 'No, on seconds thoughts, you should, I was definitely worth it. I think I'll give up the doctoring business and become a professional gigolo if beautiful women are going to shower me with expensive gifts every time I sleep with them.'

He'd made her laugh.

'Nice to see a smile,' he said.

Amelia pushed him to get him to leave.

He kissed her goodbye, she waved.

A Mistake

The affair with Ross had been a mistake. Weeks passed into months, and another year turned, and Amelia and Kieran had found a way to coexist together.

They began to live more within their means. Amelia adjusted her work to give a much better work-life balance. She'd just won a prestigious grant that meant she could delegate more to others, have less to do herself, she'd have more time for her two wonderful children.

They started to share a social life in Bath. She saw again what she had originally seen in him when they'd first met, and Kieran, for his part, seemed much more relaxed, less prone to rage.

Kristine wasn't well, her jaw had swollen.

Kieran had taken her to the GP in the week, and the GP had said he thought it was mumps, though knowing that Amelia was a consultant, he'd called that evening to discuss his findings further.

Amelia had to fly out to Houston the next day.

Kristine didn't want Amelia to leave, she cried, she begged for her mummy to stay.

'Kristine, love, you know that Mummy has to go away with work from time-to-time,' explained Amelia, 'but mummies always comes back.'

'I don't want you to go, please stay,' pleaded Kristine.

'But I have to,' said Amelia.

'Can't Daddy go?' asked Kristine.

'No, Daddy can't go,' replied Amelia, 'Only Mummy can go.'

'I want Mummy,' insisted Kristine.

It was the same every time Amelia went away, Kristine would demand for her to stay. It's what children wanted, their mummies, but Amelia had to go work, bills had to be paid.

In Houston, Amelia wore her favourite pink business suit as she stood at the podium and addressed the conference. There had been many questions, which she'd answered, and a terrific round of applause. Her speech couldn't have gone any better.

She was hungry, and made her way towards the lunch hall, though it was slow progress as every other delegate she passed wanted to shake her hand and congratulate her.

She decided to call Kieran before she had lunch, to see how Kristine was. To get good phone reception she stood near a window in the convention centre's foyer.

It took a while for Kieran to answer.

She thought he sounded a little odd, he kept clearing his throat.

'It's not mumps,' he said, 'it's a tumour. It's cancer.'

MOTHER

A Moment of Truth

Kristine was seriously ill, she was admitted to hospital immediately. Her temperature was high and the blood tests showed that her immune system was weakening.

For Amelia, the flight from Houston was torment, each and every second taking an age to pass.

She raced straight to the hospital from the airport after landing, oblivious to speed limits, her mind frantic.

Corridors, stairs, doorways, she found Kristine's ward and was directed to her bed.

Her gorgeous, bright, beautiful daughter lay strung like a puppet, tubes and wires threaded to machines.

Kristine looked up at Amelia.

'Where were you?' she screamed.

Kristine lashed out, punching and kicking.

'Where were you?' she howled.

Amelia could say nothing, she just took all that Kristine gave.

And then tears.

'Where were you?' sobbed Kristine. 'I told you not to go.'

Amelia knelt by the bed and clasped her daughter's cold hand between hers.

Amelia felt as if the earth was about to open up beneath her, and the very fires of hell consume her. How could she atone for what had happened?

A week passed. Kieran and Amelia shared Kristine's bedside vigil. Tests and more tests, Kristine continued to deteriorate. Victor was with a babysitter.

It was thought best to transfer Kristine to a specialist children's unit in the main regional hospital. Kieran and Amelia followed the ambulance as it flashed and wailed its way through the heavy traffic. They said nothing, their eyes transfixed on the road ahead.

The following day, Dr Wallis called them into his office.

'Please, sit,' he said.

He described Kristine's current state with numbers relative to normal limits. None of the numbers lay within them. He talked about the various tests and scans. He showed images where he could, pointing out relevant features. He summarised the path he had followed to reach his diagnosis. And then he said one word.

'Neuroblastoma.'

Kieran asked what it meant.

'Neuroblastoma is a rare type of cancer that mostly affects babies and young children,' explained Dr Wallis. 'It develops from cells called neuroblasts that are left behind from the baby's development in the womb. Neuroblastoma commonly occurs in glands above the kidney, or nerve tissue along the spinal cord. It can spread to other organs such as bones, lymph nodes, liver and skin. Kristine has stage four neuroblastoma.'

'How many stages are there?' asked Kieran.

'There are only four stages of neuroblastoma,' replied Dr Wallis, his voice flat.

Silence followed.

Doctor Wallis waited before continuing with his prognosis. He wanted to be sure that Kieran and Amelia had understood what he had said.

Amelia knew what he was going to say, she was already thinking about what she needed to do.

'The outlook for Kristine is not good,' continued Dr Wallis. 'Treatment options are limited, though you can be assured that we will do the absolute best we can. However, her chances of survival are low.'

Amelia saw Kieran tense his body. He started to shake, almost imperceptibly at first. His jaw tightened. She saw a tear form in his eye.

'How low?' asked Kieran.

'At this juncture, less than even,' replied Dr Wallis and then he added, 'statistics indicate one in five, perhaps one in ten.'

Amelia could see Kieran digest what he'd been told.

'How long?' Kieran closed his eyes, but a tear escaped.

'Weeks, months, a year, it all depends on many factors,' answered Dr Wallis. 'However, I suggest that we take things day-by-day for now.'

Dr Wallis then described his recommended course of treatment and some of the options they may need to face, perhaps a little more than he would do normally, as he knew that Amelia was a respected clinician and was sure to ask.

Finally, he mentioned that there were some experimental treatments available in America, however such treatments were not available on the National Health Service and were both extremely expensive and high risk.

In the weeks that followed, Amelia devoted herself to doing as much as she could to research Kristine's condition. She tried to find out about anything that might help. She was anxious. She drove the junior staff at the specialist children's unit to distraction with constant questions, suggestions, so much so that Dr Wallis had to speak with her.

For Amelia it was simple. Life or death.

Kristine's treatment started, and Dr Wallis suggested that by the spring they would know how successful it was.

Kieran was emotionally paralysed by Kristine's illness. He struggled to focus on anything practical, his mind was wracked with fear. All the women he had loved in his life had left him. First his sister had died, when he was a young child, then his mother was taken tragically from him, and now his daughter.

He sat at the bottom of the sweeping staircase, attempting to tie his shoe laces, his thoughts lost in grief, sunlight catching the track of a tear running down his face.

'Kieran, what's the matter?' asked Amelia, impatiently. 'Hurry up, we're going to be late.'

Kieran just sat still, staring at nothing.

'Get up, and shake yourself, man,' she demanded, unsympathetically. 'We've far too much to do for this nonsense. For goodness sake get a grip of yourself. There's no way I can keep on doing everything myself.'

Kieran looked up.

'We're not all like you, Amelia.'

Amelia decided, after consultation with the hospital in America, that Kristine's best chance of survival lay with their experimental treatment, and that little would be gained by continuing with the treatment in the current specialist children's unit.

Dr Wallis was shocked by the decision, he disagreed. He felt Kristine's best hope was to stay in the unit and finish her treatment.

Amelia was determined, and after three sleepless weeks had managed to make all of the logistical arrangements to leave for America before Christmas.

December came, but under the stress of her current treatment regime, Kristine's health faltered, she caught an infection. She was put into the intensive care unit.

Within a day her white blood cell count became extremely low to such a point that Amelia thought Kristine was going to die that night.

Amelia stood, her face to the glass partition, looking at her precious daughter. Dr Wallis stepped up beside her and for a while they stood side-by-side.

Without turning, Dr Wallis spoke to Amelia. He made the hospital's position absolutely clear.

'Do not put your child on a plane if she has a temperature tomorrow,' he said. 'She is critically ill. In all likelihood such a journey would kill her. If you do such a thing, and Kristine dies, it will be entirely your responsibility.'

Amelia turned to face the doctor.

'We really have to go,' she said, in a calm assured manner. 'If we stay here, I know Kristine is going to die.'

'Well,' he responded, 'I say again, if she has a temperature, you are not to get on that flight.'

Dr Wallis walked away.

Midnight came, and Amelia had almost finished packing Kristine's things at the hospital, when the mother of Jennifer, the child in the next bed, spoke to her.

'Why are you gathering Kristine's things up?' she asked. 'Are you going home?'

'No,' replied Amelia. 'We're going to America.'

'Oh, that's nice,' said Jennifer's mother. 'Are you going on holiday?'

Amelia paused, and then glanced up.

'No,' answered Amelia. 'We're going to get treatment for Kristine in New York.'

Amelia knew that Jennifer had been diagnosed with the same condition as Kristine.

For a moment the mothers' eyes locked and they knew they had had the same thought, 'My God, Kristine is going to live and Jennifer is going to die.'

It was five in the morning.

Amelia woke Kristine up. She raised her finger to her lips. They had to be quiet, she didn't want to attract any attention, she wanted to get away before the nurses came round to carry out their checks. If Kristine had a temperature, they wouldn't be allowed to leave.

Amelia lifted Kristine in her arms and stole her out from the hospital.

Anna was waiting outside, the engine of her four-by-four running. Anna was a friend and work colleague who'd agreed to take them up to Heathrow to catch the plane.

Sat in the back of the car, Michelle Edwards was ready with all of Kristine's support equipment, including a portable ventilator. Michelle was going to travel to New York with them.

Amelia placed Kristine in the back, and Michelle hooked everything up. Amelia shut the door and sat in the front.

'Ready?' asked Anna.

'Ready,' replied Michelle.

Amelia nodded.

Anna looked to her wing mirror, and pulled away.

The car sped along the motorway.

The sun broke the horizon into a clear, crisp, winter's day.

Michelle removed Kristine's hospital gown, and put a pretty dress on her. She even managed to get Kristine to eat something.

When they arrived at Heathrow, Michelle said they should take Kristine's temperature. Amelia put her hand on Michelle's.

'Let's not,' said Amelia. 'We have to get Kristine to the States. If we don't, we won't be able to save her life. Let's just do that.'

Michelle nodded and put the thermometer back in her medical kit bag.

Anna wished them luck, and Amelia thanked her. She waved as Anna drove off.

Heathrow thronged with thousands of people.

Amelia was terrified that Kristine risked getting another infection among such a crowd.

Amelia had never felt such stress in her life.

It seemed an eternity before they boarded the plane.

Once on board, they hoped to have a spare seat next to them, somewhere for Kristine's support equipment.

The flight attendant, seeing that they seemed to be struggling to sit down prior to take off, came down the aisle.

'Can I be of assistance?' she asked.

Amelia explained.

The flight attendant looked at Kristine, the medical equipment, and Kristine's bald head.

'Come with me, my dear,' she said.

She took them to first class.

'Please, have these seats,' offered the flight attendant. 'There should be plenty of room for all your things here.'

Amelia smiled with gratitude.

Kristine slept.

'You must eat,' insisted Michelle to Amelia.

Amelia shook her head. She looked to the window and saw the vast expanse of cloud beneath, and above the sky rolled from light to dark, flawless, heaven.

'Well at least sleep,' persisted Michelle.

Amelia hadn't slept properly since Kristine had been diagnosed. Partly she was afraid that if she slept, Kristine would no longer be there when she awoke.

'Go on, I'll watch Kristine,' urged Michelle.

Amelia drifted off to sleep.

She came to as the plane was preparing to land.

She looked, Kristine was still there.

She touched Kristine, she felt OK.

After the flight had landed, they took a taxi to the downtown apartment Amelia had rented.

Kieran and Victor were there, waiting. They had flown out earlier in the week to get everything ready.

Michelle set up the medical equipment in Kristine's room, and Amelia laid Kristine down on the bed. In a few hours they had their appointment with Dr Kapoor at the hospital.

The moment Amelia stepped across the hospital's threshold she knew everything was going to be alright, she just knew.

Kristine screamed. She screamed for the whole hour of the consultation.

Dr Kapoor looked across at Amelia.

'She's gonna' make it,' he said. 'She's a survivor.'

'Dr Kapoor, how do you know? asked Amelia, surprised that such an eminent physician would make such a rash statement. 'You've only just examined her.'

'I know,' he said, 'because you can spot the ones who are going to make it. She's gonna' make it, she's gonna' be fine, Dr Allen.'

He smiled.

Amelia had total faith.

Amazing Kristine

Amelia and Kieran signed the consent forms, and Kristine's treatment began. Their apartment was only seven blocks from the hospital, and they each alternated between staying overnight in the hospital with Kristine, and staying with Victor in the apartment.

Gradually, routine was established.

Amelia had found a place for Victor in a local private school with an open and international outlook. She hoped Victor would flourish in its relaxed, inclusive community, given the pressures they were all under.

Each day Kieran would walk Victor to school, and each day Kieran would wait to collect him. Perhaps it was a father son thing, but the two drew closer, they liked what each other liked, they shared their in-jokes, they sided together when sides had to be taken.

Amelia had no time. In theory she was on leave, but in reality she was still supervising her teams in Bath and Toronto, and running a research programme across two continents. She was working to get money. The cost of Kristine's treatment was beyond anything they had. Though there had been fund-raisers, and she was more than touched by everyone's generosity, much more money was needed.

With routine came a sense of stability, almost a sense of belonging, recognition.

Amelia began to see the same faces at the same time, each day, each week. And it didn't take long before her and her family were on first-name terms with the porters in their apartment building. For Amelia the familiarity made it feel like home. Each time the porters opened the doors or helped carry the bags, there would be a conversation, a smile, a comment.

The cycle of Kristine's treatment was relentless.

The hospital's sole focus was on getting the job done. Surgery and treatment, radiation and chemo, there was no discussion of outlook.

Weeks.

Months.

Occasionally, Kristine was allowed back to the apartment, and everyone could pretend that everything was normal, almost.

Danny, one of the porters, took a shine to Kristine. Between his gruff, know-it-all New York manner and the task at hand, he would always take time to wink and smile at the small, bald girl, the girl from the hospital. He always stopped and asked after Kristine.

Danny had faith. He was a devout Catholic. One evening, about nine o'clock, he knocked on the apartment door.

Victor, who should have been in bed, but had stayed up because Kristine had come home from the hospital, answered the door.

'Who's there, Victor?' asked Amelia from the kitchen.

'It's Danny,' replied Victor.

'Danny?' said Amelia.

Amelia went to the door, Danny stood hands together, head bowed slightly. Clearly, something was up.

'Hi, Danny, how are you?' she inquired.

Danny shook his head.

'I'm not good, I'm not good, Dr Allen,' he replied. 'Can I come in? I would like to see Kristine.'

Amelia was slightly puzzled by the request, but ushered him into the apartment.

'Of course, no problem,' she said. 'Will you have a coffee?'

'No, no, no,' answered Danny. 'I just wanna' to talk to Kristine, and I wanna' talk to you because I know you're both Catholic and I know you've good faith.'

'Come on, come and sit down. Are you sure you wouldn't like a drink?' she repeated.

'No, I'm sure,' said Danny. 'Thank you.'

'I'll just go and get Kristine,' said Amelia.

'Hi, Danny,' welcomed Kieran. 'You'll have to excuse me, I've got to put this little rascal to bed.'

At which Kieran chased Victor round the couch, past the kitchen and towards the bedrooms.

'Here she is,' said Amelia holding a shy Kristine's hand in hers.

'Hello, Danny,' ventured Kristine.

'Hi there my beautiful girl,' said Danny.

Danny raised a smile, and Kristine beamed back.

They all sat facing each other across the coffee table. Amelia turned the TV off.

'Like, here it is,' said Danny, searching for how to put over what he wanted to say.

He paused and looked directly at Amelia.

'What is it, Danny?' she asked.

Danny sighed, closed his eyes, and then word by word said it.

'My wife's been diagnosed with lung cancer.'

'Oh, Danny, I'm so sorry,' comforted Amelia and reached out to him.

'She's not been well, you know, coughing and all,' continued Danny. 'The doctor sent her to this hospital in Jersey, and they told her she had lung cancer, and that she'd die. And then she went to this other hospital to get a second opinion, and they said, "You've got lung cancer, you're gonna' die".'

Danny stopped for a few moments to recompose himself.

He then continued.

'And now she says she's gonna get a third opinion, she's gonna go to that hospital you go to tomorrow. I said to her, "Kristine, the little Irish girl I've been telling you about, she goes there, it's a good sign, I'll go up and tell her". So I've come up to tell you.'

Kristine got down from the couch and toddled over to Danny.

'You just wait there a minute,' she said, and she went to her room.

A few seconds later she returned, clutching something in her hand. She gave it to Danny.

'You take this home, and you bless your wife, Danny,' said Kristine.

She'd given him a relic of Padre Pio that an old family friend from Loch Garman had sent over, the relic that Amelia used to bless Kristine on her head and on all the parts of her body that were affected by cancer every night.

'She will get better if you use this,' explained Kristine.

'Are you sure I can have this?' asked Danny.

'Absolutely. If Kristine says you can have it, you can have it,' replied Amelia. 'Tell us how your wife gets on.'

Nine o'clock the following evening, and there was knock on the apartment door.

Kristine ran to the door. It was Danny. Amelia let him in.

'How did you get on today at the hospital, Danny?' asked Amelia.

Danny just smiled and smiled. He could not speak for the tears in his eyes.

'Danny?' she repeated.

'We went to the hospital, and they did all these tests, just like the other two hospitals, and they did these special, other tests and they said...' but Danny just couldn't speak anymore, overwhelmed by emotion.

'They said what, Danny?' prompted Amelia.

'They said, they said she's got an infection, not lung cancer, an infection,' he replied. 'They found out that it's not lung cancer, it's an infection. She's gonna' live, and it's all because of you, Kristine, all because of you. It's a miracle, a miracle. You're a miracle, Kristine, a miracle. You've cured my wife! Kristine's cured my wife. It's a miracle, a miracle!'

Amelia threw her arms around Danny, she was so happy for him.

'Thank God,' she said.

Saint Patrick's Day

On those rare occasions that Amelia found she was not busy, she would go for a walk. It gave her solitude, her own space. She liked the anonymity of the city. When she went for a walk she was no one's wife, no one's boss, no one's mother, she was able to be herself.

Sometimes, if she was feeling lonely, if she needed support, she would call Ross. He was always good to talk to.

He'd joke with her when he picked up the phone.

'And the time is four twenty-seven and fifteen seconds,' he'd say. 'I know the only reason you call is to ask what the time is on my nice, new, expensive watch and to check that I'm still wearing it, and that I haven't sold it, or, God forbid, that I haven't lost it as part of my divorce settlement.'

She'd ask him how things were going with Abigail.

'Abigail?' He'd pretend that he had to try and remember who Abigail was. 'Oh, Abigail, my soon-to-be ex, I think she's fine. Though, my lawyer seems to think she's possibly criminally insane judging from the demands her lawyers are making, but that's another story. How goes it at your end, eh?'

Amelia would round up all the latest events, Kristine's progress, her and Kieran's lack of progress, Victor's latest school project, her jobs. And Ross would listen. Ross was good at listening, he never questioned, he just clarified, he was always patient, never rushed.

Invariably Amelia would have to go, her time was always short. And after they'd said their goodbyes, Amelia would sometimes reflect on what might have been if circumstance had been different.

With the coming of spring, the hospital determined that now was the time for Kristine to start the experimental drug. The drug had to be administered intravenously at the hospital, it was unlicensed and was only allowed to be used as part of a clinical trial.

Amelia knew that this was the critical stage of Kristine's treatment. This was what they had given up everything for, this was what they'd travelled across an ocean to receive.

How she prayed.

Also, with spring, came New York City's Saint Patrick's Day Parade, the biggest event of the season. Something to look forward to, a chance to get out.

Ross said he was coming down from Toronto with his kids that week,

190

visiting relatives and, if she didn't mind, would it be OK to watch the parade with them. Amelia said she'd check with Kieran, but she was sure that it would be fine.

The day after, Ross called again, or at least Amelia thought it was him when she picked up the phone. It wasn't, it was Abigail.

'Oh, hi Abigail, thought you were Ross for a moment there,' stuttered Amelia.

'No' said Abigail, calmly and then asked, 'How are you and the family?'

'Oh, we're fine. I think we've just about acclimatised to New York,' replied Amelia, somewhat hesitantly. 'Kristine has started her treatment and all seems good so far.'

'Ross says he's planning to take the kids to the Saint Patrick's Day Parade with you,' stated Abigail.

'Ah, yes, we're all looking forward to seeing Ross and the kids,' said Amelia. 'Should be a great sight to see. They say it's the biggest and oldest parade in the world. It's the day everyone claims to be Irish.'

Amelia knew Abigail, this small talk wasn't why Abigail had called.

'Was there something you wanted, Abigail,' continued Amelia, 'it's just that I've got to go in a minute.'

'I've called to tell you that I think you are the very definition of hypocrisy,' stated Abigail.

The line then went dead.

Abigail's words rang cold and clear in Amelia's head.

'Jesus,' thought Amelia, 'she knows.'

On the day of the parade the sky was bright, the air cool, and the streets were packed green behind the curbside barriers. Hats, pennants, banners, every conceivable novelty item was on display.

Ross and his kids, Leo and Beatrice, arrived at the apartment early. Amelia wasn't quite ready. Kieran made coffee and gave the kids something to drink.

Leo and Beatrice were about the same age as Victor and Kristine, and after a tentative minute or two, Victor asked if they'd like to play in his room.

Ross and Kieran were left to chat.

When Amelia finally appeared, she smiled at Ross. Although happy to see him, she felt awkward and guilty. She asked him how he was. He said he was fine. Amelia was anxious to leave, and with the children dressed, they made their way to the parade route.

The children were so excited, they pushed eagerly to the front and peered through the railings. Ross, Kieran and Amelia stood close by, but couldn't see much for the people in front of them. They compared New York to Toronto, talked sports and talked children. Amelia updated Ross on Kristine's latest treatment. Ross said it was all positive. They talked about friends in common, but they didn't talk about Abigail.

In the distance the crowd cheered, a cheer that rippled towards them. All strained to see. And then came the sound of pipes, faint but audible.

Uniforms, costumes, flags green and orange, red, white and blue, people young and old, dancers, baton twirlers, shamrocks, leprechauns, everyone was marching or watching.

'So many Irish,' said Kieran, 'there are more Irish here than in the whole of Ireland, I wouldn't wonder. Makes you proud.'

The parade had passed, and Ross and his kids had to go. They hugged and kissed, shook hands and waved farewell. Amelia knew she should get Kristine home to rest, and with the diminishing crowds they threaded their way back, Victor and Kristine still waving their flags. It was a strange feeling to be so close and so far from home.

Victor sat, engrossed in TV.

Kristine was asleep in her bedroom.

Kieran stared at Amelia as she busied herself with endless chores.

'I know,' he said.

'Know what?' asked Amelia apprehensively.

'I know about you and him,' stated Kieran.

Amelia stopped, unable to look across. She felt panicked, frightened about what might happen. She knew she didn't love Kieran the way she should, Ross had only been an infatuation, but she had to keep the family together and could see no way forward.

'I saw it at the parade,' he accused, 'the way you looked at each other, the way you couldn't stop talking to each other, your little asides. You're having an affair with him. Go on, admit it, Amelia'

Kieran's tone was flat, his gaze direct.

Amelia carried on with her chores.

'Don't be ridiculous, Kieran,' she said as calmly as she could, 'we're just good friends now, work colleagues. We've far more important things to be worrying about.'

She tensed. She knew Kieran would either say nothing or he would explode into a rage.

Kieran said nothing.

Faith

Kristine's daily experimental treatment was progressing to plan, though the hospital would make no comment either way as to its effectiveness, other than to say they expected the treatment to end in three months, the end of August.

Amelia's thoughts turned to what to do next. She had been offered the opportunity of a high-paying job in Toronto, working at the St Anthony's Teaching Hospital. They'd have a house, and the job would pay the bills. And it was only an hour and a half flight from New York, in case Kristine needed to return for further treatment.

"No" was about all she got out of Kieran. To him the argument over living in Canada was history. Not only did he not want to live there for the same reasons he didn't want to live there before, but he suspected that Amelia just wanted to be near to Ross. His mind was set, best to return to Bath.

Amelia and Kieran were in deadlock to such an extent that it took a professional mediator to settle the dispute. The choice was obvious, they had debts and mounting bills, and given the uncertainty around Kristine's condition, proximity to the hospital in New York was important. And so Kieran agreed, reluctantly.

A month or so later, Amelia flew up to Toronto and made preparations before starting her job. It was hot and busy, and the strain of the last six months was starting to tell.

She spent the first day in bed, asleep, exhausted. She awoke, looked at the clock, it was early evening. She'd missed a meeting she was supposed to attend at the hospital, she would have to make her excuses tomorrow.

She'd arranged to meet Ross in the Mission Bar at seven-thirty for dinner, even though she'd told Kieran she wasn't going to.

She got dressed and arrived on time, but there was no sign of Ross. She sat, ordered a drink, and sent a text asking where he was. No reply. She called, but his phone went straight to voicemail. She waited. She pulled a local magazine from the rack by the bar, and started to flip through it. She finished her drink.

She just knew he wasn't going to show.

She was so lonely, she needed someone, someone to be close to, someone who would listen, someone who understood.

She decided to order some food, she was hungry, she hadn't eaten all day. The food arrived and she continued to read the magazine as she ate. An article on spiritual healing caught her eye. She read it.

For Amelia faith was all. Her belief in spirituality beyond the material world was unshakeable. Without it she was certain that Kristine would not have survived. It was their faith in the will of God that had protected and saved Kristine. To Amelia, Kristine was a special child, there was something spiritual about her, something beyond the day- to-day of human experience.

Faith was what kept Amelia going even in the darkest of times. It was the light that burned to help her find her way. And when she felt low, depressed, alone, as she did now, it was her faith she turned to find solace, to revive her, to help her overcome.

At the bottom of the page, in the corner, was a small advertisement, "Spiritual Healer, Let God Help Share The Load", and there was a telephone number. In despair, Amelia decided to take the advert and tore it from the page.

The following day, and still no word from Ross. Amelia managed to reschedule the meeting at the hospital for the morning. She said that things had overrun yesterday, and before she knew it the time had gone. She could only apologise.

As she left the hospital, she searched and found the advertisement in her bag. She decided to call. The voice she spoke to had a kindness about it, a calm that appealed to Amelia. She made an appointment for later that afternoon.

The spiritual healer's practice, just off Chinatown, was signed on a brass plaque on the wall next to a doorway. Amelia pushed the door and went inside. The corridor led up some stairs, to another door, again signed. Amelia knocked.

'Come in,' said a voice, 'the door's open.'

Amelia entered.

'You must be Amelia,' said a woman, who Amelia guessed was about fifty.

The woman smiled and put her hand forward.

'I'm Teresa,' she said, 'we spoke on the phone earlier.'

'Hi, pleased to meet you, I am Amelia,' replied Amelia, and shook hands.

'Take a seat, would you like some lemon balm herbal tea?' asked Teresa.

'Well, if you're making some, I would,' said Amelia. 'That'd be great.'

Amelia sat in a high-backed reclining chair, facing the window through which she could see nothing but a cloudless sky.

Teresa passed a cup to Amelia and sat to one side on a simple wooden chair holding a cup of her own.

The tea's scent was mild, the taste relaxing.

'I find,' said Teresa, 'that as simple as it may sound, often the best place to start is at the beginning, though sometimes it's hard to know where, or when, or how it all began. Do you know, Amelia?'

Amelia thought. She thought for a while. Her mind rolled back. There were many places she could have begun from.

'I shouldn't have said "yes" when he asked to marry me,' said Amelia.

And then she told her story. She left no detail out, she told of her unhappy marriage, Kristine's illness, her affair, her struggle to be everything to everyone.

Teresa listened, occasionally asking the odd question for clarity, occasionally adding the Lord's word.

Amelia spoke openly, she spoke fully with trust.

Teresa passed no comment but to say that they should schedule another session next time Amelia was back in Toronto, a session that would look to the future, much work needed to be done.

Amelia agreed. She was surprised by how helpful it had been, she felt so much better. She did not feel so alone anymore.

Guilt

Amelia had been back in New York for just one day when Ross sent her a text. He said he was sorry for not showing up and that he'd call to explain why. Amelia replied, telling him to call at three-thirty in the afternoon. This was when Kieran picked up Victor from school.

She wondered what was going on, it wasn't like Ross not show up, nor was it like him to be so secretive. She shrugged, she had too much on to waste anymore time thinking about the matter.

Talking to Teresa had given Amelia the confidence and energy to focus on what was important and to spend less time worrying about things she couldn't control.

The phone rang at three-thirty.

'Hi,' said Ross.

'Hi,' replied Amelia.

'Look, I'm so sorry about not making it,' apologised Ross. 'I really wanted to, but things have got complicated.'

'Things?' asked Amelia.

'I think Abigail has hired a private investigator to gather as much dirt on me as she can prior to the divorce proceedings,' explained Ross. 'My lawyer says the more she can dig up on me, the more favourable the settlement will be for her. God, it's a nightmare. For all I know my phone calls are being tapped...' He then added, for good measure, 'Abigail, if you can hear me, you really are a bitch!'

Amelia listened.

'Don't worry, this conversation's fine, I'm calling from a colleague's work phone,' reassured Ross. 'Anyway, for your sake and mine, I think it's probably best if we don't see one another.'

'Oh,' replied Amelia.

'I am so sorry, Amelia,' said Ross. 'I really value our friendship, but the way things are just now, well it just wouldn't be a good idea.'

'I guess so,' agreed Amelia.

'Amelia, take care,' said Ross. 'When this is all over, perhaps we could met up again. Look, I've got to go, bye.'

'Bye, Ross,' replied Amelia.

Amelia put the phone down.

The following week, Amelia returned to Toronto to give a presentation to her new team. She had arranged to see Teresa after the presentation.

All in all, she felt very positive about her new job and her family's future in Canada. And the fact that she was so busy trying to sort out the move, meant that she was arguing less with Kieran.

Kristine appeared to be making good progress, and Victor seemed happy enough.

The second spiritual healing session proved to be very different from the first. Teresa did more of the talking. She praised Amelia for all the good things she had done, she said she could see that Amelia had a kind and generous heart, and that Amelia had true faith.

Teresa's words lifted Amelia, they made her soul shine.

But then Teresa spoke of bad things, things that cast a shadow over Amelia's soul.

She spoke of Amelia's infidelity.

To hear Teresa describe it so clearly, made Amelia realise how painful the guilt she carried was, the guilt she suppressed.

Amelia began to cry.

Amelia noticed a strange smile pass over Teresa's face as she offered her a tissue to wipe away her tears. Momentarily, Amelia's intuition made her feel that something was very wrong.

'Now stop crying. Focus. You need to atone for your sins, Amelia, if you want your daughter to live,' warned Teresa, and then continued sternly. 'I will help you, but and it's going to cost you.'

'What do mean, cost me?' asked Amelia, confused by Teresa's sudden change in tone towards her.

'You know what I mean,' reaffirmed Teresa.

'But I've said I'm sorry,' faltered Amelia.

'Sorry is not enough,' stated Teresa, 'you must pay for what you have done, and I can only save you if you promise never to tell anybody that I am helping you. Do you promise?'

Amelia was scared, she couldn't think straight, she felt so vulnerable.

'Yes, I promise, tell me what I need to do,' stuttered Amelia.

Teresa turned to face Amelia, eye-to-eye, seizing her opportunity.

'There are two things you must do to appease your soul,' threatened Teresa. 'Firstly, you must never see Ross again, or have anything to do with him. You must destroy everything from your relationship with him, immediately.'

Amelia cowered.

'Secondly,' continued Teresa, 'you must pay me one gold bar for each year you have been married.'

'But that's thousands and thousands of dollars I don't have,' panicked Amelia. 'I need the money to pay for Kristine's treatment.'

'If you don't pay she will die,' replied Teresa, cruelly. 'It's your choice.'

Fires That Burn

It just seemed to Amelia that the more she tried to talk to Kieran, and the more she tried to discuss the move to Toronto, the more bloody-minded he became. Though he'd said to her, in front of the mediator, that he agreed with the move, and that he thought it was the best option, his actions did not match his words.

Every little thing had become an argument, even who was going to drive the car from New York to Toronto.

Amelia felt exhausted, Kieran seemed to sap every bit of energy she had. He simply made things impossible.

Kieran said that Amelia just wanted everything her way, and if she didn't get it her way she made people's lives miserable.

'"Her way", indeed!' thought Amelia. 'Everything she did, she did for someone else, as a mother, a wife, a daughter, a sister, a doctor. How could he say such a thing? When was the last time she did something for herself?'

Amelia's schedule was such that she was now making weekly trips to Toronto, though she wasn't supposed to be starting work until September.

Each time she travelled, she would stay in the Tour Blanc Hotel, it was convenient. And each time she would have to make an appointment to see Teresa to pay a gold bar for her salvation. She didn't have the emotional reserves to question Teresa's motives. She had to believe that Teresa was trying to help her, she had to save Kristine, and if this was what it took, so be it.

Staying in the hotel had become such a routine for Amelia, that she was mostly oblivious to the comings and goings of the other guests, so much so that when she saw Ross waiting in the foyer, she had to do a double take.

She didn't know what to do, he wasn't supposed to be there. Amelia knew she had promised Teresa never to have anything go do with him again.

Ross stood, she couldn't avoid him, she walked across to him.

'I wanted to see you,' he said.

'I thought we agreed that it wasn't a good idea,' replied Amelia.

'Look, let's go for a drink,' he suggested.

'I'd rather not, said Amelia.

'Just one drink,' insisted Ross, 'it would be great to catch up, I miss you.'

Amelia considered, he smiled.

'Just one drink,' he repeated.

'OK,' agreed Amelia, reluctantly. She needed an opportunity to sever all ties for Kristine's sake.

When she awoke, Amelia tried not to remember the previous evening. She busied herself, and set her mind to other things.

Today was the day she had to collect the keys to her new house.

Later, she took a taxi out to see it in the suburbs.

It reminded her of their first house in Toronto, the house near Ross and Abigail's, but this house was much larger, much more grand.

She loved it.

Like their first house, this house had a steep-sided roof, and was set in a tree-lined avenue, but this house was more traditional. It had a chimney, which meant a fireplace, and a real fire. The drive circled round in front. There were trees giving shade and privacy, and there was even a swimming pool.

The kids would love it.

It was perfect, a family home.

A Family Again

With August came the last of Kristine's daily treatments. Dr Kapoor had finished running his tests and confirmed that everything was good. It was the best news Amelia and Kieran could have heard. They could be a normal family again, and do the things normal families do.

Amelia and Kieran agreed to make the most of the end of summer, and decided that they would stop off for a few days in Vermont, en route to Toronto. Kieran had booked them into a resort hotel with all the facilities, golf, spa, swimming pool, lake and best of all, a kids' camp.

The hotel was just as they imagined, wooden beams, stone fireplaces, uneven floors, and framed pictures from an age past. The kids loved the pool and open grounds, it was such a release after the confines of New York.

After much protest, Kieran made Amelia switch off her cell phone.

'Just this once,' he said. 'If the world ends, so be it, the world ends, but at least we'll have had a holiday. And if I see you using it, I swear to God that I'm going to throw it into the pool. Understood?'

For once, Amelia knew that Kieran was right, and so she lay by the pool and read a book. It was the best thing she'd done in a long, long time.

Kieran ambled off to the bar to get drinks.

It was hot, the kids' wet footprints evaporated as they made them. Amelia moved into the shade. She wondered where Kieran had got to with the drinks, caught in some conversation she didn't doubt.

'Mummy, mummy,' said Victor, 'can we get an ice cream?'

'Sure, love, sure,' said Amelia.

Amelia shielded her eyes with her book, and routed around in her bag. She gave Victor a ten dollar bill.

'I want the change,' she added as she saw the look of delight in his eyes, 'and take your sister, don't just leave her.'

Victor reached out his hand, Kristine took it, and the two of them walked off towards the refreshment stall.

Amelia wondered if Kristine had strained her ankle or something, she seemed to have a slight limp.

'Drinks,' announced Kieran, and thrust something tall, brightly coloured, with one miniature umbrella too many, into her hand.

'What is it?' she asked.

'Good for you,' replied Kieran.

Amelia smiled. Kieran could be such great company. Now, after months of day in, day out argument they seemed to be getting on. Was this all it took, a simple family holiday?

Victor returned face-deep in chocolate ice cream with Kristine in tow. He passed a couple of dollar bills and some coins to Amelia's outstretched hand.

'Thank you,' she said.

Victor sat down, and Kristine came into view.

She was definitely hobbling.

'Kristine, sweetie, are you OK?' asked Amelia.

'I'm fine, Mummy,' she replied.

'Have you hurt your ankle?' queried Amelia.

'No,' answered Kristine.

'Have you twisted it, or banged it?' continued Amelia.

'No, why?' wondered Kristine.

Amelia beckoned Kristine to come to her.

'Turn round, let me see,' she said.

Kristine turned round.

Amelia put her drink down and sat up.

'Come nearer, dear, let me have a look,' she asked.

Kristine came close and Amelia tested her leg and foot. Nothing, Kristine did not wince at all at her manipulation.

'Sweetie, walk up and down, will you,' requested Amelia.

Kristine did as she was told. Her gait was uneven.

Amelia said nothing.

'Is everything OK, Mummy?' asked Kristine.

Amelia nodded, pensively.

'Go play, dear,' she said.

Kristine grinned, and tried, unsuccessfully, to stuff the rest of her ice cream in her mouth all in one go. It dribbled down her swimsuit before landing on her foot.

'Why, you are the muckiest muck monster I have ever seen!' observed Kieran.

Kristine giggled.

'And do you know what happens to mucky muck monsters?' he said.

Kristine shook her head from side to side.

'No,' she replied.

'They get tickled!' exclaimed Kieran, at which he leapt from his lounger.

Kristine screamed, and turned tail.

That evening they ate in the restaurant.

For Amelia, something so ordinary, so day-to-day, would have been a joy after the fragmented lives they had been forced to lead these last months, but she was worried, and the worry would not go away.

It didn't take much to get the kids to sleep, though even so, Amelia made

Kieran step outside of their room.

'What is it?' asked Kieran.

'We need to go back to New York now,' said Amelia.

'What! Why?' he said. 'You're mad, woman.'

'Shssh! Keep your voice down, people are sleeping,' whispered Amelia. She could see Kieran's frustration simmer, she pulled him close. 'I think Kristine's limp may be symptomatic of the cancer's return.' She felt Kieran physically rock back on his feet.

'We must go back to New York and get her tested,' she repeated.

Kieran closed his eyes.

'Please tell me you're not serious,' he muttered.

'If the cancer has returned, every day, every hour will matter if she is not treated,' explained Amelia.

'What do you mean?' he asked.

'I mean that...'Amelia took a moment to think about how to phrase what she wanted to say, 'it's potentially very serious.'

Kieran put his head in his hands.

'Look,' said Amelia, 'first thing tomorrow I'll call and try and make an appointment, and we'll drive back.'

She put her arms around him, and pushed her head to his chest. He dropped his hands and held her.

Belief

The aluminium-framed glass doors swept back automatically, and Amelia strode across the hospital's foyer to the reception desk. The receptionist looked up, recognised Amelia and Kristine, and smiled.

'Good afternoon, Dr Allen,' said the receptionist, 'how may I help?'

'We're here to see Dr Kapoor,' replied Amelia.

'Thank you, I'll just book you in.' The receptionist flicked through the booking screens on the computer, and then flicked through them again. 'Um, Dr Allen, I don't seem to have an appointment on the system for Kristine. There must be some mistake.'

'There's no mistake,' said Amelia.

'But if you don't have an appointment, I can't book you in,' stated the receptionist. 'I was told that Dr Kapoor was too busy,' said Amelia, 'and wouldn't be able to see Kristine until next Monday. Next Monday is too late, Kristine needs to be seen now, so we're here today.'

'Ah,' pondered the receptionist, 'let me call Dr Kapoor's secretary and see what I can do. Why don't you take a seat, I'll just be a minute or two.'

Amelia took Kristine's hand and they sat on the row of steel-framed chairs against the window.

People came, people went.

'Mummy?' ventured Kristine.

'Yes, dear,' replied Amelia.

'Mummy, have I got cancer again?' she asked.

Amelia turned and looked face to face at Kristine.

'That's what we're here to find out,' explained Amelia.

'But I feel all well again, well, like I did before,' replied Kristine.

'That's good, Kristine,' said Amelia. She didn't know what else to say.

The receptionist managed to catch Amelia's eye.

'Dr Allen,' she called.

Amelia got up and walked over.

'Dr Allen, I've got Dr Kapoor's secretary on the line,' said the receptionist holding her hand over the telephone receiver, 'and she says that he is completely booked-up for today. If you could come back on Monday, she'll make sure you have the first appointment.'

Amelia leant over the receptionist's desk.

'Listen,' said Amelia, her tone as controlled as she could be. 'You see my little girl over there, I believe her cancer has come back in her brain, and that she needs to be treated as soon as possible.'

'I understand, Dr Allen,' said the receptionist, 'but there's nothing I can do.'

'Pass me the phone,' instructed Amelia.

'But...' began the receptionist, unsure, clearly torn over what to do.

Amelia reached across and took the receiver.

'Dr Allen, you can't just...' insisted the receptionist, but it was too late.

'Is this Dr Kapoor's secretary?' asked Amelia. 'Well, tell Dr Kapoor, Kristine is waiting in reception to see him.'

And with that, Amelia slammed the receiver down and returned to her seat.

Within five minutes one of the hospital's administrative supervisors was stood in front of Amelia.

'Dr Allen, I'm really sorry, but I'm going to have to ask you to leave,' said the supervisor in a polite but firm manner. 'Dr Kapoor can't see Kristine today. Please come back on Monday.'

'The only way I am leaving this hospital, without seeing Dr Kapoor, is if that security guard physically drags me outside kicking and screaming,' declared Amelia, pointing at one of the burly security guards posted by the front entrance. She then added, 'A sight I'm sure you'll wish to avoid.'

Amelia folded her arms and stared.

'Me too,' added Kristine, folding her arms and staring just like her mother.

Dr Kapoor was not pleased and made his feelings quite clear to the administrative supervisor. However, he agreed to see Kristine, and she and Amelia were shown up to his office between appointments.

Amelia opened the door, stood where she was, and then told Kristine to go and say "Hi" to Dr Kapoor.

Kristine limped across the room. She ran her hand along the edge of Dr Kapoor's desk as she went around it to see him.

'Hi, Dr Kapoor,' she said.

He smiled.

'Hello, Kristine,' he replied, 'and how are you?'

'I feel fine, Dr Kapoor, but Mummy thinks I've got cancer again. Do I have the cancer again?' she asked.

'I'll tell you what, Kristine,' he confided, 'if you go and get your mother and come and sit back down here, we'll talk about it.'

Kristine turned and hobbled back to the door.

Dr Kapoor watched her, and then, momentarily, shot a knowing glance to Amelia.

Amelia saw he suspected too.

Over the next few minutes he checked the articulation of Kristine's limbs, commenting as he did so, "Excellent", "Fine", "Good".

'Can you stand on one leg for me, Kristine?' he asked.

'Yes, Dr Kapoor,' replied Kristine, and duly stood on her good leg.

'And the other?' he continued.

Kristine stumbled, became unbalanced and tipped over. Amelia managed to catch her before she hit the floor.

'Well done, Kristine,' said Dr Kapoor. 'Shall we see if Mummy can stand on one leg too?'

'Yes,' giggled Kristine.

'Well, I don't know if I can,' said Amelia, standing up.

'Go on, Mummy, let me see you try,' urged Kristine.

Amelia lifted her right leg.

'There you go,' she said.

'And the other one,' said Dr Kapoor.

'The other one?' replied Amelia.

'The other one,' instructed Dr Kapoor.

'Yes, Mummy, the other one,' demanded Kristine.

'OK, here goes.' Amelia swapped legs, began to sway, and rolled onto the floor. Kristine laughed and jumped on top of her.

When Amelia and Kristine had clambered back into their chairs, Dr Kapoor turned to Kristine.

'Now as one last check today, I'd like to take a special picture of you, Kristine, a picture called a scan,' he said. 'Do you remember having a scan done before, Kristine?'

'Yes,' she said, 'it was very noisy and a bit scary. Can Mummy come too?'

'Of course she can,' said Dr Kapoor. He picked up the phone, spoke for a while, and then said to Kristine, 'A nurse is going to come and collect you and get you ready.'

'OK,' replied Kristine.

'Now, I need to borrow Mummy for a few minutes, and then she'll come straight down to see you. Is that alright with you?' asked Dr Kapoor.

'OK,' answered Kristine.

There was a knock at the door.

'Enter,' said Dr Kapoor.

In stepped a nurse with a broad smile. She held out her hand towards Kristine.

'Hi, I'm Elaine,' she said, 'and you must be Kristine.'

Kristine remained in her chair and nodded.

'Come with me,' said Elaine.

Kristine looked to Amelia.

'Go on, I'll be with you in a minute,' said Amelia.

'Promise?' asked Kristine.

'Promise,' agreed Amelia.

Kristine got down from her chair and limped across to the nurse. She held her hand, and then waved back.

'See you in a minute, love,' said Amelia.

A World Apart

Amelia looked to the window and stared. She could see the edge of the building across the street, flat-faced, with copper coloured glass, and beyond that, a flat sky, blue, almost washed to grey.

Kieran sat next to her, but they did not hold hands. They sat legs crossed. Kieran had his arms folded, Amelia rested her hands on her knees.

Knowing what Dr Kapoor was going to say didn't make it any easier for Amelia to hear. He talked facts not sentiment. He built the evidence to its inevitable conclusion.

Kieran shook his head.

Amelia continued to stare through the window at the empty sky devoid of clouds, or birds, or planes. Perfectly empty.

Kieran unfolded his arms, his hands upturned, open, fingers frozen, grasping. He leant forward and asked questions. Dr Kapoor gave answers.

Amelia looked at Dr Kapoor as he explained. His face was clean shaven, his hair neat, parted to one side, and behind his heavy rimmed glasses he had dark eyes. If he wanted to be seen to be listening, he would sit back, pull his glasses off and hold them to one side. But when he put them back on and sat upright he would regain control of the conversation.

At the end, Amelia found herself standing, shaking hands, saying thank you.

Dr Kapoor showed them to the door with a reassuring hand.

The door closed.

And as Amelia propped herself against the elevator's back wall she watched the numbers change above the doors. Kieran stood in front of her. She thought how much he'd changed since they'd first met. His hair was mostly gone, and he carried quite a few more pounds these days.

The elevator rested to a halt and its doors slid open.

They stepped into the foyer as others brushed past.

The doors to the street swung open.

Kieran stood to one side to let Amelia pass through first, out into the world outside.

In the instant she stepped onto the sidewalk, that world outside crashed into her mind.

Her head clamoured, screamed, a cacophony of noise, words, thoughts, sound.

She shut her eyes, not to see.

She wrapped her arms around herself, not to feel.

But Amelia knew that in this maelstrom of emotion she had to find the strength to help Kristine see it through.

She would not, could not, let her die.

She must not lose faith.

The Day After

Dr Kapoor said that the thirteen hour operation to remove Kristine's brain tumour had been a success, but the treatment that was to follow would be extremely intensive, more intensive than the first treatment Kristine had had. He said they should prepare themselves, her recovery was unlikely to be easy, it would all take time.

But the day after surgery, Kristine was up and about, her tubes unhooked. She said she didn't need to be in bed. She played with Victor.

'Kristine's recovery is simply miraculous,' thought Amelia. She could think of no other word for it, as she remembered the events of the evening before Kristine's operation.

Knowing of Kristine's illness, Christopher and Hiruni Moretti, friends from church, had invited them to dinner at their family home. Christopher was a New Yorker, and Hiruni was originally from Sri Lanka. They had two young daughters.

Christopher was ardently catholic, and a strong proponent of Padre Pio.

That evening he had led them in prayer.

After they had all prayed, and while the children were playing, Christopher had explained that when he was a young man, he'd been to see Padre Pio just before Padre Pio died. Christopher had said that he had confessed to Padre Pio, but Padre Pio had not forgiven him his sins. Padre Pio had told him that he must spend the rest of his life making amends and doing good deeds.

Amelia had wondered what sins Christopher must have committed for Padre Pio not to have forgiven him.

'Perhaps he'd killed someone,' she'd thought.

Christopher had said that Padre Pio had given him his glove, and had told him to do good with it.

He wanted to bless Kristine.

He'd brought the glove out, but when he'd tried to bless Kristine with it, he couldn't speak. Kristine had taken the glove from him and had put it on her own hand, and then had put her gloved hand over where the tumour was. She had closed her eyes, and had rubbed her head.

When Kristine had finished, the room was silent, nobody had been able to say a word.

Amelia had felt like the Lord God himself had been in the room.

Kristine had taken the glove off her little hand, and had returned it to

Christopher.

'It was a miracle, truly a miracle,' thought Amelia.

In the weeks that followed, Amelia started her job at the St Anthony's Teaching Hospital in Toronto. She and Kieran had planned for Victor to start school there too, so it was agreed that Victor would travel to Toronto with Amelia. Kieran would stay in New York with Kristine.

Dr Kapoor suggested that Kristine would need up to a year's worth of chemo, experimental and radiation outpatient treatment.

Soon a routine developed. Amelia would fly down to New York once a week, while Victor stayed with friends. She would visit the hospital with Kieran and Kristine to follow up on Kristine's progress, and she would try to be there for any of the key tests, or when a new treatment started.

It was the beginning of October, leaves had started to colour and fall. Amelia and Kieran were waiting in a room with Kristine to be called for a blood test.

As ever Amelia was on her phone dealing with the endless demands of work. Kieran thumbed a magazine, and Kristine seemed bored.

The nurse appeared at the doorway.

'Kristine Boyle?' she asked.

'It's OK, I'll take her,' said Amelia. 'Come on Kristine, let's go.'

Amelia grabbed Kristine's hand, and they followed the nurse out of the room.

Kieran looked up from his magazine and noticed that Amelia had dropped her cellphone. He reached down and picked it up. There was a text from Ross, "Missing you".

Kieran thought back to the St Patrick's Day Parade when he'd confronted Amelia, and she'd told him to not be so "ridiculous", and that Ross was just a "good friend and a work colleague".

He didn't believe her then and certainly didn't believe her now.

She'd lied.

Enraged, he threw Amelia's cellphone back on the floor.

Half an hour later, Kristine appeared at doorway, ran across to Kieran and sat on his lap.

'Look,' she said. She showed him her sticker.

'Who's my brave princess?' said Kieran.

'I am,' declared Kristine.

'That's right, you are,' he agreed.

'Daddy, Daddy, did I tell you about the doggy?' she asked.

'The doggy? No, you didn't tell me about the doggy,' replied Kieran.

'Well, in the hospital they have this doggy,' explained Kristine, 'and he comes and plays with all the children, He's big and fluffy and has this tail that goes swoosh, swoosh, swoosh.'

Kristine waved her arm from side to side to illustrate.

'And what might this dog's name be now? asked Kieran.

'Alfie,' replied Kristine. She leant in and whispered in Kieran's ear, 'He licked me!' 'Like this?' and Kieran licked Kristine across her cheek.

'Urghhh!' exclaimed Kristine and giggled.

'Or was it like this?' This time Kieran tickled as he licked. Kristine burst into fits of laughter.

Amelia came back into the room.

'And what's happening here?' she asked with mock concern.

'Daddy's trying to lick me,' said Kristine, attempting to push Kieran away.

Amelia was a somewhat bemused.

'Lick you?' she asked.

'He thinks he's a doggy, like Alfie,' said Kristine.

'Does he now,' said Amelia. 'Come on everyone, time to go.'

Kristine got down, and raced ahead to the elevator.

Amelia spotted her cellphone on the floor, and walked over to pick it up. She saw the message open, and she saw Kieran's face.

'I was going to throw it in the trash where it and you belong,' he said bluntly.

'I can...' Amelia stopped before she started.

Kieran brushed past her, and then turned.

'You lied to me,' he said, 'you two-faced, two-timing bitch.' 'Kieran, I'm so sorry, I didn't...' began Amelia.

'I'm not interested in how sorry you are,' he snorted.

'But Kieran, I... I love you,' stammered Amelia.

Kieran stared.

Amelia knew her words did not reflect her thoughts. She didn't love Kieran, she wanted to leave him, but she didn't have the courage to walk away. All her life she had wanted to have a family. If she left, the family she had built would be devastated, but if she stayed she would be destroyed. Tormented, she just couldn't reconcile her emotions. Amelia wanted love.

'Well, you sure have a strange way of showing it,' said Kieran. He shook his head and went to find Kristine.

Amelia followed.

My Sins Revisited

Amelia was apprehensive, she had avoided seeing Teresa since meeting up with Ross in Toronto. She stood at the doorway of the spiritual healer's practice, and looked at the brass plaque on the wall. Amelia opened the door and walked up the stairs.

She knocked.

'Come in,' came the reply.

Amelia entered.

'Amelia, come sit,' ordered Teresa, gesturing to the high-backed chair, facing the window. 'Take a seat.'

Amelia sat.

'You've seen Ross, haven't you?' accused Teresa.

'Yes,' murmured Amelia.

'And bad things have happened,' continued Teresa.

'Yes,' confirmed Amelia.

Amelia struggled to speak, but eventually she told Teresa about seeing Ross again, even though she'd meant not to. Then, tearfully, she told Teresa about Kristine's relapse, Padre Pio's glove and the operation. Finally she spoke of Kieran's words, and that she'd told him she loved him, but he'd said he did not forgive her, nor did he trust her.

'Amelia, you must listen to what I have to say,' insisted Teresa. 'I told you to atone for what you have done, you ignored me, and now you see the consequences. You will need to pay me more so I can protect you, an extra five gold bars.'

Amelia hung her head despondently, she knew that Teresa spoke the truth, and that she had to do all that Teresa demanded to absolve her from her sins and save Kristine.

'You must repair your marriage, and then make the best of life with Kieran,' ordered Teresa. 'Do as he asks, if only for Kristine's sake. If you ever deviate from this path again, you will have to leave Kieran immediately.'

And so Amelia became resigned.

Her life in Toronto centred on Victor, her job, and her weekly flight to New York.

Amelia enjoyed the plane journey, it felt like the only chance she ever got to sit down and have time by herself. She was using a new airline, which offered executive travel at budget prices. The seats were deep and comfortable, and the flight attendants brought endless tea, coffee and snacks.

'I'm going to write to the owner of the airline and tell him what a nice airline he has,' thought Amelia.

So she wrote a letter, on headed paper from the St Anthony's Teaching Hospital, saying that though she was going through a difficult time, what a really great experience her commute to New York had become. She then asked whether it would be possible to purchase a bundle of ten flights.

Two weeks later she received a reply from the owner of the airline. He thanked her for her letter and said that it was good to hear positive things about his airline. He also added that, given the circumstances of her journeys, he wanted to offer her travel at cost.

It was only later that Amelia found out the owner of the airline was a neighbour and golfing partner of Ken Scott, her boss and Chief of Medicine at St Anthony's. Apparently, when the airline owner asked about her story, and the "difficult time" she was going through, Ken had told him all about Kristine's cancer, and the extraordinary challenges and sacrifices that Amelia had faced.

In Black and White

Kristine was released from the hospital, but remained an outpatient. This meant that she and Kieran could now relocate to Toronto, though there would be regular trips to New York.

At last the whole family was together, and they settled into their beautiful home, set amid its shading trees. Life started to become normal, stresses eased. Victor was delighted to have his father and little sister around again.

Amelia followed Teresa's instructions. She worked hard to repair her marriage. She did as Kieran asked and tried to avoid confrontation. For his part Kieran looked for work, but the impact of the global financial crisis had hit hard and there was little around.

Amelia received a letter stating that she'd been awarded a Fellowship of the Royal College of Physicians. It was a great honour. The graduation ceremony was to be held in Edinburgh.

Arrangements were made. Victor and Kristine were to stay with some doctor friends, while Amelia and Kieran made the trip. Amelia thought that time away without the kids would be good for their relationship. Flights and hotel were booked, as was a dinner at one of the best restaurants in Edinburgh. Amelia had invited her parents, who booked flights from Ireland.

On arrival, they all met at and checked into the hotel, and in the evening, Amelia, Kieran and Amelia's parents had dinner at the restaurant they had booked. It was every bit as good as the reviews had suggested.

The following morning, Amelia and her mother went and had their hair done. It was wonderful, Amelia couldn't remember the last time she and her mother had spent time together doing something so ordinary.

After lunch, they all took a taxi to the Royal College of Physicians for the ceremony at three o'clock. They pulled up outside the ornate Victorian facade and walked up the front steps under the double tiered portico.

The door was open, and they entered the building, looking for signs or directions to the ceremony. None were obvious. Across the chequered marble floor, sat an official- looking man at a wooden desk. He seemed busy.

Amelia introduced herself and asked where the graduation ceremony was. The clerk seemed puzzled.

'I'm not aware of a graduation ceremony today, Dr Allen,' he replied.

'That can't be,' said Amelia. 'I have the invitation here.'

Amelia opened her handbag, and began to search for the letter.

'I'll call the main office and double-check,' offered the clerk, and he picked up the telephone receiver, dialled and started a conversation.

Amelia found the letter eventually, crumpled. She smoothed it out and held it in her hand.

The clerk put the telephone receiver down.

'Dr Allen, there are no graduation ceremonies at any of our sites in Edinburgh today or anytime this week,' said the clerk.

'You must be wrong,' insisted Amelia. 'Look here's the invitation, in black and white. We've flown all the way from Canada to be here. My parents have flown in from Ireland.'

She handed the clerk the crumpled letter. He unfolded it carefully on his desk and read it. He then read it again.

'Um, Dr Allen, I'm afraid you're in the wrong city, you should be in London,' he said quietly, and passed back the letter, pointing to the appropriate paragraph.

Amelia dared not look, but there it was in black and white.

'Thank you,' she said, and returned to Kieran and her parents.

'Where is it then?' asked Kieran.

'London,' mumbled Amelia.

For several moments Kieran stared blankly at Amelia, and then he laughed, uncontrollably.

Amelia and Kieran returned to Canada. Everyone wanted to know what the graduation had been like, and how it went. Indeed, Amelia found almost without exception that it was the first question everyone asked.

Kieran just said that he was, "Delighted for Amelia", or, "It was great to have met up with the in-laws after so long", or "We had a wonderful time and...", with some truth, "...I've never laughed so much".

Amelia couldn't bring herself to say what had actually happened. Where she could, she avoided answering directly. She would say things like, "Edinburgh was brilliant, thank you so much", or, "Scotland was fantastic", or, "We had wonderful weather, not a drop of rain".

In the months that followed, Kristine's appointments became less frequent as her health improved. She began to enjoy being a normal little girl again. Kieran would take her to the park or down by the waterside, she loved the boats. And with the recovery of her immune system, she became able to socialise with other children.

Amelia was, as ever, all-too-busy, but managed to find time to be with Victor and Kristine, on the weekends mostly. She was always conscious of the risk of relapse, though she tried not to make Kristine aware.

Kieran remained unable to find work, and soon began to press for the family to go back home. Canada was nice enough, but he missed his friends, his social life, his sport, and he didn't like the fact that they lived where Ross

Byrne lived.

He told Amelia they should move back to England, he'd have a better chance of finding work. And though Amelia knew the real reasons why Kieran wanted to return, she knew she must also leave Canada if she was ever going to break free from Teresa's control.

The decision was made, Amelia felt secretly relieved.

Lost and Found

Amelia did not have to spend long searching for a job in England. No sooner had Kieran said they should relocate, than she was asked whether she would consider a senior consultant post at a newly built hospital near Bath, the Midstone Foundation Hospital. It wasn't so much an interview as a discussion, and within a three months she had left Toronto, much against her better judgement.

It made sense for Kieran and the children to stay on in Canada for a while longer. Victor had his school year to finish, and Kristine had one more treatment course to complete in New York.

In their old apartment in Bath, Amelia stood surrounded by all their furniture and belongings. It seemed strange to find herself here. It was almost like going back to a long lost past, so much had happened since.

In the haste to get Kristine treated, they'd decided to let the apartment out, with a plan to sell when the future was a little clearer, but a combination of uncertainty and the recession had meant they'd never sold it.

Amelia walked from room to room, stopping and touching, looking and remembering. Amelia rarely reflected and yet merely being in their apartment brought so much back to her.

The present soon subsumed the past.

A friend had offered her a car to help her find her feet. She needed the car to commute to work. It was an old Ford, and a horrible shade of off-blue. It must have been twenty years old if it was a day, but she was too polite to turn down her friend's kind offer.

It didn't take long for her concerns about the car to be realised. Within two days it broke down. It was the worst car ever, and after a three hundred pound repair bill, Amelia collected it and drove it home, but the next morning it refused to start. Amelia called the garage again, and they came, lights flashing, and towed it away. The mechanic had smiled, and said they'd fix it, no problem.

Amelia stood beside the road, car-less, cursing when she heard a familiar voice.

'What's going on?' It was Martin Sharpe, a hospital colleague.

'Oh, my car's broken down, again,' replied Amelia. 'It's just been towed away.'

'I didn't know you lived round here, we're just round the corner. Why don't you hop in and I'll give you a lift?' he offered.

'You don't mind?' said Amelia.

'Not at all,' replied Martin.

He pushed the passenger door open from the inside, and Amelia got in. Compared to her clapped-out Ford, the car was absolute luxury, quiet, smooth, comfortable.

They talked.

Amelia knew his wife, Vicky, very well from before they went to Canada. Amelia told Martin about getting everything ready for Victor, Kristine and Kieran, and said she hoped they would be over from Canada just as soon as school finished.

Martin said he would give Amelia a lift back from work later on that evening. He said that he and Vicky were away for the weekend, going up to London. He then offered Amelia the loan of his car, until hers was fixed.

'You're too kind, I couldn't,' said Amelia.

'Not at all,' he insisted, 'it'll just be standing idle otherwise, go on, you need it.'

'Are you sure?' checked Amelia.

'Certain,' he confirmed.

'Thank you,' said Amelia.

That evening, Clare Markham had invited Amelia to her divorce party, at her house a few miles outside of Bath. Amelia had bought an outfit especially for the occasion, though she wasn't quite sure what one wore to a divorce party.

Amelia filled Martin's car with fuel, she wanted to be sure she gave it back to him with a full tank. She managed to overfill the car, and sprayed petrol on her new outfit. She stank, and decided to go back home to change.

She couldn't find a parking space outside the apartment and ended up driving round and round until she found a spot at the north end of St Peter's Square. She parked the car there, and walked back.

While changing, Amelia decided it would be better to call a taxi, rather take Martin's car. If she knew Clare half as well as she thought she did, then there was certain to be too much drinking at the party.

There was.

Amelia awoke in her bed, her mouth dry, her head throbbing. At least she'd made it back home. Tea and half a piece of toast did little to revive her, and she still smelt of petrol even though she'd changed her clothes. What must everyone have thought? Though, thinking about it, most were probably too drunk to have noticed.

As the morning wore on, and her mind cleared, she realised she'd left her work bag in Martin's car. It had her computer, her passport and several files she needed to look at.

She'd have to go and get her bag.

Oh well, fresh air would do her good.

She stepped outside, the day was bright and clear, somewhat in contrast to how she felt. It was something of a walk to St Peter's Square, and it was uphill, but eventually she came in sight of the trees that marked the small park at the square's centre. With relief, she reached the top of the square, and turned into the north side. She walked all the way along, looking for Martin's car. Strange, it wasn't there. Perhaps she'd parked it on the other side of the square. She continued to walk around.

No car. She walked around again.

Still, no car. But she was sure she'd parked it in the square.

'Oh no, don't say it's been towed,' she thought, though she was sure she'd parked it legally. 'Or it could have been stolen.'

The thought that Martin's car, that he'd so kindly loaned her, together with her work bag, might have been stolen sent Amelia into panic. She walked around the square again, but it was to no avail. Martin's car had vanished. She didn't know what to do. She didn't have Martin nor Vicky's mobile number.

She'd call Kate, she'd know what to do, she was sensible about these things. Kate was away, but said she should call Jason. Jason was Kate's latest boyfriend.

Amelia called Jason.

Some minutes later, Jason arrived in his hatchback. They searched for Martin's car, but it was nowhere to be seen.

'I think you need to ring Martin, and tell him his car's been stolen,' concluded Jason.

'Oh God,' said Amelia, 'but I don't have his number.'

'Oh,' said Jason, 'you had better ring the police then.'

Amelia decided that the telephone call would be best made from her apartment. Jason dropped her off, and she thanked him for his help.

Amelia called the police to report the car stolen together with her computer and passport. The police took details, but promised nothing.

'It's going to be a nightmare,' she thought. 'Without my passport I can't return to Canada,' as she had been planning to do next week. And her computer had her whole life on it.

By Sunday, Amelia was feeling depressed. If it could go wrong, it had gone wrong, and then the telephone rang. It was the phone call she'd been dreading, it was Martin, the police must have managed to get a hold of him.

'Amelia, really great news,' he declared, 'they've found the car. The car's been found.'

Amelia was delighted. At last something had gone her way.

'Fantastic,' she said. 'Where was it?'

'Well, it was three doors down from my house, Amelia,' ventured Martin.

'Pardon?' she said.

Amelia didn't believe what she was being told.

'Yes,' he repeated, 'three doors down from my house.'

'But that can't be because I didn't park it there,' said Amelia.

'Well, that's where it was found, ' he replied, 'and that's where it is now, if you want to come round and have a look.'

'I will, I will,' said Amelia.

Amelia was out of breath, she had run round to Martin's house.

'Oh my God, there it is,' she said. 'It must mean that people who stole it, put it back.'

'Well, there's that, or there's another explanation,' suggested Martin, and held up Amelia's work bag.

'They didn't take my bag!' exclaimed Amelia.

'Indeed,' chuckled Martin.

'I don't believe it, they must have just taken the car for a joyride,' explained Amelia, 'and then parked the car back where they found it...'

Amelia realised what she'd done. She must have moved the car when she got back, drunk from the party, thinking it would be better for it to be parked outside Martin's house, than left in St Peter's Square. And then she'd forgotten all about it.

'The police said it was one of the most unusual car thefts they'd investigated in recent times,' continued Martin. 'Not a scratch on the car, tank full of fuel, contents untouched, and left neatly parked three doors down from the owner's house.'

Amelia blushed.

Hillside

Kieran wanted to sell the apartment and move to a larger house in Bath. It was too small, and they couldn't have a dog. Kristine wanted a dog desperately. Amelia didn't want to move, but agreed to put the apartment on the market.

Within a week there was an offer. Kieran told Amelia to find a house. "Take Roland, he knows property and can do a deal" was Kieran's instruction. Roland was a family friend and local businessman.

Amelia organised to meet Roland on Saturday morning in order to visit estate agents and start looking at houses. Roland, ever the gentleman, insisted on collecting Amelia from her apartment.

Smart and stylish were two words that Roland owned absolutely. Nothing out of place, everything matched. Amelia, who always thought she dressed well, felt positively frumpy as he opened the car door for her. And Roland loved his cars. Amelia sat cocooned in an immaculate interior of leather and veneer.

The car glided off.

'I have the perfect house for you, Amelia,' announced Roland, as they turned to go up the hill. 'I've arranged for the estate agent to meet us at the premises.'

Amelia didn't know quite what to say, given she hadn't discussed what she was looking for with Roland at all. But that was Roland, he was very much "can do".

'Sounds wonderful,' said Amelia. 'Where is it?'

'Oh, not far,' replied Roland enigmatically as he parked the car.

'We're here?' she asked.

'We're here,' he said.

The estate agent recognised Roland immediately and came over to greet them.

'Morning, Mr Zane,' he said and shook Roland's hand. 'Fine morning.'

'Indeed it is,' said Roland. ' This is Dr Allen.'

The estate agent introduced himself and shook Amelia's hand.

He showed them inside, and while the house wasn't particularly large, it had a great garden with views out across the city, and it was close to the children's new school.

Amelia imagined Victor and Kristine running around in the snow, playing fetch with the family dog.

The estate agent said he'd go and wait in the hallway, so they could explore the property by themselves.

'Do you like the house, Amelia?' asked Roland.

'It's lovely,' replied Amelia. At which Roland disappeared inside.

Some ten minutes later, Roland reappeared in the garden.

'It's yours,' he said.

Amelia was a little taken aback.

But it turned out that Roland had done a fantastic deal. He'd knocked fifty thousand off the price by saying that Amelia was a cash buyer.

'Um, Roland, I'm not a cash buyer,' said Amelia. 'I've only just had an offer on the apartment. Kieran wants to sell it, but I haven't decided if I want to yet.'

'Well, the house is yours if you want it,' said Roland. 'You won't get a better one for the money, just make sure you sell your apartment in two weeks.'

Amelia knew it was a really good price, they wouldn't get anything like it in the area. She decided to take it. It was a lovely house, and she wanted everything sorted out before the kids came back.

She thanked Roland. It really was kind of him to spend his Saturday morning helping her.

It was only when Amelia was sat in her apartment drinking tea that she realised what she'd done.

She'd gone and bought a house and Kieran didn't even know!

She knew she had to tell him, but was afraid of what he might say. But, in the end, she could put it off no longer.

She rang Kieran.

'Hi, Amelia,' he said. 'How's it going?'

'Fine,' replied Amelia. 'And you and the kids?'

'We're all doing well here,' said Kieran, 'looking forward to coming over, can't wait.'

Amelia hesitated.

'Was there something you wanted to say?' asked Kieran.

Amelia took a breath.

'Well, I went to go see a house with Roland this morning,' she said. 'It was lovely, and Roland did a fantastic deal, so I bought it.'

For a moment there was silence.

'You what?' exclaimed Kieran.

'I bought a house, just like you said to do,' replied Amelia. 'I took Roland and he said we wouldn't get anything better for the price.'

'Without the rest of us looking at it?' questioned Kieran.

'There isn't time, Roland did a deal,' explained Amelia. 'We've two weeks to sell the apartment.'

'You're joking!' gasped Kieran.

Amelia could sense Kieran's exasperation.

'I'm not,' she replied.

And then he started swearing and cursing. She held the phone away from her ear.

Eventually he calmed down, and Amelia described the house. He said little, but finally agreed it was a good deal, so told Amelia to go ahead.

The day of the move came. Amelia had arranged for removal men to take their furniture and belongings up to the new house. However, she had managed to double- book herself, and had a keynote lecture to deliver at the University.

The removers were halfway through emptying the apartment, when she came down in an elegant cream satin suit, with pencil-thin skirt.

'Goodbye now, lads. I'll be back in two hours,' she said. 'I'm off to give a lecture. How do I look?'

The removers stared at her, speechless. But before they could say anything, she had toddled off down the road in her high heels.

When she returned, the removers had finished loading the trucks and were about to head up the hill to the new house. She exchanged her high heels for more comfortable shoes and followed them in her car.

The scene was chaotic. The first truck wouldn't fit on the drive, leaving the other two trucks blocking the road, much to the annoyance of her new neighbours.

The other two trucks had to be moved, and parked some way away while the removers began to unload the first truck.

And then the first piece of furniture, a sofa, wouldn't fit through the front door. The removers had to take the door off to get the sofa in, but when it came to the antique wooden bed, no amount of trying would get it into the house.

'Put it back in the truck,' said Amelia, 'and return it to the apartment, I'll do a deal with the new owners, they can buy it.'

The removers did as they were instructed, and much to Amelia's astonishment, the new owners of the apartment bought the bed.

Home

They were home, but tired. Kieran had listened to sport on the car radio on the way back from the airport. Victor and Kristine had slept. Amelia couldn't wait to show them the new house, and the little surprise she had.

When they arrived at their new home, the kids jumped out of the car and raced round to look at the house. When they opened the front door they were greeted by the scurry of paws and over-excited panting.

'A doggy!' squealed Kristine.

Bella was a cocker spaniel, mostly black with the floppiest of ears. Kristine was in love.

'What's the doggy's name?' she asked.

'She's called Bella,' replied Amelia.

'Let's go play fetch in the garden,' said Victor.

'No you can't, not yet, she's too young,' said Amelia. 'Here's a rubber ring for her to play with, and only in the hallway.'

Kieran had wandered off to look around the house.

Amelia said she was going to put the kettle on.

He returned to the kitchen, and closed the kitchen door.

'It's way too small,' he said. 'I don't like it.'

'Well, it's the best I could get for the money,' said Amelia. 'Roland said we should be able to get planning permission and extend it out to the rear if we wanted to.'

'Knock it down and build it again more like,' remarked Kieran.

Amelia sighed. Whatever she did, it wasn't good enough. She had tried to do as he asked. She didn't want to sell the apartment, but he'd said he wanted a house, so she bought a house. And now, all he could do was complain.

'And where's our bed?' he demanded.

'I sold it,' replied Amelia. 'It wouldn't fit.'

Kieran shook his head.

'Jesus,' he muttered.

Amelia decided to ignore him and went to find the kids. They were playing tug with Bella and the rubber ring.

Kieran went into the living room and turned the TV on.

Amelia was relieved when the kids started school. Having two children, a dog, and a demanding job was simply exhausting. She and Kieran only seemed to stop to argue, and there never seemed to be a shortage of things to argue about.

The kids hated it when they argued. Victor would go to his room and shut the door to try and keep the sound of the shouting out. Kristine would tug at Amelia's clothes, or try and hug Kieran in an attempt to get them to stop rowing.

The good news was that Kieran had managed to find work, but this too led to arguments over who was going to do the school run.

As ever, Amelia hid in her work and her friends.

Every time Kieran went out for a drink, or one of his golf or rugby weekends, and she was left with the kids, Amelia made sure she went out next time. It was only fair.

Amelia and Kieran had started to get phone calls from the school. Victor was disengaged, he seemed upset. When Amelia went in to discuss the matter, the school asked if there were any problems at home.

What could she say? She and her husband were incompatible and did nothing but argue? He was a controlling bastard who didn't care about anyone except himself? She wasn't going to say any of that.

She suggested that perhaps Victor was having trouble trying to adapt to his new school, or perhaps it was just an age thing.

Victor's school teacher had just looked at Amelia.

'Perhaps,' she said.

Step by Step

Amelia's hard work had paid off. She had been promoted to the Board of Midstone Foundation Hospital, and was told that the next Board meeting was to be held at an outdoor activity centre, Green Forest.

In the true spirit of corporate team-building, "Death by Powerpoint" was to be replaced by obstacle courses, ropes, trees, raft-building, human pyramids, and anything else the trainers could conceive of to extract the participants from their office-bound lives.

The night before this day of outdoor pursuits, Clare had asked Amelia if she wanted to go out for dinner, just her and a few friends.

'No, no, no, no, no. I have to be on top form for Green Forest,' Amelia had replied.

'Oh, just come for a quick dinner,' Clare had persisted.

Amelia's resolution had folded, and she'd decided to go, but she'd vowed she wouldn't drink.

'Oh, come on, let's go listen to the live band,' Clare had urged after they'd eaten.

Clare adored live music, she'd even sung backing vocals in an up-and-coming rock band before she'd married. The photos were something else. How she ever thought that particular outfit she'd been wearing was anything but ridiculous, Amelia would never know.

'No, I have to be on good form for Green Forest,' Amelia had affirmed.

But it appeared that one glass of wine was all that was required to overcome any last vestige of good sense Amelia may have had.

They'd gone across the road from the restaurant with Jess Fitzgerald, Thomas Fitzgerald's mum.

'Well, at least she doesn't have that self-styled hairdresser of a boyfriend in tow, with his well-beyond-its-shelf-life seventies haircut,' Amelia had thought.

Jess had gone up to the bar and got Amelia a glass of wine, a small glass, her second and definitely her last.

Amelia didn't know what happened after that glass of wine. She just went a bit crazy. She thought it must have been spiked, because the next thing she knew she was the one, and only, up in front of the band, dancing, if you call whirling like a dervish, and flirting outrageously with the lead singer, dancing. She just couldn't stop herself.

The next Amelia knew, Clare and Jess had lifted her by her arms, her legs akimbo, and dragged her from her *Dance of the Seven Veils*. They'd said it was time for her to go home, much to her annoyance.

At Jess's house, Amelia had started swinging from the rafters, literally, but eventually she'd calmed down, well, that's to say she'd just conked out, and fallen like a sack of potatoes.

When she awoke, the next morning, she had just the worst headache ever in her whole life, though she knew she hadn't had that much to drink. She felt so ill. But she had to get up, and drive all the way down to Green Forest, and she had to go on the obstacle course, and swing on the ropes, and climb the tees, and build the raft, and be the apex of the human pyramid, and anything else that corporate team-building entailed.

'Dear Lord,' was all she was able to say. Not the longest of prayers, but a prayer nonetheless.

Blindfolded, and unable to talk, Amelia was guided by Adrian over the obstacle course, step by step. Trust was all that kept her from plummeting forty feet to an ignominious end, dangling, tied to a safety rope. She was certain she was going to be sick.

And then she had to build a raft.

It was the worst day of her life.

Afterwards, Amelia slept for two days. She didn't wake up. That was a Friday. She slept Saturday and Sunday, much to Kieran's annoyance as he was left with the kids. And for ten days she couldn't eat a thing. She was so, so ill. She was sure that somebody had tried to poison her, because she'd had such a weird reaction.

So, after that, Amelia decided to give up alcohol. She thought, 'I'm never drinking again, and I'm never going out with Jess Fitzgerald ever again.'

Happy

The fighting, the arguing, the bickering didn't stop, it just happened less often. Kieran and Amelia had learnt to manage their lives separately. Whether by design or by chance the opportunities for conflict had diminished.

Kieran found a balance that he could live with between Amelia, his job, the children and old friends. It wasn't perfect, but what was? He was happy enough.

Kristine was thriving at school. She had exchanged being a lonely, afraid, special little girl, engulfed in the grown-up world of doctors, hospitals and treatments, for a being just another happy little girl in a school yard full of other happy little children.

Victor had found friends and sport, and had mostly lost interest in what his parents did. He wanted them to be happy, he wanted everyone to be happy.

As a mother, Amelia was grateful that her children seemed happy and well. And as a career woman it couldn't be going any better, she had a career that had led to being on a hospital board. But was she happy? Well, she just didn't have time.

It didn't happen overnight, it must have happened gradually, but Amelia stopped reading. She stopped reading novels, she stopped reading medical journals, she even stopped reading the newspaper. She was just too busy with work. She worried. She stayed up late.

Amelia had been asked to instigate a review of the hospital's staff health and well-being policy at the last board meeting. These procedural responsibilities were part of being a board member, hardly glamorous, but were key to maintaining the hospital's efficiency.

To get the review going she went to see Dr Adrian Coles. As Human Resources director, he had responsibility for the implementation of the staff health and well-being policy.

'Good morning, Amelia,' he said. 'Come on in, it's lovely to see you.'

He smiled. Adrian was always smiling and helpful. Amelia liked him very much. She thought of him as friend since the time he had guided her over the obstacle course on that awful off-site outdoor pursuit day. They often talked, if they got the chance, and he always listened.

'Hi, Adrian,' said Amelia, and took a seat at his very clear and tidy desk. Adrian had a great view from his office, open fields and countryside.

'And how may I help you?' he asked, brightly.

'I've come about the board meeting internal reviews,' sighed Amelia. 'I picked up an action to review the staff health and well-being policy.'

'Ah, yes.' Adrian leant forward and rested his elbows on his desk. 'Have you read it?'

'Um, probably, when I joined,' hesitated Amelia.

'Perhaps you should read it again,' he suggested.

'I'm a bit pushed for time,' replied Amelia. 'It would be great if you had a list of the salient points for me.'

'For you, I do,' he said and walked across to his filing cabinet. 'How are you planning to review the policy's effectiveness?'

'I thought I'd random sample hospital employees and interview them,' explained Amelia.

Adrian pulled a sheet of paper from one of the cabinet's drawers and passed it to Amelia.

Amelia thanked him and got up to leave.

'May I suggest testing the policy on yourself first,' he ventured. 'You know, so you can answer any questions your random sample of employees might ask.'

'Ah, yeah,' said Amelia, though she seemed distracted.

Adrian stood between Amelia and the door. She looked at him.

'Amelia, I hope you won't mind me for saying this, or take it the wrong way, but you look exhausted,' he commented. 'Is everything alright?'

'I'm fine, just busy,' replied Amelia, feigning a smile.

'You know you've been working nonstop, dawn till dusk since you joined this hospital,' he continued. 'I've noticed you're always here. Your commitment is highly commendable, but you're going to burn out if you carry on like this, and that will be no good for anyone, least of all you.'

Amelia was a little taken aback.

'I've always been totally committed to my work,' she said. 'It's the way I am, it's what I've always done.'

'Everyone can see how committed you are, Amelia. That's not the point,' said Adrian, not wishing to push too hard. 'Look, read the sheet, and before you do anything, think about how it applies to you. Promise?'

Amelia thought about what Adrian was saying. His happy demeanour was hard to refuse

'OK,' she agreed.

The Walk

Amelia was surprised when Kieran said he agreed it would be a good idea for her to have some time off. Her review of staff health and well-being at the hospital had made her reflect on her own health and well-being. The simple act of completing the self- assessment form, and the resulting "highly at risk" score, made Amelia realise that she needed to start caring for herself if she was going to give others the care they deserved.

She now saw how tough her life had been, Amelia felt like an empty vessel. She knew what she needed to do for herself, she was going to have an adventure. But what kind of adventure? And then she remembered a story a patient, back in Toronto, had told her about walking the Camino Way to Santiago de Compostela, an old pilgrimage route, and the story had lodged in Amelia's mind ever since.

The coach, that had picked up Amelia and her fellow travellers from the airport, dropped them off by the side of the road next to a wooden post with a yellow arrow on a blue circle.

The post read "À Santiago" and "250 km". People posed to have photographs taken, others started on the bare earth footpath that led up into the hills.

Amelia turned around to find the coach was gone. She looked back beyond the road. The footpath threaded from some distant point on the horizon.

Amelia turned to the post once more. She stood alone. Ahead, her fellow pilgrims were dotted into the distance. She placed her hat upon her head and under the white- blue sky put one foot in front of the other, a walking stick in her hand.

To begin with Amelia concentrated simply on walking to try and gain a sense of the physical journey ahead. She gauged how long it felt to travel from one marker to the next, how tired she seemed. Occasionally her eyes would wander to the dried green landscape, drawn by a building or a copse against the hillside. And as she progressed she noticed how varied the markers were, stone, concrete, metal, old, new. Most had the yellow scallop shell symbol that radiated the direction of travel.

Amelia found herself alone, but yet she wasn't. As other pilgrims passed her by, she heard the now familiar acknowledgement of "Bon camino". She couldn't recall the last time she had been able to focus on herself this much. She hoped her journey would help her find direction, help her gain strength.

There were conversations, mostly when she stopped for the night, over dinner. People had stories to tell, most talked of "getting away from it all", and most talked with the relief of a smile, happy. Amelia listened, but she did not speak of her story, she was "just taking a break".

Before embarking on her journey, Amelia had read that the Camino Way will find for its pilgrims whatever they need, even if they don't know what that need is themselves.

How she hoped the Camino would find a way to heal her.

The open dorms of the albergues got a little getting used to, but the exertions of the day made sleep easy to come by. Amelia couldn't remember when last she slept so well, it was a revelation.

Day turned on day, her credencial filled with stamps, her feet hardened to the walk.

It seemed that all she did was walk, eat, sleep, walk, eat, sleep, walk, eat, sleep. All the while, her subconscious liberated thoughts, and these thoughts and words she'd keep with her as she walked, trying to discover insight into their meaning. Other times her mind would just meander with the footpath, or drift with a cloud.

Amelia felt peaceful and happy, finally.

Strangely, she didn't ponder over Kieran, nor her patients, nor the hospital, the things that usually crowded her mind. She thought of Victor and Kristine, and her family.

At times, when dusk had fallen over whatever remote village or town she happened to be staying in, she would look up at the stars cast across the sky. Amelia would wonder, had Kristine not survived, which star Kristine might have become in the heavens, looking down, faint in the vastness of creation. And her eyes would redden, blink, moisten. Some thoughts she could not bear.

But through it all, Amelia was grateful for the wonderful blessings that had been bestowed upon her. She was in no doubt that she had been graced by God during the trials of these last few years.

However, Amelia still felt guilty for the transgressions and the wrongs she had committed. She partly saw her pilgrimage as an atonement and hoped for forgiveness.

After two weeks, she knew her adventure was coming to an end as her destination drew into view. Amelia had enjoyed all that the Camino had given her, and she felt a calmness.

Santiago de Compostela, dwarfed by its cathedral, spread out across the low lying land. Terracotta roofs scattered atop off-white buildings, centred about the cathedral's towers.

Amelia had arrived in front of the baroque facade of the cathedral, in time for the midday pilgrims' Mass.

Amid the crowded seats, Amelia took her place to the sound of organ and voice.

The Mass started, and the vaulted ceiling echoed to those inside the cathedral's pillared walls. And then, as if it were a vision, Amelia witnessed the enormous brass Botafumeiro incensory swinging before her, and she was overwhelmed by the smell of incense percolating to her very core. With the pilgrims she gave thanks to God for the journey they had taken, and for having reached their goal.

And then it was all over. Amelia followed the congregation as they left the Mass, and found herself standing outside on the steps, in sharp relief, shadowed in sunlight.

Normal

It didn't take long for things to return to normal. Though gauging normal against the backdrop of the last few years was not easy. Perhaps the "normal" Amelia thought of was somebody else's life, some statistical average of a nuclear family, some common childhood-held expectation.

Suffice to say, Amelia soon became engulfed by the day-to-day juggle of her life, never enough time to do all that was needed to be done, always late, worried about things forgotten.

And while Victor and Kristine thrived in school, Kieran and Amelia continued to manage to find something to disagree about.

However, there was routine to their lives between the working days of their jobs and the termly timetable of the children's school. All of which was punctuated, every three months, when Kristine had to travel to the hospital in New York for her check-up.

Amelia would always go with her, sometimes Victor and Kieran would come along too. And though Amelia tried to put it to the back of her mind, like a spectre from the past, the thought of Kristine's cancer returning again was forever there, all too painful to dwell on.

Amelia placed the tea cup on the table in front of Kieran.

'Thanks,' he said. 'You're a treasure.'

He drank from the cup.

'Not bad,' he added, as he thumbed through the sports section of the Sunday paper, 'not bad at all.'

Amelia had made herself tea, and chose to sit across the table from him and his pile of papers. She cupped the tea between her hands and raised it to her mouth.

Outside the day was clear and cold. Late autumn. Victor and Kristine frolicked with Bella in the sea of leaves that had washed up in the back garden. Amelia watched through the window.

'Kieran?'

'Uh?' Kieran was lost somewhere in the rugby scores, smiling and shaking his head knowingly.

'Kieran,' interrupted Amelia.

He glanced up.

'What?' he asked.

Amelia looked back from the window and put her tea down on the table.

'Kieran,' she said, staring at him, straight, face-to-face, 'I want a divorce.'

THE END

POSTSCRIPT

That woman! I just couldn't stop reading about her. What she has created is a tapestry of her life's highlights and lowlights. It's so intimate. She tantalises me on every page. She tells me stories from her life, and finishes them without ever explaining what she thought and felt after they had happened. So I had to work hard to imagine what is going on in her mind. I don't fully understand women, but she really perplexes me. She intrigues me. How could this woman, who is so intelligent and beautiful and accomplished, be so stupid when it comes to men?

How could she have become trapped in such an unhappy marriage? Did it ever occur to her as she spent her life caring for sick people, especially her own daughter, that she was actually the person who needed the most help?

How could she have got so under my skin like this?

God, am I falling for her too?

Jeremy, get a grip on yourself man! Stop obsessing over Amelia.

I've been a journalist all my life. I've interviewed all sorts of people, and heard their deeply felt personal stories, stories that have touched me. But I've always been able to walk away at THE END.